It was time to lay
table...

"What's going on with you, Zoë?" Brad looked genuinely puzzled.

"I don't have any idea what you're talking about," she lied.

"How about the way you jump every time I get within arm's reach of you? How about the way your expression turns guilty every time I glance in your direction? How about the...the way you're looking at me right now?"

Feeling shy and as much afraid to speak her mind as afraid the chance might not come again, Zoë pushed herself to her feet. Brad's hand was on her bare arm to steady her...and his shockingly sensual touch sent longing ricocheting from her skin to the core of her body.

Without any clear sense of moving toward him, Zoë threw her heart ahead of her, thrust her body against his and pulled him into a kiss.

She had to prove to herself that nothing more than friendship was possible...or prove to Brad that something more than friendship was.

Dear Reader,

Welcome to another month of life and love in the backyards, big cities and wide open spaces of Harlequin American Romance! When April showers keep you indoors, you'll stay snug and dry with our four wonderful new stories.

You've heard of looking for love in the wrong places—but what happens when the "wrong" place turns out to be the right one? In Charlotte Maclay's newest miniseries, two sisters are about to find out...when each one wakes up to find herself CAUGHT WITH A COWBOY! We start off this month with Ella's story, *The Right Cowboy's Bed*.

And hold on to your hats, because you're invited to a whirlwind *Last-Minute Marriage*. With her signature sparkling humor, Karen Toller Whittenburg tells the delightful story of a man who must instantly produce the perfect family he's been writing about.

Everyone loves the sight of a big strong man wrapped around a little child's finger, and we can't wait to introduce you to our two new fathers. Dr. Spencer Jones's life changes forever when he inherits three little girls and opens his heart to love in Emily Dalton's *A Precious Inheritance*. And no one blossoms more beautifully than a woman who's WITH CHILD... as Graham Richards soon discovers after one magical night in *Having the Billionaire's Baby* by Anne Haven, the second story in this extra-special promotion.

At American Romance, we're dedicated to bringing you stories that will warm your heart and brighten your day. Enjoy!

Warm wishes,
Melissa Jeglinski
Associate Senior Editor

Last-Minute Marriage

KAREN TOLLER WHITTENBURG

HARLEQUIN®

TORONTO • NEW YORK • LONDON
AMSTERDAM • PARIS • SYDNEY • HAMBURG
STOCKHOLM • ATHENS • TOKYO • MILAN • MADRID
PRAGUE • WARSAW • BUDAPEST • AUCKLAND

To MJ and Tashya, who encouraged me to get better
acquainted with *Daisy Rose!*

And to Don, who knows a thing or two about life
(and the mule) on *Lazy Daisy Acres!*

ISBN 0-373-16822-5

LAST-MINUTE MARRIAGE

Copyright © 2000 by Karen Toller Crane.

Visit us at www.eHarlequin.com

Printed in U.S.A.

ABOUT THE AUTHOR

Karen Toller Whittenburg is a native Oklahoman and has lived in Tulsa for most of her life. She fell in love with books the moment she learned to read, and began to pursue a writing career in 1981. Taking a writing class convinced her that completing a book wasn't as easy as it sounded, but she persevered and sold her first book in 1983. She divides her nonwriting time between family responsibilities and working part-time as an executive secretary.

Books by Karen Toller Whittenburg

HARLEQUIN AMERICAN ROMANCE

197—SUMMER CHARADE
249—MATCHED SET
294—PEPPERMINT KISSES
356—HAPPY MEDIUM
375—DAY DREAMER
400—A PERFECT PAIR
424—FOR THE FUN OF IT
475—BACHELOR FATHER
528—WEDDING OF HER DREAMS
552—THE PAUPER AND THE PRINCESS
572—NANNY ANGEL
621—MILLION-DOLLAR BRIDE*
630—THE FIFTY-CENT GROOM*
648—TWO-PENNY WEDDING*
698—PLEASE SAY "I DO"
708—THE SANTA SUIT

727—A BACHELOR FALLS
745—IF WISHES WERE…WEDDINGS
772—HOW TO CATCH A COWBOY
822—LAST-MINUTE MARRIAGE

*The Magic Wedding Dress

HARLEQUIN TEMPTATION

403—ONLY YESTERDAY

Daisy Rose Knows...

Hi, Neighbor! You probably don't know me, but I live just down the road at Lazy Daisy Acres. It's a small farm, as farms go, but there's a lot that happens here at our place. We've got the requisite barn, complete with the barnyard glee club. Our smart-aleck rooster can't seem to tell the difference some days between dawn and three o'clock in the morning! 'Course, if he didn't wake us with his proud cock-a-doodle-doodling, I wouldn't get to spend as much time in my gardens and, oh, Friend Neighbor, I do love to garden. Flowers, vegetables, herbs…anything that can add color and definition to my own lovely little plot of earth.

It's just the three of us, here on Lazy Daisy Acres…my sweet Hubby Bee, our daughter Kate (she's six, going on a precocious twenty-two) and me, Daisy Rose. I promise, I'll do my level best to entertain you—and give you some of the tried-and-true tips on gardening, cooking and decorating I've picked up over the years. Maybe you could share with me, too. Write to the editor of your local newspaper, and feel free to ask whatever question comes to mind. We'll learn from each other. In the spirit of sharing our little corner of the world, here's my tip for today:

If you're dying to decorate with brightly colored towels but are afraid the dye will fade out in the wash, try this: Soak the new towels in the washing machine in cold water, using a half cup of salt to half a tub of water. Let them sit in the salt bath for thirty to forty-five minutes, then wash as usual. (No bleach, of course!) This really helps hold the color in. Try it!

Thanks for spending this time with me today! And in the next Daisy Rose Knows…how to make a cookbook holder that's not just pretty, but downright practical, too!

Chapter One

Oh, what a tangled web we weave…when we decide to wage chemical warfare on those pesky red spider mites and their friends! The organic approach may be more trouble initially, but it pays off for me when Hubby Bee and Daughter Kate chow down on my pesticide-free zucchini casserole. (Recipe follows.) Does my heart good to see them eating healthy, fresh vegetables that I grew myself, and I swear the benefits sure do outweigh the extra work.…

"Yo! Boss! Phone call for you!"

Brad Kenneally laid down his pencil, but kept his feet propped on the desk as he reached for the phone. It wasn't much of a stretch. The business end of this newspaper office took up less space than his efficiency apartment, and, Lord knew, there was no room to spare there. Not that his right-hand man seemed to notice the cramped quarters. Lloyd routinely yelled out like a sailor sounding the water depth. Brad occasionally toyed with the idea of buying himself a pair of earplugs, but knew ultimately it'd be pointless. Lloyd would just yell that much more loudly.

"Kenneally," he snapped into the receiver, then remembered to press the flashing red button on the antiquated phone. "Kenneally," he repeated, swiveling away from Lloyd's omnipresent, ever-tuned-in ear.

"Why don't you answer your own phone?" The bass voice was sharp, deep and irritable. As usual. "I must be paying you too much if you can afford a male secretary."

"He works for the sheer joy of reporting small-town gossip. Like me."

"I pay you damn well to report facts and community information, not gossip."

Granite Ames—the owner of an empire that included a string of small, regional newspapers, six of which Brad, as managing editor, car-hopped to and from— had a Cro-Magnon sense of humor. At their first meeting in the Ames publishing Mecca in Houston, Brad had decided there must be a pre-historic throwback in every generation and it was just his luck to be hired by this one. On the other hand, the job suited Brad's disposition and his take-time-to-smell-the-flowers approach to life. He'd lived in the fast lane once and had just escaped with his sanity, so in the big picture, Granite Ames was not such a huge burden to bear. "I was kidding," he said, although he knew it to be an exercise in futility. "Just a little light humor on a Monday morning."

"Hmmph. If I'd wanted to talk to a comedian, I'd have called Lou Costello."

"I'm pretty sure he's got an unlisted number, now."

"You like your job, Kenneally?" Ames didn't wait for an answer, just continued gruffly, "Listen up. I've checked the numbers on circulation twice now. What in hell have you been doing up there?"

Brad didn't need his job, but he did love it. He mentally reviewed the last report he'd seen, reshuffled his own rather pleased reaction and stumbled into an apologetic explanation. "Subscriptions are up six percent, sir, at the *Chicktown Scoop* and four percent over at the *Buckthorn Bugle*. The other papers are showing steady gains, and we're really pushing for a three-percent increase overall by September, when the county fair begins. I'm going to hire another Lifestyles reporter just as soon as—"

"Another reporter!" Ames roared. "What the hell happened to the last one?"

Brad shifted in his chair, crossed one ankle over the other and sighed somewhat wistfully at the thought of blond, bubbly, bouncy Darby Witham. How could he have guessed that beneath her ambitious, career-minded, on-my-way-to-being-a-star, do-not-get-in-my-way facade beat the heart of a domestic goddess wannabe? Who knew she'd be so sensitive to rejection? "Darby quit, sir. Couldn't handle the pace."

"Darby Schmarby. I'm talkin' about the reason your four-state region has increased in circulation by nearly seventeen percent overall in the past three months! I'm talkin' about Daisy Rose Knows! What the hell are you talkin' about?"

Daisy Rose? Brad's feet hit the floor with an unsettling *whump.* "Oh," he said, momentarily unable to think of any other response. "Oh, that."

"That column's the reason you're still on the payroll, Bubb. Now, what I want to know is, when can I meet the woman?"

"D-Darby?" He stalled, knowing the word sounded like just what it was—strangled desperation.

"Does she write the column?"

"Uh…no." Brad unearthed a ragged remnant of cohesive thought. "No. Oh, no, sir. Darby doesn't write the Daisy Rose Knows column. She quit, like I said, and when she was with us, she was strictly the Local Lifestyles reporter. You know, writing up any honorable mentions in the Tri-County Bake-a-Better-Cinnamon-Bun contests and what Thelma Lou Baskin wore when she addressed the Fireman's Auxiliary Luncheon. All the obituaries and birth announcements. Weddings and engagements, too. And the occasional recap of election results."

"Is this Darby person Daisy Rose Knows…or isn't she?"

"No, sir." The collar of Brad's knit pullover suddenly seemed to shrink about twenty sizes. "Daisy Rose is…well, she's just Daisy Rose."

"I want to meet her."

Brad ran his finger under his collar, stretching the material a bit. "That, uh, well, that's just not possible. Sir."

Ames's frustration came right through the phone line to grab Brad by the throat. "Don't tell me you let her quit, too!"

"Uh…."

"Is Daisy Rose still my employee or am I going to have to give her *your* job to get her *back?*"

Brad swallowed hard. "Oh, she works for you, sir. No doubt about that."

"Then I'll look forward to meeting her next Tuesday, ten o'clock, in your office. See to it she's there. Tell her to wear a dress."

A *click.* A moment of dead air. Then the *buzz* of an open line. Brad looked at the phone receiver, noted the scruffy, beat-up surface, and wondered how many editors before him had pounded the damn thing against the desk in sheer exasperation or, as in his case, pure panic. Replacing the receiver in its cradle, he glanced at Lloyd, whose tufts of white hair stood out like flags of surrender all across the top of his pink head, whose grin was knowing and smugly goofy. "Liked the new figures, did he?" Lloyd licked his lips, obviously savoring the irony of the moment. "I told you he'd read the column."

"Yeah. You told me." Brad cupped the back of his neck in his hands and massaged a new knot of tension there. "He's coming here next week to meet her. He wants her to wear a dress."

There was a moment—a fleeting instant of quiet—when he actually thought he might get a bit of sympathy. But then, Lloyd busted out in thick, hearty guffaws of laughter that bounced and splatted around the office like gelatin in a food fight.

Brad picked up his pen and made himself a note. *Buy earplugs.*

He thought about it a minute, then added, ...*and a dress.*

"UNCLE BRAD! Uncle Brad, Uncle Brad!" Laura Kate Martin launched the words and her almost-six-year-old self at Brad in a gust of welcome. "You're here! You're here, you're here!"

He stepped out of his Corvette just in time to catch her in mid-leap and gather her up in his arms like a bundle of sun-dried sheets. For an instant, he wallowed in the innocent pleasures of her fresh, sunny scent, her wiggly, little-girl warmth and her pure delight in his presence. No one had ever adored him so effortlessly or completely, and he knew he couldn't love her more if she were his, instead of his best friend's daughter. She hugged his neck fiercely, then pulled back to rain a series of sloppy kisses across his cheek. "I thought you'd never get here."

"I'm right on time…just like every Sunday." He kissed her button of a nose, loosed his hold, letting her slip, then caught her in an exaggerated grab. "And every Sunday you get heavier and heavier. Why, I can barely hold you, Larky Malarkey."

She giggled, delighted as always with the name games he played with her. She might be just Lark to everyone else, but she was a dozen different nicknames to Brad, her godfather and honorary uncle. "I'm heavy 'cause I'm wearin' all my jewelry, today," she announced proudly.

He drew back to look at the ropes of costume jewelry around her neck and the uneven rows of barrettes and fancy combs adorning every available inch of her thick, curly dark hair. She was a material girl when it came to baubles and beads and was seldom without at least a half-dozen decorative items. Usually, like now, she wore several bejeweled strands looped around her neck and several more double- and triple-twisted about her scrawny little arms. "You'd better not let your mom see this." He pulled a double strand of marble-size, pearlized pop-beads from his shirt pocket. "She's going to want to borrow it, for sure."

Lark snatched the necklace from his hand with a high-pitched shriek of excitement. "Oh, thank you, Uncle Brad. Thank you. Thank you, thank you." She wiggled with glee at her new treasure, and he set her feet on the ground as she slipped the huge faux pearls around her neck and fingered them lovingly. "These are the best present you ever got me."

"That's what you said last Sunday when I brought you a two-headed grasshopper."

"Yes, but he escaped, so this is better." She smiled happily up at him, then slipped her hand into his and started swinging their arms up and back, up and back as they walked across a small, uniformly manicured yard that was duplicated in neat, green squares all through the gated community of condominiums Lark and Zoë Martin called home. "I'm running away," Lark said brightly. "And you can go with me."

"I just got here."

"You can rest for a minute if you want to," she offered.

"It may take more than a minute. It's an hour's drive down from Joplin, you know." He smiled into blue eyes so very much like her father's and felt a familiar pang of loss. Tim had died more than three years ago, but occasionally, like now, Brad experienced the pinch of memory and the sad sweetness of seeing his lost friend in the face of this precious child. He recognized, too, the solid line of determination in her familiar smile, and knew Lark was a lot like her mother, as well. "Where are you running away to this time?" he asked.

Tipping her head to the side, her tresses swinging like a beaded curtain, she considered. "McDonald's."

"Hungry?"

She nodded rather fiercely. "An' I'm gonna get a job there, too."

"You are, huh?"

Again came the determined nod. "I'll give you French fries, too. An' burgers and chicken nuggets and cookies and strawberry milk shakes. As many as you want."

"Wow, that would be a good deal for me. Maybe not so good for McDonald's."

"I'll tell 'em you're my godfather."

"Think that'll impress them, huh?"

"It 'presses me," she said with simple truth and no small amount of winning manipulation. "You could drive me there right now and I could have a Happy Meal and you could have one, too."

"What about your mom?"

Signs of a storm settled on her elfin brow. "It won't be runnin' away if *she* has to go."

He glanced toward the red painted front door that, like the postage stamp lawn, was duplicated around the complex, and wondered, not for the first time, why Zoë had chosen to move from the cozy house she'd shared with Tim in the Tulsa suburbs to this nice but unimaginative condo near the city's center. It wasn't as if she'd have had to keep up with the yard work, or tend to any of the small maintenance details of home ownership herself. Brad would have taken care of all that for her, just as he had while Tim was sick. But two months after the funeral, she'd sold the house, bought this place and moved, with stoic disregard for his opinion. Not that Zoë had ever had much use for his counsel.

Lark, on the other hand, believed him infinitely wise. Stooping, he rested his arms on his thighs so he could be eye to eye with her little-girl logic. "If we don't invite her, she'll get all upset, and you know how much she scares me when she's mad."

Lark's smile arrived as quickly as any pout. "You're not scared of her," she said firmly. "You're not scared of nothing 'cause you're a—" she threw back her head and made the Tim Allen ape sound ''—HE-Man! Aren't you, Uncle Brad?''

He smiled, too. ''Yeah, Larka Lou, I am. Let's go in and beard the lioness in her den.''

''She's in her bedroom,'' Lark informed him studiously. ''And she doesn't have a beard 'cause she's a *girl* and girls don't have hair on their faces.''

''You should meet my Grandma Tildie.''

''You're too old to have a grandma.''

''That'll come as a shock to Grandma Tildie. She thinks I'm still a young whippersnapper.''

Lark laughed, and the sound of her amusement was soft and pleasurable to his ears...a sound he could never be too old to enjoy. Straightening, he grabbed her hand and led her up the two short steps to the porch—if a square of concrete and matching square of roof qualified as a real porch, which it didn't in Brad's book. ''All right,'' he said. ''Let's go in and ask your mom if she's old enough to run away with us.''

''She's old 'nough, but she won't go.'' Lark stuck out her tongue and made a disgusted face. ''She's got a *date*.''

A date? Brad made a face, too. ''Is that anything like a fig?''

With a thoughtful tilt of her head, Lark studied the question, then said, ''I can't know,'' which was her catch-all version of *I don't know* and *I can't remember.* ''He could be a fig, but I think it's just Noodle Roni from her office.''

Newton Rooney. Brad knew that name and the pompous bag of self-importance that went with it. He could not for the life of him figure out what Zoë saw in the guy. Lark was not quite six, and she already had the man pegged as a piece of elbow macaroni. "Is that why you're running away?"

Lark nodded firmly. "He's taking us out to dinner."

"You and your mom?"

The storm on her brow darkened ominously. "She says I have to be on my best manners and I can only wear one necklace and one hair barrette and I can't take extra ones in my pockets and I can't talk when the adults are talking and I can't order a burger 'cause it's not that kind of rest'rant, and I have to sit still until everybody's through eatin' and say 'please' and 'thank you' and not ask twenty questions and that's why I'm runnin' away."

Sounded like ample reason to Brad. "Now that I'm here, maybe you can stay with me."

She brightened for a second, then gloomed over again. "She won't let me. She wants me to like him and be friends with him. But I don't like him and I'm not gonna like him and I wish Mom didn't like him, too."

"Maybe she just likes going out to dinner."

"Why couldn't she just like going out to dinner with you?"

It was an innocent enough question, but Brad didn't have a good answer. The truth was, he'd never thought Zoë liked him all that much, whether they'd been sitting at the same table or on either side of Tim's bed during a bad night. She was nice, laughed at his jokes—well, most of the time, anyway—and seemed genuinely appreciative of his long friendship with Tim. If her welcome wasn't always enthusiastic, it was at least always warm. But on a personal level? She kept her distance. "I say, we march in there and tell her you'd rather stay with me and ask her if she minds if you do."

It was a long shot, but Lark latched on to it. "Okay. You go in and ask her. But if she says no, then we're runnin' away to McDonald's."

He contemplated the all-or-nothing nature of that ultimatum and its probable outcome. "Well, what if she says *be-bop a re-bop a bip-bam-boom?*"

His nonsense startled a giggle right out of the child. "She won't say that, Uncle Brad."

"She might. Let's go ask her."

But Lark balked at the door. "You go. I'll wait in your car."

Now there was a vote of confidence. "Come on. Go in with me. I need the moral support."

She shook her head vigorously and wrinkled her nose in distaste even as she lowered her voice to a confiding whisper. "She smells like a French horse."

Whoa, Nellie. "Where did you hear that expression?"

"From Sonchie. He told me that when his mom comes home from getting her hair curled and her fingernails painted, Mr. Wilcox always sniffs like this—" She demonstrated by taking an exaggerated whiff of the air. "Then he pats her on the behind and says, 'Whew, baby, you smell like a French horse!' And that's just the way mom smells right now."

Hmm. Brad spared a glance at the red-painted door across the street, where the infamous Sonchie Wilcox lived. Sonchie. Brad had yet to figure out if that was a nickname, a simple mispronunciation on Lark's part, or the new trend in boys' names, but he knew for a fact that eight-year-old Sonchie picked up some not-so-proper phrases from Mr. Sonchie, Sr., and passed them on to Lark, who soaked them up like an adoring little sponge. Another reason, in Brad's humble opinion, that this neighborhood wasn't the best place for his godchild to be growing up.

"Probably best not to repeat that in front of your mother," he advised.

"I already did," Lark admitted with a long-suffering sigh. "She said she'd wash my mouth out with soap if she hadn't already used it all up gettin' ready for her date."

"A narrow escape for you, Splarky. Must be your lucky day."

"She wasn't really gonna put soap in my mouth. She just said that 'cause she wanted me to go outside and not bug her anymore about Noodle Roni. But maybe if you pat her on the behind and tell her she smells like a French horse, she won't want to go on the date anymore, and you and me can go to McDonald's and she can stay home and we can bring her back a v'nilla milk shake. Don't you think *that's* a good plan, Uncle Brad?"

Yeah, right. They'd never find his body if he did something as stupid as patting Zoë on the butt. Not that he hadn't privately and on occasion admired her slim little derriere—being Tim's friend hadn't rendered him unconscious, for Pete's sake. But he couldn't think of a suitable way to explain to Lark why her plan wasn't entirely a good one. "Listen, kiddo, no matter what your pal, Sonchie, tells you, it's never a good idea for a man to tell a woman she smells like a horse. Especially not if he's about to ask her for a special favor."

Lark's Cleopatra hairdo made a *clink-clunk* sound as she tilted her head to look up at him with a disconcerting degree of curiosity. "What special favor?"

No way was he going to confide his vague plan to have Zoë impersonate Daisy Rose for Granite Ames's visit. No way was he trusting a six-year-old to keep that stray information under her barrettes. No way was he even going to ask for Zoë's help. It was just a thought, a passing impulse, nothing he was actually going to act upon. Unless, of course, the perfect opportunity simply fell into his lap. "I'm gonna ask her to let you go to McDonald's with me while she goes on her date. Don't you think that's a pretty special favor?"

Lark narrowed her eyes, either unconvinced or skeptical of any chance for success. Then she selected a gaudy strand of green and pink crystals from the collection around her neck, carefully took it off, and solemnly handed it over to him. "You'd better wear my lucky necklace when you ask her. She's not in a very good mood."

Brad didn't really think green and pink beads went that well with his shirt, but he'd have worn a dozen more necklaces just like it if Lark asked him to. Partly because he would do anything in the world for her, but mostly because, when it came to dealing with her mother, he could use all the luck he could get. For some reason, Zoë had always had the effect of turning him into either a tongue-tied adolescent or a testosterone-empowered geek. Whichever way it went today, he should probably borrow a lucky barrette or two from Lark and clip them in his hair to go along with the necklace. But even a real "HE-man" had to draw the line somewhere.

LEANING CLOSER to the mirror, Zoë debated the merits of the two shades of lipstick. Sageplum Sugar, on the left, was a soft, barely there mauve, while Fairydust Berry, on the right, had heavier traces of pure pink. Turning her head, she examined first one color, then the other, from a sideways angle. Newton would like the Sageplum Sugar, she felt certain. He paid her numerous compliments whenever she chose muted shades, whether the colors were worn as clothing or makeup. The Fairydust Berry was iffy, with its hint of sparkle, but she honestly liked it better and thought it gave her ordinary face, with its dusting of ordinary freckles, a little pizzazz. As if it were possible for a layer of lip gloss to bestow anything other than a slight lift of the spirits that wore off long before the main course was served.

Sighing, she reached for a tissue to wipe off the Fairydust Berry…and her heart leaped to her throat in startled alarm when she caught, via peripheral vision, a glimpse of colorful plaid shirt in the doorway behind her. An involuntary scream made a pitiful attempt to spring from her vocal cords and came out, instead, as a strangled "Aack."

Brad's eyes met hers in the mirror, instantly and simultaneously apologetic and amused. "Sorry, Zoë," he said as he leaned a broad shoulder against the door frame. "It's Sunday."

Aptly put, she thought, trying not to notice just how casually attractive he looked in the mirror. Since Tim's diagnosis nearly five years before, there had yet to be a Sunday without Brad Kenneally. If it was morning, the sun came up. If it was Sunday, Brad appeared. His visits were as much comfort as intrusion, as much solace as annoyance, as much looked forward to as dreaded. She knew he came, each and every Sunday, rain or shine, because he'd promised Tim that he would. She knew—because she'd tried—that no amount of protests on her part would change his macho resolve to fulfill that promise. She knew he was a hard-headed, tenderhearted, underachieving, muscle-flexing, chest-thumping, super-studly, stubborn-as-a-mule, gentle giant of a chauvinist—and that there was no way she could ever repay him for the simple gift of his presence, whether she needed it or not.

"You might have knocked," she said, turning back to the mirror and rubbing away the swatch of Fairydust Berry.

"I said hello as I came up the stairs. Guess you were busy getting ready for your date and didn't hear me." He watched as she swabbed off the lipstick, his steady regard unnerving her to the point that the tissue in her hand disintegrated into a wad of pink lint. His presence always unsettled her, somehow kept her on edge…alert and aware of him in ways she'd never been able to define. "Aren't you supposed to put lipstick *on* instead of trying to rub it off?"

He had an irritating way of making her feel foolish, too. "I couldn't decide on the color." She decisively picked up the closest tube and bent forward to finish applying…*oops*…Fairydust Berry.

"Good choice." Brad lounged comfortably and confidently in the doorway of her bathroom. "Gives you a little extra pizzazz."

She'd have scrubbed it off right then, but explaining why would have taken more energy than she currently had. Dating—and the whole process of getting ready for a date—made her anxious. Lark had worn her to a frazzle with her questions, complaints and bargaining, and now, here was Brad to finish the job. "Thanks," she said tightly. "I live for your good opinion."

"And I am happy to give it," he replied, undaunted. Then—aggravating man—he sniffed the air like a bloodhound on the trail.

Zoë sighed. "Don't even start with the French horse comments," she warned him, wishing he might have ignored the obvious and just told her she smelled nice. Not that she wanted his compliments, or needed them, but once in a while, it would be lovely to think he noticed she was a woman, and not just Tim's widow and Lark's mother.

"I wasn't going to say a word."

That was half the trouble with Brad. He didn't have to say a word for her to know what he was most likely thinking. She could tell by the devious twinkle in his eyes pretty much exactly what was on his mind. And right now that was the strong scent of bath oils and cologne surrounding her. "I spilled some bath oil," she said. "Get over it."

"You smell very nice," he said in that most-gentlemanly manner that drove her crazy. "And I would never, ever compare you to a horse, no matter what its nationality."

"I don't know where my daughter picks up that kind of language, and I certainly don't know why she feels she has to share it with everyone."

"I'm not *everyone*, Zoë. And she picks it up from the kid across the street, although I'm thinking her rather skewed interpretations are all her own. You should keep her away from him."

"The Wilcoxes seem like a very nice family."

"When Lark is forty and living with a jerk who pats her on the butt and pays her seedy compliments every time she gets her nails polished and her hair curled, don't say I didn't warn you."

There seemed no point in dignifying that ambiguous remark with an answer. So she checked her hair in the mirror—still reasonably in place, all tucked and twisted on top of her head—and turned around. The room seemed to shrink in proportion to his overly tall, muscled body, and Zoë felt a wisp of longing she couldn't name. It was probably caused by his overbearing presence. He just walked into her bedroom as if he belonged there. Annoying male. She did fervently wish he wasn't always so comfortable in her house. She'd thought when she moved here that he'd become more like a guest, but instead the house seemed foreign to her whenever he was in it. As if she didn't belong there any more than he did, which was just plain ridiculous.

His gaze slipped to her toes, came back to her Fairy-dust-Berried lips, then met her eyes, and she went all fidgety inside, like a good little girl on the verge of giving in to temptation. "Is that what you're wearing?" he asked. "On your date, I mean."

She looked down. The pants suit was a classic. Dark brown, good lines. Casual, but not indifferent. Dressy, but not self-conscious. With a cream-colored silk blouse and the pearls Tim had given her on their first anniversary, the suit made the most of her average height and too-slender form. The fabric was a little heavy, maybe, for this late in the spring, but she always got a trifle cold in air-conditioned restaurants. Newton didn't seem to mind sitting under the vent, and she thought it would be a little petty on her part to ask to move to a different table. And she could always take off the jacket on the chance that they'd be seated somewhere other than his favorite spot. But now, here was Brad, making her worry that she looked like somebody's frumpy grandmother. She drew her gaze from the outfit to question him with a trace of attitude. "What's wrong with this?"

"Nothing," he said quickly. Very quickly. "It's a great look for you. Really."

His smile was endearing, aggravating and sexy, and altogether so appealing that it sent a little jolt of awareness spiraling down her spine. For a moment, she could understand why women lined up for a chance with the guy. Of course, he wasn't—and to her knowledge, never had been—interested in a permanent relationship. Avoiding commitment had been his major in college, and since then, he'd stayed true to that aim. Brad was a smooth operator—all smooth talk, smooth actions and smooth getaways. In all the time she'd known him—which was considerable when she added it up— he hadn't gone out with the same woman more than a half-dozen times. A great person to offer advice as to what she—a person who sincerely believed in marriage and a lifetime commitment—should wear when going out on a date with a very nice man.

"I was just thinking how great you look in a dress," he continued. "Noodle Roni would probably really like seeing you in one."

Zoë narrowed her eyes. "I wear dresses to work almost every day of the week, Brad. *Newton* has plenty of opportunities to see how I look in one. And please, *please* stop encouraging Lark to call him anything other than Mr. Rooney. It's no wonder she doesn't listen to me, when you're coaching her from the sidelines to misbehave."

"I have never encouraged Lark to call anyone Noodle. It's against my religion."

"Well, you certainly don't discourage her."

Brad shrugged. "I've got to call 'em like I see 'em. And I think you ought to wear a dress."

"If Tim were here, he'd punch you in the nose for saying that."

"If Tim were here, he'd agree with me."

Brad's grin softened in reminiscence. And, of course, he was right. Tim would have advised her to wear a dress. A softly flowing dress that had more float than fit, more simplicity than style, not like the slim-skirted, very tailored professional appearance outfits she wore to the Rooney-Gaines Real Estate offices almost every day of the week. But now that Brad had brought up what she ought to wear, she had no choice but to wear exactly what she had on—even though she was suddenly certain that it made her look like somebody's frumpy grandmother.

"If Tim were here—" she brushed past him, momentarily coming into his space, feeling the heat of his body contact the heat in hers...and dismissing the quickening *trip-trip* rhythm of her heart as irritation that he hadn't the good sense to move out of her way "—you and I wouldn't be having this conversation."

Brad made a smooth turn and wound up lounging against the opposite side of the doorway, arms crossed over his muscle-bound wall of a chest, lazily watching her pace about the bedroom. "You seem a little nervous, Zoë. You're not expecting old Newton to pop the question tonight, are you?"

"No," she said abruptly, because the mention of marriage and Newton together made her unaccountably anxious. All the more so because Brad had mentioned it. "No," she repeated more firmly. "And even if I were, it wouldn't be any of your business, now would it?"

"Since when has that ever stopped me from asking?" he countered. "And I do think I ought to have some input into a momentous decision like marriage. I am, after all, Lark's godfather."

"Tim never intended for you to take on the role of guardian angel."

"No, that's his job. Mine is to try to keep you and Lark safe from bad situations, whether that's a leaky roof or a lousy idea. Which, by the way, dating your boss definitely is."

"You just don't like Newton."

"There's that, too." He came out of the doorway to shrink even that good-size room with his presence. She retreated, for no good reason that she could ascertain other than that it seemed safer to keep her distance. "Come on, Zoë. You can't really *like* the man. He lives with his mother, for Pete's sake!"

"That's temporary, just until she recovers from her hip surgery."

He gave her a look she knew very well. A look that said, *Wise up, Zoë, you're smarter than that.*

She didn't know when, exactly, Brad had gotten so comfortable in her life that he felt he could and should say whatever he wanted whenever he thought of it. She didn't know how she'd come to let him take on the man-of-the-house role. She did, however, know why. When Tim had gotten sick, there hadn't been anyone else she could turn to. Brad had proven himself a harbor during those long and awful days. He'd been the only shelter she could find, the only completely dependable anchor in the storm that suddenly became her whole existence. And day by day, one little "Let me help" at a time, he'd become the only father Tim's daughter could remember.

But Tim had been gone a long time now, and despite her believing life wouldn't go on for her, it had. Presenting her with a *fait accompli* she couldn't keep ignoring. "Brad, you know I appreciate all you've done for us. I really do. And I don't want to offend you. But you're not my father, my brother or my guardian, and whom I date—or even marry—is none of your business."

He took the declaration of independence in without a blink. It didn't even seem to register. Certainly, it didn't faze him. "But you're not going to marry Newton."

It *sounded* like a question, but she heard it as he'd meant it—as a statement of fact. "He hasn't asked me. When and if he does, and when and if I say yes, I'll let you know." Brad frowned, and she could feel an I'm-only-trying-to-protect-you-and-Lark lecture coming on, so she moved to divert it. "Look Brad, I know you promised Tim you wouldn't let me marry some jerk, but give me a little credit. I know what a good marriage is. I had one with Tim. I'm not going to risk Lark's happiness and future—or my own—with someone I don't truly love. Okay?"

"But you will talk to me first before you go and do it."

Again, the sound of a question with the underlying tone of injunction. "I'm perfectly capable of making my own decisions, you know. With or without your input."

"I'm a guy, Zoë. I know how guys think. And basically, what we think about is sex and what we have to say and do to get it. Newton is too unoriginal to do anything *except* propose, if that's the only way he can get you into bed."

"Not every man is as...uncomplicated as you, Brad."

He grinned, completely unaffected by the verbal jab. "Sure they are, but for some reason, you women want to think there's a hidden reservoir of meaning in our actions." He shrugged. "But that doesn't change the fact that we guys are mostly motivated by the sex drive."

"You're such a philosopher." There was more to him, she was sure—well, pretty sure—but he always took great pains to keep her believing he was a shallow, insensitive, my-way-or-the-highway-type male. She'd come to the conclusion a long time ago that Brad just didn't know how to handle a male-female relationship based on anything other than the purely physical. Which was a shame, considering the fact that she thought he might have made a very good friend if he hadn't been so fixated on protecting her as if she were a hothouse rose. "And what makes you think I haven't already had sex with Newton?"

He ticked off the reasons on his fingertips. "You're nervous. You're dressed like a missionary...except for the lipstick. Your voice is pitched in the Minnie Mouse range, and you're wearing your pearls."

"That's ridiculous," she said, touching the necklace and taking care to moderate her voice. "None of that has anything to do with whether I have or haven't had sex with Newton."

"Sure it does. And for the record, I don't think Lark ought to have to chaperone you on dates."

"'Chaperone'?" The pitch went up again and she consciously brought it down. "You think I need my daughter to chaperone me? Please."

"Why else would you make her go along?"

Argument was on the tip of her tongue when she belatedly recalled that *she* was Lark's parent, that godfathers didn't get a vote, and that she didn't need to defend herself, as she always seemed to do with Brad. "Because I want her to go. I want you to go, too. Home. Or downstairs. Or wherever you want that isn't my bedroom. You're so pushy, Brad, you make me crazy. I'd give anything to have you visit us just once—just one time—without my having to defend something I've either done or want to do."

He looked surprised, or possibly startled. Then a barely discernable tinge of red crept up his neck, and he seemed to consider what she'd said. Which surprised her. "Am I that bad?" he asked, then quickly added, "You'd do *anything?*"

"Anything," she answered just as fast, then corrected. "Within reason, of course."

"Of course." His deep brown eyes lit up beneath a newly furrowed brow. "Would you let Lark stay here with me while you go on your date?"

For no good reason, she was disappointed. Of course, he'd ask a favor involving Lark. It wasn't as if Zoë thought *she* was of any interest to Brad. Not that she wanted to be. Not even close. She'd like to be of *less* interest to him, if possible. "I'll think about it," she said. "I'm not sure you could keep from pestering me with your opinions for five minutes, much less a few hours on Sunday."

"You know I'm a man of my word."

True. Witness his often misguided means of keeping his promise to Tim. "And if I let Lark stay here with you tonight instead of making her go with me, you'll give me one Sunday without an opinion?"

A crooked grin tipped the corners of his mouth.

"You know and I know you were going to let her stay with me anyway, so that doesn't seem like an even trade. I...uh, do have a favor in mind, though. A *small* favor that could net you a whole month of congenial Sundays, if you're willing to—"

"A whole month?" Her eyebrows went up. She couldn't help it. "What would I have to do?"

He hesitated. "Well, it would involve wearing a dress."

The fidgety sensation increased to a serious flutter and her heartbeat unaccountably picked up speed. "I am not going on a date with you, so don't even ask."

"A date?" He couldn't have sounded more stunned if she'd suggested a suicide mission. "With you? And me? *Together?*"

She gave him the full force of a good frown. He didn't have to make it sound so completely out of the question. "Okay, so that's a little over the top. But you have been standing here fussing at me for not wearing a dress on my date tonight when normally you wouldn't care if I went out in a bathrobe. It was a natural assumption."

"I would definitely care if you wore a bathrobe for your date with Newton," he said.

Zoë wanted to change into her natty old robe right then, just to spite him, except that she'd just have to change back into the pant suit before Newton arrived, which would, basically, defeat the whole purpose. "So what exactly is this small favor?"

He rubbed the lucky necklace Lark had obviously insisted he put around his neck—her daughter was always looking out for the underdog—and gave a half-embarrassed shrug. "It's a long story...which you don't have time for now, and probably wouldn't really find all that interesting, anyway."

"But you will explain thoroughly later."

His expression turned a wee bit obstinate. "Well, sure. If you're interested, that is."

Oh, she was interested all right. "What exactly will I have to *do* while wearing a dress?"

"Smile. Nod. Say as little as possible. Just agree with me."

"And...?"

"Wear a dress. I swear, Zoë. That's all there is to it. Ten, fifteen minutes in my office next Tuesday morning. And afterward, I'll buy you lunch."

"I'd have to take the day off to come to Joplin."

"It would mean a lot to me, if you would."

Curiouser and curiouser. He never asked for help. Ever. It was an unwritten law of tough guys or something. "This isn't anything illegal, is it?"

"Of course not," he said, brushing off any concern. "It's just a little, uh, reception for...a newspaper columnist, that's all. Nothing fancy."

"A reception?" she repeated. "So I'd be there as your—for lack of a better term—date?"

He looked uneasy. "Something like that."

She hadn't had much experience with shady real estate deals, but she could spot an overeager seller from the get-go, and she knew there was more to this deal than he wanted to tell. "Look, Brad, I'm not sure this is such a good—"

A long blast from a car horn cut her off in mid-refusal, and he grabbed the easy way out. "Newton's here," he said. "I told you the guy has no class."

"Newton would never just pull up and honk his car

horn. He comes to the door and rings the doorbell. Like a gentleman.''

Brad looked unimpressed as he moved toward the bedroom door. "If it isn't your date, it must be mine. She gets pretty impatient when it comes to her Happy Meals."

She didn't want him to get away that easily. "Lark has no business being in that macho machine you call a car, you know. It could slip into gear. There could be an accident. You should keep it locked."

"You know, you're right. I'd better get down there before she drives off with that young Wilcox boy you think is so 'nice'." Brad walked smoothly through the doorway and out of argument range. "Have fun on your date—if that's possible—and don't worry about Lark. I'll make sure she has a well-balanced meal, with lettuce and tomato on her burger, and a milk shake." His words floated back to her from the stairs as he went down. "Oh, and don't stay out too late. I've got to be on the road for home by ten."

The front door opened and closed with a *thud,* leaving Zoë—who'd never actually *said* Lark could stay with him instead of going with her—frustrated, and curious and no longer looking forward to her evening with Newton. Leave it to Brad to make her formerly anticipated date seem as appealing as an overripe banana. Leave it to Brad to get her all stirred up and then dangle some carrot to keep her wondering long after he was gone. Leave it to Brad to make her wish she could stay home and hear the whole story—interesting or not—as to why he needed this little favor from her.

A favor that sounded, bottom line, like a date—no matter what he chose to call it. Brad, who could slant a long look at a woman and make her yearn for him, needed a date for a small reception on a Tuesday morning and thought Zoë wouldn't find the reason *all that interesting*. Well, she was interested, all right. She probably wouldn't be able to think about anything else the rest of the evening, no matter how charming Newton tried to be. Just the idea of a "date" with Brad made her shiver with excitement.

No, that was wrong. It wasn't, couldn't be excitement. Had to be something else...something to do with being so curious she could hardly stand the thought of having to wait several hours to hear the whole explanation. Taking her Sleeping Beauty watch from the jewelry box, she clasped it around her left wrist and smiled at the idea that, whatever the "long story" turned out to be, it made Brad uncomfortable.

And Zoë was one hundred percent in support of that.

Chapter Two

Chickenheart never won first prize at the county fair, so get out the pruning shears and snip, snip, snip those rosebushes! (See Helpful Hints for successful pruning, below.) Hubby Bee is ruthless when it comes to thinning the foliage (although it takes serious supervision on my part to ensure the survival of our plants, let me tell you!) But when he shyly presents me with a bouquet of Angel Face roses straight from our own garden, my heart spills over with love for nature's gifts…and, of course, for my dear, dear, so-very-sensitive husband. Oh, Friend Neighbor, I am blessed to have an impetuous pruner as my soul mate.…

The soft blue dress was made of cool cotton and sprigged with tiny white flowers. The style was loose and lilting, its folds draping around Zoë like a cloud. It was the dress she'd worn the night Tim proposed. It was what she'd been wearing when the doctor confirmed she was pregnant with Lark. It was the outfit she'd worn home from the hospital after giving birth and the one she'd worn for seven straight days after

Tim's memorial service because choosing to change into anything else seemed, somehow, so final. It was a dress with memories, bittersweet and tender, a dress that made her feel young again, resilient and hopeful...and she should never, ever have banished it to the back of her closet for three long years.

She didn't know why it had caught her eye this morning or why it suddenly seemed the perfect dress to wear to a reception for a small-town newspaper columnist, but without giving the idea so much as a moment's consideration, she'd pulled it out of the dry cleaner's plastic wrap, given it a quick pressing and put it on.

It had felt right when she'd looked in the mirror, too...a soft foggy float of a dress that heightened the contrast of dark hair against rosy skin and made her feel feminine and feisty. Even Lark, who hardly ever paid attention to anyone's appearance but her own, told Zoë she looked good. Of course, that could have had more to do with the necklace—a thirty-inch rope of faux pearls—she'd lent her mother for the occasion. Lark never missed an opportunity to accessorize and, although Zoë usually had to decline similar offers, this morning she'd dropped the necklace over her head with a smile of appreciation, and no small surprise when she discovered she liked the result.

But now, too far down the road to turn around, too close to Brad's office to reconsider, she was having second thoughts. Everyone else would be dressed for business, or at least wearing something more professional than frilly. She'd be out of place. A wallflower in what was essentially a house dress. Why had she agreed to take a day away from her own office to drive all the way to Joplin for a fifteen-minute reception and lunch with Brad, which would probably consist of a packaged sandwich from a convenience store and a bottled juice, if she was lucky? Brad didn't get in a hurry about most things, but he wasn't particularly inclined to enjoy a leisurely lunch at a real restaurant, either. At least, not with her. He probably suffered through civilized meals only if he was convinced it was the only way to get a woman into bed with him. Honestly, the man was such a Neanderthal at times. Sexy as a steamy shower, true. But still more male than Zoë felt comfortable thinking about. She should never have agreed to do him this small favor. But how could she have refused?

"I'm having fun," Lark announced from the back seat, where she was surrounded by costume jewelry, several stuffed animals and enough coloring book activities to occupy her attention for about a thousand miles. "I wish you took a v'cation every day."

Guilt arrived in a landslide. Here Zoë had been wishing she were safely at work, begrudging Brad this solitary day and her daughter these few hours away from the dull sameness of her normal day-care routine, when she ought to be focused on how to make the most of these golden hours with Lark. Brad, too. For all his shortcomings, he'd been Tim's best friend and a true friend to her. Fifteen minutes of smiling, nodding and agreeing with what he said, wasn't much to give in return. "I'm glad you're enjoying the trip," she said to Lark. "I'm having fun, too."

Her daughter smiled at her in the rearview mirror, and as easily as that, Zoë stopped fretting about the dress.

BRAD PACED THE SIDEWALK in front of a plate-glass window on which large, black letters boldly proclaimed the office inside as an Ames Publications Affiliate. It would have been nice if the lettering were a little less obtrusive. Slightly smaller than a business card would have worked. People in passing cars didn't need to know the office was here. He knew. Lloyd knew. The Post Office must know, because a short, round man in a blue uniform delivered their mail Monday through Saturday with all the *joi de vivre* of a toothache. Who else really needed to find this place, anyway? Delivery was handled separately by each of the newspapers. Printing was done at a central, regional location. Brad oversaw office and editorial operations from here for each of the six papers, and Lloyd took care of sales and most other activities associated with advertising. Other than that, not much went on at this location.

Granite Ames, certainly, hadn't seen any reason to drop in before now, although he made harassing phone calls on a regular basis and sent a regional supervisor to rattle cages every few months. If those incriminating black letters on the glass weren't so glaringly obvious, it was possible the boss man could drive right past today and miss the place entirely. If not for the mile-high lettering, even Zoë, who had been here before, could easily sail right past the office and never, ever have to know what an idiot Tim's best friend had turned out to be.

Keeping an eye on the traffic, Brad paced some more and thought about one of Lark's favorite bedtime stories. When it came to courage, the Little Billy Goat Gruff had nothing on him this morning. He was weak-in-the-knees, scared-to-his-marrow panicked and would have thrown Big Billy Goat Gruff to the mean old troll without a second's hesitation. Which was, maybe, what he was about to do to Zoë. Luring her here with a murky story, not telling her much of anything, playing the trump card of friendship. He shouldn't have asked her to come, should have given Granite Ames the truth skewered with a sense of humor, should never have conceived the idea of an anonymous columnist in the first place. But all of it had been self-preservation, pure and simple—with, perhaps, a faint trace of reprisal tossed in for one-upmanship.

Oh, who was he kidding? When Darby had flung her challenge at him, had said he couldn't write his way out of a paper bag, had the editorial skills of a myopic garden snake *and* wouldn't know a good human-interest story from his—well, from a part of his anatomy he felt she had absolutely no reason to belittle— he couldn't help but take up the gauntlet. He'd never misled her about their relationship and he certainly hadn't wanted her to quit her job. But quit she had, jerking her column at the last minute and leaving him with white space to fill and about ten minutes' lead time to fill it. He'd meant for it to be a one-shot deal, to prove his point and give Darby a cleverly disguised comeuppance. He'd never expected readers to *like* the column and ask to see more of it. He hadn't expected to get real fan mail after only one appearance of the Daisy Rose Knows byline. He certainly had never thought he'd feel a genuine responsibility to and affection for the people who took the time to write a chatty note—or a newsy three-page letter—to the fictitious Daisy Rose. That hadn't been his plan at all. Bottom line, this whole fiasco could be laid at Darby's door.

Except, of course, for the fact that he was responsible for being the numbskull who wrote the dang column himself just to prove that he did know a thing or two about all the things she'd accused him of *not* knowing. Not that anyone would ever *know* he knew, since he'd taken some pretty long steps to ensure that Miss Daisy Rose's true identity was never revealed. *Dumb*, he thought. *Dumb, dumb, dumb*.

He looked up the street again and then down, wondering why there couldn't have been a traffic jam on Tuesday mornings instead of Friday nights when the college and high school kids rode Main Street like a restless ribbon. No such luck. Only a few cars slid past the newspaper office on their way downtown. Maybe it wasn't too late to thumb a ride and get the hell out of Joplin...before he had to explain to Zoë that he'd sort of, almost unintentionally, modeled Daisy Rose after her. Not as she was now, but more as she'd been when Tim first introduced them—shy, reserved, all big eyes and megawatt smile, timid but tough, with a smoky laugh that was contagious and irresistible.

Oh, yeah. He'd love to be on the other side of the world about now...before she arrived and he had to admit he knew somewhat more about certain subjects than he'd ever wanted anyone—especially her—to know he knew. Before he had to confess that he'd talked her into making the trip this morning in the hope of passing her off to his boss as the author of Daisy Rose Knows.

An evil-looking sedan turned the corner, and the faint hope of a reprieve was whisked away, replaced by a sinking feeling that life as he'd come to enjoy it was over. Resolutely, he squared his shoulders. Granite Ames had arrived and any hope of getting out of this meeting gracefully vanished as the limo pulled to the curb in front of him. "Kenneally!" Then Ames was on the sidewalk almost before the car stopped rolling, giving Brad a succinct handshake and heading into the office. "How the hell are you? Is she inside?"

"Not yet, sir." Which was, technically, the truth on both counts.

"She's late, is she? Typical female." He winked as he reached for the door handle with a beefy hand. "Can't expect a woman to watch the clock when she's getting all gussied up for us, can we, Bubb?"

"Zoë is usually right on time," he said in defense of all women, gussied or not.

Ames nodded knowingly. "Just naturally pretty, is she? Good. I don't like too much makeup. Makes a woman look cheap." He paused, frowned, didn't open the door. "Now, I hope she's not on the chubby side. Not that I, personally, find a few extra pounds objectionable. But the camera can really plump up a female, you know."

"Zoë's not plump," Brad said indignantly, intending to add that it'd be perfectly okay with him if she were. "Camera?" he repeated instead. "What camera?" His glance flew to the sedan's opaque windows, checking for a tagalong photographer who might still be inside with the driver. "She's not going to like having her picture taken. She's very shy, sir. I had a hard enough time just persuading her to come today. Photos aren't really necessary…are they, sir?"

Ames's frown deepened, his face folding into bulldog wrinkles. "You're awful jumpy, Kenneally. What's wrong with the gal? Buck teeth? Flat bosom? Freckles?"

"No…well, she does have freckles." He could have bitten his tongue for admitting that, as if it were some kind of flaw, when, in fact, he'd always found Zoë's spattering of freckles completely charming and not just a little bit sexy. "But only a couple of them. Half a dozen at most."

"No problem. We can airbrush out a few freckles. Just so long as she's not peppered with specks."

His boss was a throwback. No doubt about it. And it was up to Brad to set him straight. At least, in this instance. "Zoë is attractive, sir. She has nothing that needs 'covering up.'" Perhaps that was a tad *too* inclusive. "Well, except the normal body parts."

"Ah…not much of a figure, huh?" Ames considered that for less than half a second. "Well, we can work with figure flaws…unless it's a big butt. Now, that could be a problem."

Brad was offended on behalf of Zoë, Daisy Rose and their gender in general. "There's nothing to work with, sir."

"No butt at all, huh? Well, don't worry about it. We can pad her out."

"Zoë looks fine just the way she is," he said, feeling indignant and out of sorts. "Just fine."

"Then what are you so worried about? I've dealt with my share of shy country girls. Trust me, I know how to handle our little Daisy Rose, and I'll do it with velvet gloves…providing she gets here before I have to vamoose, that is." With a hearty—and a particularly unsettling—chuckle, he pulled open the door. "I'll be inside, making some phone calls," he said. "You keep watch and let me know the minute she arrives."

Then he stepped inside the office, letting the door close behind him, leaving Brad as he'd been, only now with the assigned duty of keeping an eye out for Zoë and about ten times as much to worry about as before. There was nothing to do but pace…and entertain the urge to march into that office and inform Granite Ames that Daisy Rose was, in fact, six feet four inches tall, weighed a whopping two hundred and forty pounds, and had buns like a linebacker. That would cinch her fate, but good. Unfortunately, it would seal his, too, and while he knew he could find another job, he didn't like the idea of disappointing the Daisy Rose Knows readers. And they *were* out there, those fans. He had the letters to prove it. Plus, he genuinely enjoyed writing the column.

"Uncle Brad! Uncle Brad!" Lark yelled and waved out the window of a moving Toyota half a block away. "Hi, Uncle Brad!"

He could see Zoë motioning to her daughter to sit down as the back window rolled up, then down, then up again in a silent tug-of-war. Although he figured this was his last, best chance to rush over and shoo them away with some quickly improvised tale of the Black Plague or an invasion from outer space, Brad felt better just knowing his girls had arrived. Wait a minute. *His girls?* Okay, so that was a slip of the brainwaves. Zoë was his best friend's widow and Lark was—signed, sealed and baptized—his goddaughter, but neither one of them belonged to him. Nor did he want them to. Responsibility wasn't exactly his forte. Witness the disaster currently in the making.

He waved as the Toyota zipped into a parking space, then looked both ways before crossing the street to meet them. Zoë stepped out of the car and walked around to the other side to release Lark from all the safety gadgets. As his brain registered that first wispy glimpse of her, all of Brad's hastily composed explanations for this impending meeting slammed into oblivion. *Holy Hamlet, what is she wearing?*

And what had she done to her hair? And lipstick?

Was she wearing that luscious, kissable shade of pink pizzazz again? Ames would trip over his chauvinistic feet in lecherous delight at first sight of her. Even Brad's normally plodding pulse rate zigzagged as if he were jumping hurdles, instead of merely walking. He had to suck in a couple of deep breaths just to keep moving forward. It felt strange to be looking at Zoë and thinking she was so damnably beautiful. Not that he hadn't noticed in the past, of course, but suddenly it was so obvious, so unavoidable, so...conspicuous. He couldn't decide if what he was feeling was more akin to astonishment, or fascination.

Today of all days, he'd been counting on her to wear one of those crisp little business suits she favored. Skirt to the calves, back slit just to the knees, tailored jacket, lapel pin, no-nonsense clunky heels—a true poster girl for equal rights for women. It had never once occurred to him that she might wear a softly feminine dress or pull her hair loosely back at her nape and tie it with a simple blue ribbon. It had never entered his mind that she might arrive looking fresh as a daisy, shyly appealing and so wholesomely pretty that it took his breath away. It was something of a shock to his system to discover she could look so innocently seductive, too. This wasn't good. The absolute last complication he needed was for her to show up looking like...well, a whole lot like he'd pictured Daisy Rose!

"Uncle Brad! Uncle Brad!" Lark burst from the back seat, flew around the back of the Toyota and flung her small self into his arms, heedless of any traffic and of her mother's exasperated, "Lark! For heaven's sake, be careful!"

Brad caught the child, gave her a quick hug and repositioned her in the cradle of his left arm as he stepped onto the sidewalk and shifted his attention back to Zoë. "You didn't have to dress up," he blurted out because his tongue felt thick and his thoughts went haywire the moment she walked toward him. The sway of the dress about her ankles drew his gaze up to the sway of the dress about her hips and directed him to the sway of the pearls between her breasts—and the smile on her mauved lips swayed what otherwise would have been a normal hello into an awkward greeting. "You should have worn something else. Something not so…pretty."

She sighed at his clumsy compliment, and he wanted to take it all back and begin again. "You said wear a dress, Brad, and this *is* a dress."

Boy, was it ever. "I, uh, was thinking more of one of those starchy outfits you wear to work, not a seductive little number like that."

She glanced down at the dress, then curiously back at him. "You think this is *seductive?*" A gurgle of laughter bubbled past her lips. "And here I was thinking I'd be mistaken for your country bumpkin of a cousin."

Tact, belatedly, kicked in. "You look terrific, Zoë. Really. Very pretty. You just surprised me, that's all."

"Thanks…I think. It isn't as if you've never seen me in this dress before. It's just been…a while."

"Must have been a *long* while." Even at that, she couldn't have looked this good in it before. He would have remembered. Definitely. "Because you look great today. Different, I mean. You look *different.*"

"She's wearing my pearls." Lark tapped him on the ear to claim his attention. "And I'm wearing my ruby necklace, Uncle Brad. Don't I look pretty, too?"

He pulled back to take in the little-girl frills that,

even at not-quite-six, she had perfected to an art. Zoë swore—and Brad believed her—that she bought color-matched outfits and that, somehow, Lark managed to take the pants from one and the top from another, accessorize the whole ensemble, and wind up with a fashion statement all her own. Today she had on an orange flowered top over green-striped capri pants, topped off with sparkly yellow sandals and, around her ponytail, a slew of colorful ribbons. Madonna should have looked so good when she was six.

"You, young lady, are more bea-u-ti-ful than a lady-bug on her way to Sunday School." He exaggerated the syllables, glad to be focused on something other than Zoë's unexpectedly sexy and unsettling appearance. "More beautiful than a rainbow over Niagara Falls, more beautiful than an oyster on the half-shell, more beautiful than a monkey in the zoo, more beautiful than a—"

"Uncle Brad!" Lark giggled. "You're silly. Monkeys aren't beautiful."

"They are, too…to another monkey."

"But I'm *not* a monkey."

He blinked in fake surprise, then pretended to check behind her ear. "Well, excuse me. You're right. Your name tag clearly says that you're not a monkey, you're a radish."

Her innocent laugh made him smile for the first time since Sunday. "I'm not a radish," she corrected him. "I'm a *girl!*"

"So you are…and a very pretty girl, too."

"Prettier than mom, even?"

"Well, that'd be a close call, but you're prettier than me, for sure."

"You can't be pretty, Uncle Brad. You're

han'some.'' Lark squeezed his neck and gave him a smack of a kiss on the cheek.

''Thank you,'' Brad said, giving her cheek a kiss in return. ''Thank you, very much.''

Zoë slipped the woven strap of a summer purse across her shoulder and gave Brad a questioning look. ''Now that I'm here, could you please tell me what this is all about?''

Ah, truth. He could run from it, but he couldn't hide. Although, it was still worth a shot. ''Didn't I already explain all that?''

''You know good and well you haven't explained one bit of it, other than the fact that there's a small reception in your office. But I've been in your office and it's not big enough for five people and a plate of cookies, much less a bowl of punch.''

Brad's mood dipped back into a respectful panic. ''Well, perhaps *reception* wasn't quite the right word— it's really just a meeting. A very short meeting. You'll really be helping me out.''

Zoë wasn't thrown off the scent. ''This sounds suspicious to me, Brad,'' she said.

He lifted his shoulder in a persuasive shrug. ''Sounds like fun to me.''

''I like fun,'' Lark pointed out. ''And cookies.''

''See?'' he said to Zoë. ''Lark knows the ingredients for a party.''

''Look, I'm here to help because you asked me to, but it would be easier to help if you'd just give me a reason as to why I'm supposed to smile, nod and agree with you.''

''That's easy. I'm a man, and men like agreeable women.''

''That does not answer my question.''

He glanced across the street, wondering if there was a chance in hell this dumb scheme could work, debating whether he'd rather die of humiliation or get hit by a Mack truck. No contest. Unfortunately, there wasn't a Mack in sight. "It's sort of a long story."

"So you've said." Zoë crossed her arms. "Come on, Brad. Out with it. The whole story. *Before* we go in there."

He shifted Lark's weight, a stalling tactic that didn't alter the determination in Zoë's expression one iota. "The whole story, huh? I did mention it's not all that interesting, didn't I?" If anything, she looked as if she were ready to reach in and yank out the truth along with his tonsils. Brad sighed, accepting that there was no way he could come out of this with a shred of dignity. "Okay. Here goes. I haven't told you any of this before because I thought—well, that doesn't matter. It's just that there's this column in all six of my newspapers, and, well, the truth is...." He stopped to clear his throat. "The truth is, you see...my boss is—"

"—right behind you." Ames's booming bass thundered out like a blast from a bazooka. "And I must say, I am mighty tired of waiting on you to introduce me to this little lady." His hand reached out to close over Zoë's, and Brad knew the jig was up. In a matter of minutes, his career as a newspaperman would be over, his macho persona exposed as a fraud. He could all but hear the collective gasp of disappointment from the community of Daisy Rose Knows readers. Humiliation loomed and it was his own damn fault. His and nobody else's.

"I'm Granite Ames, Ames Publishing, and you must be—"

"Zoë," Brad interjected quickly. "This is Zoë, sir."

"I *know* who she is, Kenneally," Ames said, his voice slick as polished cotton, his admiring gaze entirely focused on the woman at the other end of his hand. "I cannot tell you, *Zoë,* what a great pleasure it is to find out you're every bit as breathtaking as I'd imagined you'd be. Not like this numbskull described you at all."

Zoë's blue eyes flashed momentarily to Brad's, conveying about a zillion questions, but her smile was easy and gracious. "What a lovely thing to say. I'm afraid, though, that I'm a bit at a disadvantage. Much to my chagrin, he has neglected to tell me anything at all about you."

"Warn you, you mean." Ames held her hand as if it were a juicy pomegranate and he were king of the fruit flies. "No, no. Don't defend him. I know Kenneally brought you here under false pretenses. Not that I approve of his devious methods—that's just the way he thinks. Backward little guy that he is."

"I hardly think that's a fair description," Zoë said, and Brad silently applauded her for defending him, at least until she added, "There's nothing *little* about him."

Ames laughed and continued to hold her hand. "You're right on that one. He played professional football for a year, did you know that? Bunged up his knee, though, and had to quit. Cost the team a shot at the Superbowl. Isn't that right, Kenneally?"

It hadn't been quite like that, but Ames preferred his version of the facts, and Brad had long since given up trying to correct him. "That's right, sir."

"As I remember," Zoë said, "the team lost its shot at that year's Superbowl about six games into the season. I'm not sure even Superman could have saved the day.''

Ames arched his caterpillar eyebrows, obviously charmed to the cockles of his wicked heart by Zoë's killer smile. Brad didn't know why she was wasting it on the old lecher.

Oh, that's right. He'd asked her to.

''Well, well,'' the publishing prince continued. ''So you know a little about sports trivia. And here, Kenneally had me thinking you were an awkward, shy little lumpkin.''

Zoë's gaze flicked to Brad again, a few of the questions in her eyes giving way to an outright frown. ''He's been talking about me?''

''Sure has. Said you had freckles and not much of a figure.'' Ames gave his head a sad shake. ''What'd I tell you? Backward as a barn door, as our Daisy Rose would say,'' he continued, with a broad wink. ''The man's been spending too much time looking at Barbie dolls to appreciate the genuine article.''

Zoë frowned at Brad. ''You told him I had freckles?''

It was a sensitive area for her, Brad knew. She didn't try to cover up the freckles, but she'd never really liked having them, either. ''He was afraid you might have specks,'' he began, only to be cut off by Ames again.

''Boys don't respect girls who have specks, and gentlemen never make passes at lasses in glasses.'' Ames's laugh was broad and hearty. ''Now, how in hell—excuse my French—did a babe like you hook up with Kenneally? Bad karma?''

Zoë raised her eyebrows at Brad, then, with a slight shrug, she nodded and offered the old goat another hint of a smile. "We met in college," she said. "I was dating his roommate."

"Ah-ha. The plot thickens." Ames nudged Brad with a hefty elbow, and got caught by Lark's forthright stare. "Well, well, well. Who is this? Is it…? Could it be…Daughter Kate?"

Lark's beribboned head shook from side to side, and her clinch on Brad's neck tightened just a trace. "I'm Lark," she said. "Who are you? The mean, old troll?"

All right, kiddo! Brad thought.

"Lark!" Zoë scolded. "That wasn't nice. Apologize, please, to Mr. Ames."

"Sorry," Lark responded obediently, then added, "But you do kind of look like him."

Ames puffed his cheeks and his chest and laughed robustly. "Oh, I think you're a lot like Daughter Kate, all right." He gave her a wink. "And I may look like a mean, old troll, but I could turn out to be your fairy godfather."

"Uncle Brad is my godfather, and he's real good at it, too."

"*Uncle* Brad?" Granite Ames shifted his attention from Lark to Zoë to Brad. "You mean *this* fella?"

Lark nodded and hugged Brad fiercely. "He's the best uncle in hell—excuse my French."

Ames roared with laughter. Zoë flushed crimson with embarrassment. Brad fell in love with his godchild all over again. But the moment passed and Ames turned his bulldog frown on Brad.

"Let me get this straight," he said. "You're related to Zoë and Lark?"

"I'm sort of an, um, honorary uncle." Brad didn't like the calculating look in his boss's eyes. It made him uneasy, and certain that disaster was standing in his shadow right there on the sidewalk. "Maybe we could get out of this sun, go inside the office and, uh, have a cookie before we all, uh, break out in freckles."

"I want a cookie," Lark said. "A marshmallow cookie."

Ames shook his head like a dog with a dinosaur bone. His gaze moved back to Zoë with new interest, and he gave her hand a last, deal-sealing shake. "Now, isn't this a cozy little bird nest, as someone we all know and love would say?"

Brad swallowed, hoping he'd headed off calamity for the immediate future. "Cookies," he said jovially. "Let's go in and have some cookies."

Ames glanced at his watch, let his gaze make another calculating pass over the three faces, then let loose with a broad and mysterious smile. "Wish I could stay, but I've got to be on my way sooner rather than later. It was a delight to meet you, Miss Lark. And you, *Zoë*. I have a feeling we're going to be seeing each other again real soon. All of us. You included, *Uncle* Brad." With a conspiratorial wink, Ames finally released Zoë's hand and raised his arm in a sweeping motion, which immediately brought the limo angling across the street as if it owned the right-of-way. "I'll be reading your column with new interest," he said to Zoë as the back door opened from within and he slid inside. "Keep up the good work, Daisy Rose. And Kenneally, you'll be hearing from me."

"Guess he doesn't like cookies," Lark said as the black sedan pulled away from the curb.

"He's just in a hurry." Brad repositioned Lark onto his shoulders, where she perched like a queen overseeing her kingdom, her fingers curled tightly into his hair. "Men like him are always in a hurry." Brad looked

up the street and down, as if he were an animal testing
the wind before stepping onto open ground. In reality,
he was just trying to get across that street before Zoë
started asking questions. "Mr. Ames is a very busy
man. He owns lots and lots of newspapers. And he
lives in Houston, Texas, and he just doesn't appreciate
the finer things in life...like marshmallow cookies and
pretty girls and—"

"Sounded to me like he appreciates the value of a
quick getaway." Zoë stepped up beside him, her gaze
following his up the empty street. "I can't believe you
were talking to him about my freckles."

"It wasn't the way he made it sound at all."

"That's good to know, because he made it *sound*
like he reads *my* newspaper column. You wouldn't
think a man in his position would make that kind of
mistake."

Brad forced a laugh. "I've always said too much
responsibility can cause a man to say the dumbest
things." He started across the street and had to step
back as the only car in sight in either direction came
out of the blue to honk at him. "Oops," he said, making Lark giggle at his sudden and exaggerated moves.
"Almost got us squished like bananas. Squashed like
peas. Strained like carrots. Squeezed like a tube of
toothpaste."

"Mashed like potatoes." Lark wiggled, leaning forward to clasp her hands over his eyes. "Don't worry,
Uncle Brad. I can see just fine. Go straight. No turn."
She giggled. "Not that way, silly. Look." The blind-
fold of hands flapped open, closed over his eyes again,
and he felt the warmth of Zoë's hand as she took his
arm and guided him unobtrusively, safely forward. If
only she could lead him out of the mess he'd made of

Daisy Rose's career. "Do you really have marshmallow cookies, Uncle Brad? 'Cause I'm hungry."

"Well, I don't know about the cookies, but there's a package of chocolate doughnuts in my desk drawer."

"Are they crumbed up?" Lark was particular about her doughnuts.

"There's got to be one whole one in the bunch. And I know there's at least one root beer left in the pop machine, for sure. It's yours, Malarkey, for the measly sum of a great big hug."

"It's a little too close to lunchtime for doughnuts and root beer," Zoë said, as they reached the office door. Her hand slipped away and his arm felt, somehow, lonely again. "And you are taking us out to lunch, remember?"

"Oh, lunch," he said, wondering what maggot of poor planning had led him to make that offer. "Of course, I remember."

"McDonald's?" Lark bounced on his shoulders. "Can we go to McDonald's?"

"No," Zoë answered firmly. "Uncle Brad is taking us to a quiet little restaurant where we can talk."

Off the top of his head, Brad could think of about a dozen more appealing options. "I have the perfect place already in mind," he said, thinking of the noisiest, nastiest greasy spoon in town. "And you, my little radish, can order a cheeseburger, French fries, and talk with your mouth full." He pulled open the office door and offered Zoë a big smile as she strolled past him. But she stopped in the doorway and gave him The Look. The kind of singeing zinger of a look that told a man he was in trouble before the first word was spoken.

"I think I'm going to order the Daisy Rose special," she said sweetly.

Against all odds, he kept his smile in place. "Well, okay, Zo. But trust me, you'd be better off with the cheeseburger."

A stray wind lifted the blue ribbon at her nape and fluttered it in his face like a silky challenge. "Don't tell me," she said with a coy little tilt of her head. "Let me guess…you're going to have the crow platter."

"Look out, Uncle Brad!"

The interruption was heaven-sent, and he ducked low so Lark wouldn't bump her head on the door frame, then followed Zoë into the office where only Lloyd and a package of chocolate doughnuts awaited them.

Thank goodness for small blessings, he thought. For a moment there, he'd almost blurted out that he was planning to order chicken.

Chapter Three

Don't be afraid to embellish that ho-hum bedroom with passionate color. Forget everything
you've read about how *not* to decorate this very
important room in your home, go right ahead and
indulge your romantic nature. Choose fabric that
is sensual and exciting. Paint the walls and ceil-
ing with pleasing texture. Surround yourself (and
that special someone else) with stimulating hues
and touches of whimsy. Don't worry about going
overboard on the femininity—if ever there was a
room that begged for a woman's touch, this is the
one. My own, dear Hubby Bee paled the first time
he saw the Dragon Lilies bedspread, but since
then, Friend Neighbor, (and I blush to see this in
print!) he's grown *extraordinarily* fond of our
bedroom....

Lark propped her chin on one hand and kept the other
hand clenched around her hamburger. She didn't know
why grown-ups had to talk so much. Or why kids
couldn't talk, too. She had plenty of 'portant stuff to
say, but every time she tried to say it, Mom said it
wasn't her turn to talk. And she wanted it to be her

turn. She wanted to tell Uncle Brad that Lloyd hadn't put money in the pop machine. He'd pushed something and hit something else and *pop!* out came the soda. Lark didn't think that was right. You were s'sposed to put money in first. But she did like the root beer, except she didn't know if it was okay about the money. She wished Uncle Brad would quit talking so she could ask him. She wished Mom would stop being mad at him, too, even though it wasn't the mad kind of mad, like the time they found the puppy and he thought she should get to keep it and Mom said, *"No, absolutely, positively N-O, no!"* and they both got real mad and didn't speak for ten hundred minutes, until Sonchie came and said it was his friend's puppy and then no one was mad anymore. But Lark had felt real sad that it couldn't be her puppy, and she'd sorta thought Uncle Brad felt sad, too.

This time wasn't like that time. It was more of a happy mad, like Mom wanted to laugh, but couldn't. And Uncle Brad kept trying to esplain why Mr. Ames wasn't a mean, old troll, even though he sorta was, too. Lark could have told them he wasn't a bad man—not like Dudley Doom on the *Kid Force Avengers* television show, who was evil to his rotten core. Mr. Ames wasn't bad like that. But he had called Uncle Brad a numbskull, and Lark didn't think that was very nice at all.

The hamburger tried to slip off its bun, and she squeezed it harder, causing ketchup to dribble over her ruby necklace and down the front of her shirt. "Mom...." She drew the word out, like she had a mouthful of rocks. But Mom said, "Just a minute, Lark," and kept on listening to Uncle Brad, who kept on esplaining to Mom even as he dipped the corner of a napkin into his water glass and wiped the ketchup from the ruby beads. "Mom...." Lark tried again, bored with her hamburger and lunch in general, and in need of some attention. "When's it gonna be my turn to talk?"

"Do you have something you want to say, Larkaburger?" Uncle Brad asked, polishing the sparkle back into her necklace before proceeding to dab away the blob of ketchup on her shirt.

That was the thing Lark loved about her godfather. He understood jewelry was important, and he listened to her. Or maybe he just didn't want to keep answering Mom's questions anymore. Lark didn't care, as long as she got to talk. "My French fries are too salty," she said, as an opener. "And I need lots more ketchup."

"Well, that's because you're trying to wear the ketchup instead of eat it." Uncle Brad winked at her. "You gotta remember—we eat ketchup and we finger-paint with mustard."

She giggled, because he was so silly and funny and because he was talking just to her. "I like to paint with pickles!"

He made a dumb face. "Pickles? Did you say pickles?" Snatching one off her plate, he popped it into his mouth and chewed it up. After he swallowed, he made a sour face. "Whee, that's a dill pickle! Anything you paint with one of those is going to be very wrinkly."

"Can me and Uncle Brad fingerpaint when we get home, Mom?" Lark bit into her hamburger again, not caring when more ketchup splattered onto her shirt. "*Please,* Mom?"

"Maybe." Mom, as usual, meant *Probably not.* "And Uncle Brad isn't going home with us, Lark. He has to stay here and work."

She hadn't thought about that and suddenly wasn't having much fun again. "I wish we could all have v'cation at the very same time," she said with a big sigh. "Wouldn't that be good, Uncle Brad? You and me and Mom on v'cation at the same time?"

"My idea of heaven," he said, giving her mouth a fast wipe-off. "And I'm always available for finger-painting when it involves sour pickles."

Lark laughed, wishing with all her might that Uncle Brad could live with her. And Mom. But mostly, her. Then Mom could go out with Noodle Roni every night if she wanted to, and Lark could play with Uncle Brad. But even fairy godfathers didn't get to live in the same house. "Sonchie said godfathers are Muffin Men and they shoot people."

Her mother looked up from her salad.

"I think you mean Mafia, not muffin." Uncle Brad repositioned the burger on her bun and smushed it together to seal in the ketchup before putting it back into her hand. "And real godfathers don't shoot people unless they're using a camera." He looked across the table at Zoë. "You see? Just like I've been trying to tell you for the past three years. *Not* a good neighborhood."

Mom put down her fork. "She could have picked that little gem up anywhere."

"Anywhere Sonchie is, sure. He's a *H-O-O-D-L-U-M* in the making."

Lark wasn't about to let him get away with that. "Sonchie isn't either a *H-O-A-B-C*. He's an *L-M-N-O-P* and I like him."

"That's what I said." Uncle Brad snatched another pickle from her plate. "You like Sonchie and you listen to everything he says."

Lark nodded, somewhat appeased. "He's a very smart boy."

Uncle Brad looked across at Mom and ate the pickle in one crunchy bite. "My point, exactly," he said.

"He's an eight-year-old boy," Mom said. "And you probably see Mafi—*Muffin Men*—behind every tinted window."

"Ames could be Mafia, you know," Uncle Brad said. "He has the limousine for it."

Mom rolled her eyes, and Lark knew what that meant. It wasn't going to be her turn to talk again, for a long time. "Oh, right," Mom said to Uncle Brad. "He's probably driving all over Joplin at this very moment, shooting people with infrared film so he can blackmail them if they don't renew their newspaper subscriptions."

"You could be on to something there," Uncle Brad said. "Are you sure you haven't been talking to that *H-O-A-B-C* kid, too?"

"All I'm saying is that it's not really fair for you to be upset with your boss when *you're* the one who set up that meeting and then couldn't get your columnist to agree to show."

"I told you, she's really, *really* shy."

"You could have told Mr. Ames that and saved me a trip to Joplin. You also should have told *me* what you had in mind before you just threw me out there to sink or swim without so much as the bare minimum of information. Not smart, Brad. Not smart at all."

Uncle Brad looked at his chicken sandwich, and Lark knew he was about to tell another fib. He'd been telling a bunch of fibs ever since they got to the restaurant. She could always tell…and she'd have said so, too, if it was her turn to talk. But it wasn't. It was still

Uncle Brad's turn. "I was only trying to save my...uh, columnist...some embarrassment, that's all. And I did tell Ames she's shy. Or I tried to, at any rate. You must have noticed that his conversation tends to be a little one-sided."

"Maybe so, but for someone who was trying to pull the wool over his boss's eyes, you weren't very articulate. Except, of course, when you were telling him about my freckles."

"Look, that wasn't my fault. He thought you'd be speckled with freckles and I was just trying to set him straight."

"You try to pass me off as this Daisy Rose person, but you think it's important to set him straight about my freckles?" Mom shook her head. "Has the truth any appeal for you at all?"

"Of course, it does, Zoë. Sometimes, though, feelings matter more. Daisy Rose doesn't have anybody except me to stand up for her, and I'm not going to feel bad because I tried to give her a little protection."

"The world would be a nicer place if you'd stop trying to protect every female who crosses your path, and give us a little credit for being able to run our own lives."

Uncle Brad opened his mouth to argue, but Lark, who had done enough listening, reached up and tugged on his sleeve. "Can I talk now?" she whispered. "'Cause I really, really hafta go to the bathroom."

He scooted back his chair and hers in a hurry, no questions asked. "Come on, Peanut. I'll escort you there and back."

Lark happily hopped off, godfather in hand, pleased that, at least for the whole trip across the restaurant and back, it would be *her* turn to talk.

"AMES PUBLISHING," Brad rasped into the phone receiver at 8:00 a.m. on the dot, the following morning. "Kenneally, here."

"How come you never told me you had a first name?"

He winced at the energetic bass tone and reached for his coffee mug. No way, no how was he answering any questions until he'd had that first, vital sip of caffeine.

"Whatsa matter?" Ames, of course, was never in the mood to wait for an answer. "Cat got your tongue, Brad-with-a-B, my boy? Or were you out partying with our little Zoë Rose until the wee, small hours?"

"Ah." The coffee was good. Luckily. Since the morning was already on its way downhill. "No, sir. I have not been out partying with or without Daisy Rose. What about you...sir?"

"Ha." Ames laughed. Or maybe it was just his way of making conversation. "I liked her, B.K. You picked yourself a winning ticket with that little gal."

B.K.? Brad took another fortifying swallow from his cup. "Thank you, sir." *I think.* "I like her, too."

"Well, I should hope so." Again the laugh—and the accompanying anxiety. "What's not to like, heh? And you were worried about her looks. Hell, I'd like to know who you consider a *real* babe, that's for sure. She's pretty, Kenneally. Even with the freckles and the skinny rear. If anything, she could use a little fattening up. Course, the camera will add a few pounds, so no need to worry overmuch about that. We might want to see if she'd blond-up her hair...or dye it red. Now, there's an idea. I like that better. Blondes may seem more wholesome, but redheads add spice to life, you know. So send her to a hair salon and tell them to— nope, never mind. I'll send somebody from here.

Somebody who'll know exactly the shade of red I want. She won't mind, now, will she, son?'' Ames paused, but Brad couldn't get a word of protest out before he moved on. "Well, even if she does mind, I know her sweet, sensitive *Hubby Bee* will be able to convince her, won't he?''

Sheesh and Shinola. There wasn't enough coffee in Joplin to save him today. "Uh, sir. You have this all wrong, sir. I'm not Hubby Bee. I'm not, uh, anyone's hubby. Never been married. Never plan on getting married…sir.''

Ames guffawed at that one. "You may fool some of the people some of the time, son, but don't think you can fool me. You looked at her like she was paradise with a V-8 engine. I'm on to you, hotshot. You've been hiding Zoë's light under a bushel 'cause you want to keep her all to yourself. But I'm here to tell you, I'm going to uncover her for the world to see. She's going to be big, Kenneally. Bigger than Martha Stewart. Bigger than the Galloping Gourmet. Bigger than Elvis. She's a gold mine, Bubb, and her first official duty is to show the crew from *Home and Hearth Magazine* around the farm. By the way, *is* there a Lazy Daisy Acres?''

"No. No, sir, there isn't. And there's no—''

"Well, you've got three weeks to find one and get her on it. Three weeks. Got it, B.K.?''

Oh, yeah. Got it. Just like a migraine. "Mr. Ames. Sir. I have to tell you…Zoë isn't…. I'm not—''

"Come on, boy, quit stammering around, trying to convince me you're not that sweet, sensitive Hubby Bee she's always writing about. I may be short, but I'm not stupid. And you may not be married to the gal, but it's plain as a loaf of Wonder Bread that it's only a matter of time until you are.'' Ames's voice growled with good humor. "Have I ever told you you're as backward as a barn door? If she's *writing* about you, it means she *wants* you! Don't you know anything at all about women? No, of course you don't. You jocks never do. But don't worry, you'll have plenty of time to show her what a 'sweet, sensitive' hubby you'll make during those two weeks on the farm. Three weeks to get situated. Two weeks to show your stuff. Got it, kiddo?''

Desperate times called for desperate measures. "Sir,'' he said in hoarse and hurried desperation. "Zoë isn't Daisy Rose, sir!''

There was an infinitesimal hesitation before Ames's laughter echoed like thunder through the phone line. "Now, that's a good one,'' he said. "Do you think I just fell off the fertilizer truck, Kenneally? Of course she's Daisy Rose. Who else could write that column. *You?*'' He laughed as if that was the funniest joke he'd ever heard.

"But, sir, I'm telling the truth. *I'm*—''

Ames broke in forcefully. "The magazine crew will arrive at Lazy Daisy Acres two weeks from Saturday. I expect you to be wearin' your overalls and a straw hat when they arrive.''

Brad clenched the phone receiver. "You said three weeks. That's only—'' he tried to count the days through his panic "—nineteen days.''

"That's only eighteen days, Einstein. Today's already half over with, so you'd better get a move-on, now, hadn't you?''

And with a *click,* the line—and life as Brad Knew It—went dead.

HE'D QUIT. RESIGN. Clean out his desk. Move to New Zealand and raise kangaroos. Or was that Australia? Couldn't be harder than working for a lunatic like Granite Ames. Had to be easier. And he could too write the Daisy Rose Knows column. Just look at how popular it had become. Practically an overnight sensation. Why, right now, in front of him was a stack of fan mail any writer would be proud to claim. He read the letters daily. He also cut out every mention of Daisy Rose Knows in the Letters to the Editor section, and they made an impressive file all their own. People asked him for recipes and advice. Of course, they didn't know they were asking *him*, former linebacker and self-proclaimed macho man. They thought they were asking a nice lady with a romantic husband and a precocious child, who lived on a lovely little farm somewhere in their neighborhood. But the fact remained…readers loved Daisy Rose. Disappointing them would be the worst part of this rotten deal.

Brad folded another paper airplane and sent it soaring toward Lloyd's vacant and messy desk. What a disaster. The situation, not the desk, although Lloyd could do with some organizational tips. Brad didn't keep his own desk all that neat, but at least he had a workable system. For all the good it did him, now that Daisy Rose had sprung full-blown and fetching from his imagination and stirred up all this trouble.

Another plane nosedived to the floor, and he ruled out a new career in aviation. Truth was, he wanted to keep the career he had. Not that his position was imbued with fame and glory. Or even much of a salary, for that matter. But it gave him the chance to write, gave him a connection with people he might never meet face to face, gave him the freedom to enjoy the life he'd chosen…and that was worth more than all the rest. *Remember yesterday, Dream tomorrow, Live like crazy today.* That was his motto. Time was the one thing Tim hadn't had, the one thing no friend could give up for him, the one thing he'd taught Brad never to take for granted.

Letting his feet drop from the desktop to the floor, Brad looked at the round disk of a clock on the wall over the door, and wondered if there was any point in trying to get Ames on the phone again. He'd already left half a dozen messages and received nothing more satisfying than a secretary saying she'd certainly pass along the information. Odds were better than even, Ames wouldn't even bother to call back. He'd given his orders and he had every expectation they'd be followed. That's what Muffin Men did. Trolls, too, probably. And, at least in this office, there wasn't a Big Billy Goat Gruff ready to challenge him, either. Other than typing up his resignation, Brad didn't see anything he could accomplish by staying in the office. He might as well go for a drive, see if he could get the Corvette's speedometer out of its sixty-six mile per hour slump.

It was fate, pure and simple, that the road took a detour, and he took a wrong turn and wound up two hours later in front of that For Sale sign. Certainly, he hadn't had a thought—well, okay, maybe a vague sort of yen, but definitely, no more than that—of chancing upon a way out of his dilemma. But there it was. Like manna from heaven. Like finding an unopened carton of milk in the fridge and a whole package of Oreo cookies at the end of a long day. Like seeing the taco stand nearly hidden between the health food store and a ritzy Italian restaurant. A farm. "Forty acres," the handwritten information continued. "Farm house, outbuildings, some furniture, good laying hens and a mule.''

No phone number. No real estate agency or agent listed. Brad looked across the overgrown field at the green roof of what he guessed would be the farmhouse. Hard to tell from here. Did they just expect people to drive in and take a look around? An interesting approach to selling a piece of property. He wasn't exactly sure where he was. North of Joplin, and east, most likely, probably still in Missouri, although he could have wandered across any of the nearby state lines and wound up in Oklahoma or Arkansas, or even Kansas for all he knew. He'd just been driving, alternately writing up the next column in his head and then editing it into a pithy letter of resignation, imagining the Daisy Rose Knows fans taking to the streets—well, the back roads, anyhow—and rioting when their favorite column up and disappeared. But suddenly, out of nowhere... another option. Maybe not a good one. Maybe not even a plausible one. But what harm could it do to drive in, see the place, find out if a real, working farm looked the way he'd always imagined it would? Taking a look around wasn't even in the same ballpark as making an offer. No, sir.

CASPAR RENFROE OPENED the back door of the farmhouse and stuck his head into the kitchen. ''Put your apron on, Mother. There's a live one comin' down the driveway.''

His wife, Alphie, kept right on kneading the bread dough. ''What's he drivin'? Pickup truck or car?''

''Corvette,'' Caspar said. ''A yellor one.''

She stopped working the bread. ''A *Chevrolet* Corvette?''

"Yep."

"New or old?"

"New enough...and it's a convertible."

With a smile, she dusted off her hands. "I'll get my lace apron and light the gingerbread-scented candles."

Caspar withdrew, letting the screen door shut with a squeaky creak. City folks loved a creaky hinge, he'd discovered. Same thing with a whiny floor plank and a bit of scuffing on the porch rail paint. A little dressing down in the right places made them think the place was quaint, 'stead of jest old. With a weathered hand, he slicked back the remaining strands of his wiry gray hair, slapped on his straw hat and went out to meet the prospective buyer. After seventy-odd years, he'd learned there was just no accounting for taste.

KELLEN, THE ELDER of Brad's twin kid brothers, picked up the telephone on the first ring. "Yo," he said. "Give it to me."

"Yo, yourself," Brad answered, grinning. The twins had been born when he was fourteen, an intense, fairly well-adjusted only child, just old enough to be completely embarrassed by his mother's pregnancy, still young enough to be totally captivated once the babies arrived. If he'd had any idea how much fun being a big brother would be, he'd have campaigned for siblings a long time before. "Guess Mom and Dad aren't home, or you wouldn't be answering the phone, trying to sound like some macho stud."

"Brad! Hey, man, I am a macho stud. There's no *trying* to it."

"So who are you impressing this week? Allison or Amy?"

"Who? Oh, Chris and I haven't dated them since

basketball season.'' Kellen's confidence rippled through his voice. ''You're about fifty girls behind the eight ball, dude.''

''*Fifty?* What's that? Inflation?''

Kel laughed. ''Ah, don't get your jockey strap in a twist. Even together, Chris and I haven't come close to beating your old record. Your name is still considered Holy Grail in the girls' bathroom.''

''My high school exploits were greatly exaggerated.''

''Yeah, right. Quit trying to sound modest. I know you're the man.''

His brothers looked up to him, Brad knew. Trouble was, they looked up to him for all the wrong reasons. They admired him because of all his athletic achievements, his supposed prowess with women, not for who he was.

In the background, Brad could hear Chris, Kel's younger brother by all of seven minutes, thundering down the stairs, hollering at the top of his lungs, ''If that's Sarah, I'll have to call her back!''

''Tell that yahoo to slow down and not to slam the door.'' The door slammed all those hundreds of miles away, and Brad was newly aware of the energy levels of teenage boys.

''Too late,'' Kellen said. ''Baseball practice.''

''You're not going?''

''Tennis tournament finals. Coach said I could skip ball practice as long as I win the tennis match.''

''Mom's a honey of a coach, huh?''

''Yeah, if she wasn't my baseball coach this year, I'd probably have had to choose between baseball and tennis. Man, I don't think I could do that.''

In the Kenneally family, sports wasn't so much an

activity as a grand passion. Larry and Jonna Kenneally had met at the University of Texas, where both were on full-ride athletic scholarships. It had been an Oklahoma-Texas football game and a common mania for competition that brought them together, but it was definitely a fierce devotion to all things athletic that had kept them together for so many years. Brad couldn't recall a time when he wasn't competing in one sport or another. He'd played football, basketball, baseball, and soccer. He'd run track, been on the swim team, the golf team, and had lettered in high school so many times in so many different arenas that he'd been awarded two letter jackets instead of only one—an accomplishment that was nothing short of a legend, the way his parents bragged about it. Athletic prowess, they understood and admired. Education, too, was stressed, as even football scholarships required the maintenance of a decent grade-point average. One way or another.

Brad had figured out early—probably before he could walk—that the way to win his parents' affection was to make them proud of his physical abilities. He had innate talent, sure, but he'd excelled because he was born to parents who didn't acknowledge weakness, much less failure. He'd excelled because he didn't know he had an option. It hadn't been a bad way to grow up—being a jock had its advantages, especially when it came to getting girls—but he would have traded all the glory for one long summer without the discipline or responsibility of competing. However, that idea was as foreign to his parents as the possibility that any one of their boys might have other interests: gardening, perhaps, or cooking. Meals were always simple—protein, carbs and calcium. Nothing fancy.

The Kenneallys were building strong bodies, not eclectic tastes. It wasn't that they wouldn't have let Brad cook or garden or even study ballet, for that matter, if he'd asked. It was simply that anything not connected to sports was of no interest to them, and they just naturally assumed it was of no interest to their sons, as well.

In thirty years, Brad hadn't found the words to tell them otherwise, and now the twins were following in his footsteps and proud of it.

"Dad around?" Brad asked.

"Nope. He drove over to Lubbock to check out some high school sophomore who's supposed to be a big-deal quarterback next season. You know Dad, always trying to get a jump on the scouts. I think he'll be home tomorrow or the next day. You want me to have him call you when he gets back?"

"No. It's nothing important." Just a son who wished he knew how to talk to his dad about farms, gardens and phantom columnists. Just a man who wanted to confess that he loved flowers more than football. Just a lonely man, who still, on occasion, sorely missed his best friend. But it was one thing to believe in "Live like crazy today," another thing entirely to explain to his parents how that belief translated into buying a farm for a phantom named Daisy Rose. "Good luck tonight, Kel."

"Thanks. I'll send you a picture of the trophy."

"That's what I like about you, kid. Positive thinking."

"Learned it from you, big bro. Gotta go. Oh, but, hey, we're coming by to see you next week."

"You are?"

"Yeah, stopping by your office on our way to Sports Challenge Camp. So I'll see ya then."

"I'll look forward to it," Brad said, but his brother had already hung up the phone. People seemed to be doing that routinely all of a sudden. Whatever had happened to a good, old-fashioned goodbye?

NEWTON ROONEY answered Zoë's phone, so Brad hung up and called right back. When the man answered a second time, Brad clicked the connection and said, "I'm dialing the right number, but keep getting the wrong answer."

"Hello, Kenneally," Newton said with a long and patient sigh. "Zoë's not here."

"That pretty much cancels out any reason for you to be there, then, doesn't it?"

"She had a late closing. I'm keeping an eye on Lark for her."

Brad didn't like that. Not because he thought Rooney wasn't capable of baby-sitting, but because he just flat out couldn't stand the guy. "Let me talk to Lark," he said, making it sound as if he had to make sure she was okay.

Rooney was offended, just as Brad had intended. "She can't come to the phone, Kenneally. She's playing outside with Sonchie."

"It's dark outside, Newton."

"It's barely twilight, Kenneally. You're just *in* the dark."

"Keen eyesight," Brad said. "Improves my hearing, too. There's no need for you to yell."

"I'm speaking normally."

"You know, you might want to get your hearing

tested. Men your age often have significant hearing loss."

"I'm not *yelling,* damn it."

The guy was too easy to rile. Almost took the fun right out of it. "Okay, if you say so. Now, can I talk to Lark?"

"I told you, she's outside playing with Sonchie."

"Then you should be outside with them. Zoë doesn't want Lark playing with that gangster of an eight-year-old without some supervision."

"*Zoë* doesn't have a problem with Sonchie Wilcox. You do. In fact, Zoë quite likes the young man. As do I."

All the more reason to worry, in Brad's opinion. "So, how can you be keeping an eye on Lark when she's outside and you're inside answering the telephone?"

"Magical powers," Rooney said with no hint of humor. "But if I hang up the phone, then it won't be a problem, will it?" And so saying, he hung up.

Brad frowned, tapped redial and waited, half expecting the call to go unanswered. But Rooney was nothing if not predictable, and answered on the first ring. "What can I do for you, Kenneally?"

"You can open the door and tell my goddaughter that her Uncle Brad is on the line and wants to speak with her." Brad stressed the possessives and silently dared Rooney to refute them. He didn't. The man had *cojones* the size of rock salt.

"Uncle Brad!" Lark sounded breathless when she came on the line a few minutes later. "Hi, Uncle Brad! Guess what I'm wearing?"

"Two tons of diamonds," he guessed, and she giggled.

"Nope."

"Forty pounds of pearls?"

"Nope."

"A gallon of emeralds?"

"Nope."

"I give up. What are you wearing?"

"A wedding dress."

"Don't tell me you got married and didn't invite your favorite godfather."

She giggled again. "I didn't get married, silly. I'm just wearin' the dress to practice bein' a flower girl. B'sides, I'm going to marry you when I grow up."

"Oh, good, because I'm going to be *real* old and grouchy by the time you're grown up, and I'll need somebody to take care of me and visit me in the nursing home."

"You're already old and grouchy," she said with yet another giggle, and Brad wanted to tell her it wasn't nice to be so happy when Noodle Roni was the babysitter. But at least he knew the Noodle wasn't mean to her. Which was good, because Brad didn't want to have to hurt the guy. He just wanted a lower life-form to drop-kick him off the face of the earth. Actually, just out of Zoë's life would be far enough.

"That's right, Sparkle Larkle, and don't you forget it. When's your mom going to be home?"

The giggles turned into a grumble. "I don't know. She's been gone all day and Noodle Roni had to come and get me at day care and he wouldn't take me to McDonald's and I had to eat macaroni-and-cheese in a box!"

Now, *that* was what a godfather wanted to hear. "Well, of all the nerve," Brad sympathized. "I think you should tell Mom that you don't want him to baby-sit you ever again.''

Lark sighed. ''I do tell her, but she doesn't listen to me. Would you tell her, Uncle Brad? 'Cause I don't want him to live with us and be married even if I get a new dress for the wedding and get to be the flower girl. You can tell her when you get here, okay? When are you coming, Uncle Brad? Can we go to Mc-Donald's when you get here? I really want to go to McDonald's, 'cause I don't like macaroni-and-cheese in a box and I'm really hungry. Can we go, Uncle Brad? Can we?''

Brad's heart was thudding with new dread. ''Wait a minute. Back up there, Powderpuff. Who said anything about getting married? Who said anything about a wedding and you being a flower girl?''

Lark lowered her voice to a rough whisper, which Brad couldn't make out, no matter how hard he listened.

''Say that again, Lark. Did your *mother* tell you she's going to marry Noodle Roni?''

Again the garbled whisper, which sounded as if the phone receiver was covered by a small hand.

''Take your hand off the phone, Lark,'' he instructed. ''And speak up.''

He heard a *ka-lunk* as she dropped the phone, and then her voice coming from a distance as she yelled, ''Noodle Roni said he's gonna marry us whether I like him or not!''

Then, there was a far-off, but clearly gruff ''Lark! Quit yelling at the phone like some little heathen!''

Then Lark's hurried, but softer ''Oops…I gotta go, Uncle Brad. Sonchie wants to play honeymoon with me!''

That did it. He was going to Tulsa, as fast as the Corvette would get him there. "Lark," he said, "don't—" But she'd already hung up.

Brad didn't want to, but he hit redial and told Rooney, who answered yet again, not to take his eyes off Lark until Brad could get there.

"I'm perfectly capable of taking care of her," Rooney said loudly. "And of Zoë. She's going to marry me, Kenneally. As soon as I can make the arrangements. You're not needed. You're not wanted and you're not the dang Lone Ranger. And yes, *now,* I'm yelling." Then, amazingly, he hung up again.

Brad was there in just under an hour.

Chapter Four

…and protecting our tender plants from predators is not necessarily without its difficulties. Why, just last week, Daughter Kate and I were laughing at the antics of those cute little bunnies out back, but today the leaves of my tomato vines have been nibbled back to the nub and, Friend Neighbor, Hubby Bee was not amused. Neither, I'll confess, was I. For the sake of Daughter Kate, we made a pact to come up with a way—however complicated and time-consuming—of allowing the tomato leaf eaters and the tomato fruit eaters to coexist in peace. It was my dear, sweet hubby who first thought of the idea (step-by-step attack plan below), and Kate and I are so pleased that he did, because the bunnies are a lovely part of country living.…

"All right," he said when Zoë opened the door to his knock, "this probably seems a little odd."

"Odd?" She leaned against the door, arms crossed, looking exceptionally fetching in the worn blue chenille robe she'd had as long as he'd known her. Loose tendrils of curly dark hair curved along her hairline, escapees from a carelessly clipped topknot. Her lips were poised in a patient half smile, but he was certain there was a sparkle of delighted welcome in her eyes. "Driving down from Joplin at ten o'clock at night because you don't like the man I'm dating?" She shrugged. "Now what would be 'odd' about that?"

Okay, so maybe he'd overreacted a little, but now that he was here, he felt unusually happy to see her and glad that he'd made the trip. "I don't care if you date him, Zoë. Well, yes, I do, but mainly I just mind that you leave him alone with Lark."

She nodded, stepped back so he could enter the house, then closed the door behind him and put a finger to her lips. "I just got her to bed, so keep your voice down until we get into the other room. If she figures out you're here, it'll be midnight before I get her settled down again."

He glanced up the stairs, half hoping to see his goddaughter on the landing, knowing the task before him was daunting and that Lark would be wholeheartedly in support of it. But the landing was clear, and he was on his own as he followed Zoë across the tiled entryway. He couldn't help but note the slim turn of her ankles, her bare feet, and—despite knowing he shouldn't be noticing anything above the hem—the seductive sway of her hips beneath the blue chenille. He was more than a little sorry, too, that the view changed when they reached the black, white and copper-trimmed kitchen.

She motioned him to sit at the glass-topped table. "Coffee?" she asked, and set about making it even before he nodded gratefully and said yes.

The room smelled like violets and dish soap…that would be lemons, he decided. Violets and lemony dish soap. He wondered why he was always so happy in her home and why it felt so right to be in her kitchen, watching her pad barefoot on the black and white tile. His parents' house smelled of outdoors, sweaty teenage boys and high expectations. His apartment smelled faintly of long-ago cigars, fried onions and discount perfume. The office smelled like stale coffee and old tires. The farmhouse had smelled like fresh-baked gingerbread.

"I don't like Newton," he said even though, on the trip down, he'd told himself to avoid the subject altogether and to not, under any circumstances, put her in a position of defending the Noodle. "But that's not why I'm here."

"Really?" She switched on the coffeemaker and turned toward him, her hands braced against the countertop behind her. "Then did you come to tell me *again* that you don't like the kid across the street?"

"I don't like him, either," he said, trying not to stare at the soft curve of a breast, the cleavage easily visible where the robe lapped. Zoë was his friend, Lark's mother. His best friend's widow. He was not supposed to notice she *had* breasts, much less how perfectly shaped they seemed to be. "Or rather, I don't like Lark spending so much time with him. I'm telling you, Zoë, he's not a good influence. Did you know they were playing honeymoon?"

A smile crooked the corners of her lips. "As a matter of fact, I asked Lark about that. I've told her that Tim and I went to Disney World on our honeymoon, so in her mind, riding a roller coaster is a honeymoon. She and Sonchie were pretending to take a trip and ride the roller coaster."

He still thought any pretending with Sonchie required adult supervision. "Why don't we take her?" The suggestion sent Zoë's eyebrows into a questioning arch. "We could go to Six Flags in Dallas on a long weekend. Let her ride the roller coaster for real, explain the difference between a vacation and a honeymoon. She's old enough to understand."

The coffeemaker steamed and coffee began to drip into the pot. Zoë moved from the counter to sit across from him at the table. The lapels of her robe gaped even more. "Old enough to understand that a trip to Six Flags isn't a honeymoon? Or old enough to understand that you want to get us both away from harmful influences?"

She always suspected him of having a hidden agenda. And so what if he did? He'd promised Tim he'd protect her, no matter what. He just hadn't expected her to be so damn independent. "You can't really want to marry your boss," he said, certain he was right. "He's not anything like Tim."

"No, he isn't. And I'm not much like the girl who married Tim, either."

"Don't say that. You've been through a lot, Zo." He looked at her, loving the sweet cream hue of her skin and the dusting of freckles across her nose. "You deserve someone extra special, and Rooney is so…ordinary. Worse than ordinary. He doesn't even have a sense of humor."

"Well, he thinks you're pretty funny."

"I'm happy to entertain him—just so long as I don't have to dance at his wedding to you."

Zoë didn't offer any reassurances, and Brad took that as a bad sign. "So," she said. "If you didn't come here to fuss at me about Newton or about the neighborhood, why did you drive all this way so late?"

"Oh...well, I, uh, wanted to see you, talk about something." She eyed him carefully, and he almost lost his nerve. But she was clearly thinking about marrying Rooney. And he was just as clearly about to lose the job he loved. He had to do something to save them both. "Coffee's done." Pushing to his feet, he walked around the table to set out cups, even though the coffeemaker was still perking. The actions postponed the moment of truth—or rather, untruth—for another couple of minutes, gave his conscience room to argue this one last time.

Once everything was set out and ready, he turned and braced his hands on the countertop, looked at the top of her head, where her dark hair was piled in loose curls and held with a butterfly clip. Her hair looked soft and appealing and the slender slope of her nape looked damn kissable. For a second, he thought about leaning down and kissing her neck, maybe trailing kisses down the small peaks and valleys of her spine, working his way around to...

Whoa. Wrong woman for that line of thought. What was the matter with him? Noticing things about her that he had never noticed before? Well, okay, so he'd always noticed in a boys-will-be-boys, hands-off kind of way. But suddenly, it seemed to be all he was capable of thinking about...and that simply wasn't okay. He must be really on edge if that was the sort of distraction his frenzied brain provided. "Coffee's not done," he said, still rattled by the creamy glow of her skin and his totally inappropriate reaction to it. "Guess I'm a little anxious for that caffeine."

"It's decaffeinated. I, at least, am planning on getting some sleep tonight." She looked over her shoulder at him. "So with that thought in mind, why don't you tell me whatever it is you came here to talk about."

He could do this. He had to do this. It was more of a fib than a lie, really. And he was only doing it for her own good. To get her away from Rooney long enough for her to realize she didn't want to marry a macaroni. So what, if it helped out him—and Daisy Rose—in the process? Not every heroic act had to be completely unselfish. Superman must have realized at least once that saving the world meant he wouldn't have to get out and hunt himself a new home. "I…well, I bought a farm today."

Zoë stared at Brad as if he'd just proclaimed that he was, indeed, Superman, just returned from a successful mission to destroy the evil Emperor Zorg and save the world from certain destruction. "What did you say?"

"A farm. I bought a farm." He waited for her smile, but watched as her forehead wrinkled with a frown.

"A farm," she repeated, obviously struggling with the concept. "You bought a farm."

"Yes, which is better than buying *the* farm, which, of course, if I had, I wouldn't be sitting here telling you about."

She gave her head a little shake and repeated, "You didn't buy *the* farm, but you bought *a* farm."

"Yep."

"A farm," she said again, her tone changing only in its degree of astonishment. "As in 'Old MacDonald Had a Farm'?"

"E-I-E-I-O." Brad lifted his shoulder in a good-humored shrug. "Wait 'til you see it, Zo. It's perfect. The owners are moving to a retirement community and they're willing to sell me a bunch of the furniture, and nearly all the livestock. They'd already sold two of the

cows, but I talked them into throwing in the last one as part of the deal. Plus, there are a bunch of ducks— Did I mention the pond? No? Well, it's back behind the house. There's a chicken house, a barn, a couple of pygmy goats and a mule—Elmer. That's the mule. Plus, Mr. Renfroe said he'd just give me the tractor since it's old and not worth much and he can't exactly drive it around the golf course.

"You bought a *farm?*" Zoë repeated, stunned into repetition.

"Yes," Brad said, infinitely hopeful but wondering how in hell he'd ever thought he could carry off this charade. "Well, technically, I only signed an agreement to buy, but I've made up my mind. I'm going to do it."

"You're buying a farm." She was frowning in earnest now. "Don't take this wrong, Brad, but…why?"

To save Daisy Rose for the readers who believe in her. To save my job. To save you from a whopping mistake. To live in a place with space all around, with room for a dozen gardens. He answered, instead, with a shrug, adding, "I guess it does sound crazy. I just…liked the idea."

"You liked the idea," she repeated, obviously still speechless over the possibility that there could be more to this than momentary insanity, that there might be more to him than muscles and a Pez-head brain. "Where is it?"

"Where's what?"

"The farm."

"Oh. I'm not exactly sure." He was on firmer ground as long as they were talking about location. "I only just stumbled onto the property today. But don't worry, they gave me directions so I can get back there. Mr. Renfroe drew it out on the map for me.''

''Where is it…generally speaking, then?''

''Missouri. Well, I'm pretty sure that's where it is. Guess I should have asked, huh? Funny thing, though—the Renfroes? They don't even have a phone.'' She shook her head at that, as if she, too, thought it a quaint and appealing idiosyncrasy of country living. ''And there're phone lines right up by the road, too. Guess they just prefer living the simple life.''

Zoë blinked, surprised, perhaps, that he could be this excited over forty acres and no phone. ''Brad, shouldn't you think about this for at least a month or so before you haul off and jump into a thirty-year mortgage for a *farm?*''

''I have thought about it,'' he said, thinking she didn't have to make him sound like a complete imbecile. ''And I'm going to buy it, outright. No mortgage. I'm paying in cash and car. They want my Corvette as part of the deal.''

''What? You can't trade in your Corvette for a farm.''

''Sure, I can. What does a farmer need with a sports car, anyway?''

''But you love that car. You've always driven sports cars. What are you going to drive?''

''A mule team.''

''Be serious.''

''Okay…a pickup truck.''

''Look, nothing personal, but I'm going to have to have you committed this time. You cannot buy a farm.''

''Why not?''

She was at point nonplus...but only for a second. "Well, for one thing, you can't afford it."

He raised an eyebrow. "Zoë, I can. My current salary may not support a posh life-style, but it more than covers my expenses. You know I got an obscene amount of money to sign with the Chiefs and an even more obscene amount as compensation for the knee injury, and it's all still just lying around earning interest. You won't let me spend any of my ill-gotten gains on you and Lark, so what's wrong with spending it on a few acres and a mule?"

"I can think of at least forty reasons, beginning with, What in heaven's name are you going to do with a mule?"

"Teach Lark to ride sidesaddle?"

"Oh, no. Don't even think about putting that idea in her head. Mules are stubborn and mean and—"

"Elmer's a good old guy. I met him this afternoon. But if you don't want her riding a mule, we'll get a pony. I'll even buy one for you, if you want."

"I don't want a pony."

"Okay, so you'd rather have a full-size horse. I think forty acres is big enough for a horse, a pony and a mule, don't you?"

"Are you *hearing* the words that are coming out of your mouth?"

He grinned as he moved to pour coffee into a cup for her and one for him. This couldn't work. Didn't have a prayer. She'd see through him within an hour of setting foot on Lazy Daisy Acres. On the other hand, his main objective was to get her there. What was wrong with enjoying himself a little bit in the process? He placed her cup on the table in front of her and stood behind her chair, looking down at the curve of her lovely neck, breathing in the soft flowery scent of her recent bath, telling himself to stop it, stop it, *stop it.* "Did I mention the place has three gardens? One for vegetables, one for herbs, one for flowers."

She choked on her first swallow of coffee. "Careful, there," he said, and thumped her on the back before pulling out the chair at the end of the table and sitting in it.

"What do you know about gardening?" she asked in a strangled whisper.

It was on the tip of his tongue to tell her he knew quite a lot about gardens, life on a farm and several topics in between. But if he did that, he'd wind up confessing that he was Daisy Rose, and a sweet, sensitive guy to boot, and, well…he needed to stick to his original plan. Get her on the farm, persuade her of some earth-shattering reason she should again pretend to be the columnist, and try not to lose his whole persona as a macho man in the process. Saving Daisy Rose and his reputation was going to be a real challenge this go-round. "I can read," he said. "I don't mind asking questions. I can learn."

"Usually people learn about farming *before* they go out and buy a farm. Are you sure you want to do this? I thought you loved your job with the newspaper."

"What does that have to do with this?" Of course, one had everything to do with the other, but he wasn't going to say so. Not at this early stage of the negotiations, anyway. "I can commute. I can even hook up a computer and work from home."

"No phones, remember?"

Oh, yeah. "Well, I can put one in. Two."

She cocked her head, reminding him with that single gesture that she had known him a long time and that elaborate schemes often had a way of backfiring. "You're teasing me, aren't you?" she said finally. "There's no farm. There's no mule. You made it all up to save face, because you really did drive all the way down here tonight just to fuss at me about Newton."

He took a sip from his cup, wondering why coffee always tasted so good whenever he was sitting across the table from Zoë. "I couldn't make up anything so elaborate," he said. "Invent a farm? Okay, sure, I could probably do that. Add the chickens, the cow, the pygmy goats? In a pinch, I might come up with that kind of detail. But a mule? No, I'd never have thought of Elmer. And for the record, I believe I've shown admirable restraint in fussing at you about Newton. I haven't said even one of the things I said to you on the way down here when you weren't even there to hear them."

She narrowed her eyes and looked at him over the rim of her cup. "Somehow, I just can't see you in overalls and a straw hat."

Okay, so Noodle Roni was off the schedule as a lecture topic. Onward, then, with Plan A to Save the World. "Then you ought to love this idea. Why don't you and Lark come out and spend the summer?"

"The whole summer?" Zoë laughed as if he'd made a joke. "I can't take off work all summer, Brad. Besides, you won't…"

You won't make it half that long. That was what she'd been about to say. He could hear the words hovering there, unspoken, just behind her belatedly tactful smile. "You *wouldn't* want two city girls in your way for the entire summer," she finished lamely.

"Two weeks, then," he bargained in a persuasive

tone that said he couldn't think of anything nicer. Which, to be honest, he couldn't. "Come out for a couple of weeks at the end of the month. Two weeks from Saturday would be great. You can help me get settled in. Or just supervise while I get things squared away. Lark can go barefoot, and we'll have home-grown tomatoes for supper. It'll be the closest thing to a vacation you've had in years."

"Helping you move isn't exactly my idea of a—" She stopped. "Two weeks from *this* Saturday?"

"Make it Friday. You can come after work." He felt a little guilty, but he had to move quickly. For her own good. And, of course, because of the magazine crew. "I know it's soon, but the Renfroes are ready to move. They said they'll be out a week from Monday, and it's not like I have to do much more than pack a few boxes. I just can't see any good reason to wait."

"I guess waiting for sanity to return is clearly out of the question?" She set her cup on the table and eyed him with curious concern. "You're really rushing into this, Brad. Are you positive you want to live on a farm?"

"My heroes have always been farmers. Well, cow-boys, really, but this is pretty close. Forty acres. Just think of it, Zoë. No neighbors on the other side of a wall. None even close enough to know we're there. No speed bumps because tractors don't move that fast. No traffic noise. No noise, period. Well, except for birds and normal country sounds like that. It's a great spot. Green and picturesque. Just like I pictured it." *Oops.* "I mean, just like I always thought a farm should look."

"This is a whole new side of you, Brad. I had no idea—"

"I know. You didn't realize I even knew how to pronounce the word *picturesque,* much less what it meant." He smiled persuasively. Because he really did want her to want to come. Because she really did need a vacation. Because this time, he really needed her help. "Please say you'll come, Zoë. Think of it as my new adventure. One that I really want to share with you and Lark. For a couple of weeks, at least."

"We can drive out for the day once you're settled. There's no need for us to be underfoot while you're moving in."

"It's not a day trip. Once you've seen it, you'll understand. You need the full experience."

She laughed again, but this time with a soft, husky amusement. "From the rooster crowing at dawn to evenings on the porch watching the stars? Didn't you read *Animal Farm?*"

"All the more reason for you to come out and protect me. Say, yes, Zoë. You know Lark will have a grand time, and I promise you will, too."

She hesitated. "I still think this is just an elaborate plot to keep me away from Newton while you convince me to dump him."

"If two weeks on the farm will do that, I'd be crazy not to buy the place, wouldn't I?" He finished the coffee and grinned. "So, it's settled. You'll come."

"I'm always amazed at how you're able to make the nuttiest idea actually sound rational and appealing."

"But…? I definitely heard a *but* at the end of that sentence."

She sighed and, finally, smiled. And damn if he didn't feel like Superman. "*But…*" she said. "Okay. We'll do it. Lark and I will spend a little vacation time at your farm."

"Yippee! We're going! We're going to the farm!"
Lark flew through the kitchen doorway like a wild pitch
and flung herself first at her mother, then at Brad, dis-
tributing slider kisses, fast hugs and even faster sen-
tences. "I get to ride a mule! Can I have a dog *and* a
pony, Uncle Brad? What are 'piggy goats'? If I plant
a tomato, will it grow as tall as me? Can I tell Sonchie?
He'll say I made it up. But I didn't make it up, did I,
Mom? I'm going to Uncle Brad's farm! When're we
goin'? I should pack!" She bounced toward the doorway, a whole year's worth of excitement packed in
every quick little hop, her little-girl soprano singsong-
ing in and out of melody. "A far-arm, a far-arm! We're
goin' to a far-arm!"

"Lark," Zoë said, effectively stilling the song, if not
the enthusiasm. "Remember our talk about eavesdrop-
ping?"

Lark nodded vigorously. "I was real quiet this time,
Mom. Just like you said."

Brad grinned. Zoë tried to look stern, and said, "I
said, it's not polite to eavesdrop no matter how *quiet*
you are, and I also said that eavesdroppers seldom hear
anything good."

"But this time I did hear somephin' good, didn't I,
Uncle Brad? I heard somephin' *real* good."

"That you did, Larko Polo. What color pony do you
want?"

Her blue eyes rounded wide with options. "Purple!
No! Poke-it dots! No! Purple!" She nodded, the matter
decided.

"You asked for that one," Zoë said to Brad.

Brad winked at his godchild and wished Tim could
be here to see her now. "I tell you what, kiddo. We'll

get one of each—and we'll get your mama one with stripes. How's that?''

"Oh…!'' She clapped her hands. "That's just what she *always* wanted!''

He definitely liked being Santa Claus more than Superman. Less stress. At this time of year, anyway. "It's settled then. We're going to have the best vacation in the history of the world, agreed?'' He held out his hand, palm up, and Lark slapped hers, palm down, on top of it.

Slowly, with an outward show of reluctance, but a sly gleam of excitement deep in her eyes, Zoë clasped her hand over theirs, closing the deal. "Here's to impulsive decision-making,'' she said. "And polka-dot ponies.''

"And v'cations!'' Lark divvied up another round of fierce hugs. "I *always* wanted a v'cation with you and Mom! Plus, know what, Uncle Brad? I always wanted a puppy, too. Can we get a puppy, too?''

It was Christmas in June—despite the less than positive expression settling onto Zoë's features. "You know, I was thinking the exact same thing,'' Brad agreed. "Every farm needs a farm dog.''

"We'll name him Noodle Roni!''

Brad had a fleeting glimpse of Tim whispering the words into Lark's fertile imagination and was just opening his mouth to say the name was perfect, when Zoë pushed back her chair with a scrape and stood up. "You will not name him that,'' she said firmly, speaking to Brad rather than Lark. "Farm dogs need farm dog names. And you, little lady, need to be in bed.''

"I got to pack.''

"You'll have plenty of time for that, later. Upstairs,'' she directed. "Now.''

"But Uncle Brad's here."

"I'm sending him to bed, too. Now, hop, skip. Off we go."

Lark dodged, darted around her mother, and launched herself into Brad's arms. Hugging with all her small might, she thanked him without words. "I'll see you in the morning, Uncle Brad. Mom'll fix us some pancakes, won't ya, Mom?"

Zoë raised her eyebrows, but whether it was at her daughter's assumption that he would sleep over, or that she would fix breakfast, was hard to tell. Since spending the night wasn't an eyebrow-raising event—he'd been sleeping on the Martins' sofa or in their extra bedroom for longer than Lark had been around—breakfast must be the main objection. On the other hand, now that he'd won his objective, he should probably take the high road and avoid any second thoughts his hostess might entertain. "I have to get back," he told Lark. "Because bright and early tomorrow morning, even before you've started eating your pancake, I'll be out looking for that purple pony."

Any trace of pout vanished at the thought. "And the puppy, Uncle Brad. Don't forget the puppy."

"Not a chance. I'll see you Sunday, okay?" He kissed her on the cheek and she hugged his neck, in return.

"G'night, Uncle Brad."

"Good night, Laura Kate."

Zoë grasped Lark's hand, even as she glanced back at him. "You'll be here when I finish tucking her into bed?"

He shook his head. "I think I'll head on out."

"You're welcome to stay."

"I know. Thanks, but I'm a little keyed up. Too

much excitement for one day, I guess. The drive home will be good for me.''

"Me, too," she said, her lips curved into a teasing smile. "I won't be there to hear all your misguided advice."

He smiled back, glad all around that he'd made the trip, happy at the thought of having the girls to himself for a few days. "I'll write down the best parts, so you'll know what you missed."

"Great idea, Brad. You can read it all back to me on one of those starry nights out at the farm."

"What about 'Three Billy Goats Gruff?'" Lark asked. "Can we read that at the farm, too? Can we read it now? Can we, Mom? I promise I'll stay in bed this time if you read the 'Three Billy Goats Gruff' again."

Zoë urged her charge forward. "I've already read all the bedtime stories I'm reading tonight, and you promised *then* that you wouldn't get out of bed again, remember?"

"But, Mom, it's Uncle Brad." Lark said it as explanation and self-defense all in one sentence...and Brad loved being so special in her eyes.

"We've got a date," he reminded them both, trailing after them from the kitchen into the foyer, and letting his voice follow them as they headed up the stairs. "Two weeks from Friday, we'll be living high off the hog at Lazy Daisy Acres."

"Yippee!" Lark's voice carried clearly back.

Zoë's floated back from the landing, muffled but unmistakably musical. *"E-I-E-I-O...."*

ALPHIE RENFROE PUSHED the wad of flowered fabric back inside the old suitcase and closed the lid. She snapped the latches and stretched the black elastic bands around the brown tweed sides. The suitcase was a Trailblazer brand, bought new at Olsen's Sundries more years ago than Alphie could recall, certainly before she'd married. It had had more use during the last four years than it had had in all the years before. Leaving it there on the bed, which had been stripped of all but its mattress ticking, she looked around for anything she might have forgotten. She'd left doilies on the bed tables and an embroidered scarf on the chest of drawers. No point inviting water rings and scratches. She hoped the new tenant would get the message and take good care of her bedroom suite.

"You ready, Mother?" Caspar came to the door, a mismatched suitcase in each hand. "Time to head into town, hand over the keys, and pick up our car and the vacation money."

"You sure this'll go like last time?"

His smile was looser than it once was, but she still thought he was a handsome man. "'Course, I'm sure. I've not been wrong about any of the others, have I?"

"No, you haven't." He'd been right four times out of four so far, which was a pretty good record.

"Well, then, let's go." He shuffled on ahead, whistling tunelessly, happy to be leaving the farm behind. Caspar was always that way—eager to go, eager to get back.

Alphie sighed and took another last look around what had been her bedroom for more than fifty years. Then she lifted the brown tweed suitcase with the black elastic straps off the bed and headed out the door, gladder than she wanted to admit about leaving this place behind.

Disney World, here we come!

"IT'S ONLY TWO WEEKS, Newton. I have that much vacation time saved up and more." Zoë held the phone away from her ear, expecting him to raise his voice. Which he did. Which he'd been doing on a regular basis ever since she broached the idea.

"Two weeks is a long time in this business, Zoë. Besides, we have a date on Sunday."

Newton was big on standing dates…every Sunday, whether he remembered to ask her or not. Come to think of it, he'd begun taking a lot of things for granted lately. "We don't have a date," she said. "And even if we did, I'm giving you plenty of notice to find someone else to have dinner with."

He sighed impatiently. "Zoë, I want to have dinner with you. I'm not interested in anyone else. You know that."

She did…and somehow, the knowledge made her weary. "I need this vacation, Newton. I deserve it."

"You're right," he said, his tone softening, becoming persuasive. "But I'd hoped we might take one later this year. Just the two of us. We could go to Cancun or Jamaica, someplace exotic and relaxing. Not a farm, for Pete's sake."

As if she'd go off on a trip and leave her daughter behind. Besides that, Zoë was really looking forward to the time away from the office, away from her condo, away from Newton. "Lark wants to go and I think two weeks on a farm will be good for her. And being on Brad's farm will be relaxing for me, too. He'll take care of everything."

"Which you'll hate. You're always complaining about how he tries to do things for you all the time. Come on, Zoë, you don't really want to spend two weeks with Farmer Bozo, do you?"

Zoë thought about it for all of a second. "Yes," she said. "Yes, I do."

Newton's pause was long and unhappy, and his tone was distinctly cool when he spoke. "You'll leave a phone number of course, so I can reach you."

It wasn't a question and Zoë took instant exception to his subtle demand. "No, actually, I can't leave a number because there aren't any phone lines going to the farm. But you'll manage without me just fine, Newton, because that's the kind of guy you are."

"No phone lines? You're kidding. It figures Kenneally would go off and buy some backwater acreage without electricity or running water just so he could pretend to be Old MacDonald on a farm."

Zoë saw no reason to stop him from thinking the worst. "It'll be an adventure, Newton. And you know how I crave adventure."

He laughed, although not with much real humor. "Right." His voice was sceptical and somewhat derisive. "All right, Zoë. Go off with that lunatic if you must, but I will expect to hear from you every few days."

Zoë didn't care for his controlling attitude. "I rally just want to get away, Newton. I'll see you two weeks from Monday. 'Bye!"

Without waiting for any further protests, she hung up and turned her thoughts toward the farm...and Farmer Brad.

Chapter Five

It's very important to use a thick coat of softened, not melted, butter when preparing the mold and be careful not to leave any finger smudges in the sugar crust. Soufflés (or soof-fulls, as Hubby Bee likes to call them) have an undeserved reputation for contrariness, so be advised that there are moments in the process when anything that can go wrong, will. Daughter Kate may jump like a jumping bean through the kitchen, or Hubby Bee might open the oven door at precisely the wrong instant in pursuit of that delicious aroma…and *poof!* The airy soufflé you worked so hard to create falls flat as a fritter…and let me tell you, that's darn flat! So beware of the pitfalls, Friend Neighbor, when you set out to make this Lighter Than Heaven Ladies' Chocolate Soufflé, but prepare yourself for the happy *oohs* and *aahs* of success.…

Zoë took one look at the boxy, green-gabled farmhouse and fell in love. Brad was right. Picturesque was probably the best description available, although there was more to it than that. The whole place—house, weathered barn and gardens—reminded her, somehow, of the home she'd shared with Tim. Not that they had lived in similar surroundings—not even close. But this house had a lived-in-and-loved-in look that felt...*familiar,* for lack of a better word, like coming home.

Yet, Zoë didn't believe Tim would have liked the farm much at all. He'd been a scholar, a student of life, a recorder of seasons. The tending of a garden was of interest to him only in its final product—food for the body or a visual feast for the soul. It was Zoë who secretly yearned to know the therapy of working the soil, of participating in the creation of food and flower, of experiencing the quiet satisfactions of simply nurturing Mother Earth. But before those inner longings even had a chance to take on a definable form, Life had set about to teach her the much larger lessons of caring for others...in sickness and in health.

She and Tim had been married only a brief while before the question of starting a family became a moot point and there was a baby to tend. Just after Lark's birth, the question of living happily ever after became a simple question of just living and there was an illness to tend. Since Tim's death, the questions of getting on with her life had been answered one sunrise, one sunset, at a time—and there were always, *always,* details to tend.

Maybe, though, Life was offering her a respite, a reward for good behavior. Two weeks. Three gardens. Her fingers fairly itched to get started.

"Look, Mommy. A real barn." In the back seat of the Toyota, Lark had her hands and nose pressed against the window. She was a child who before today had seen barns only as part of the changing scenery from a fast-moving car speeding down the highway.

Zoë pressed the automatic switch, and the window purred down to afford Lark an untinted view of the weathered barn and the rolling green pasture on the other side. Her daughter's awed intake of breath was reward enough, but Zoë pulled farther up the dirt driveway, shifted from "Drive" into "Park," and turned off the engine. Quiet assailed her ears on every front. Except, wait…there was noise. Lots of it. Birds. Crickets. Tree frogs. A host of other less identifiable, but infinitely *quiet,* sounds. *Oh, thank you, Brad,* she thought. *Thank you, thank you, for insisting we get the "full experience."*

"Mommy, look! It's Uncle Brad! And he's got a purple pony!"

Zoë looked. It was, indeed, Brad, clad in Union-striped overalls, a T-shirt underneath that was just tight enough and white enough to show off his tanned and muscular body. A renegade thrill shivered down her spine. He could have been a genetic blueprint for athletic engineering, his body beautifully formed for professional sports with built-in speed, endurance and unexpected grace. He'd changed some since leaving the game, of course, but she didn't know anyone else in better physical condition, or anyone who maintained it with such effortlessness. A sculptor could have turned him into a bronze Adonis—a full-scale version—he looked that good. Even in the overalls. At moments like this, Zoë was struck anew with the knowledge that inside his linebacker's body beat a tender and true heart. Why else would he have gone to the trouble to find a purple pony for a fatherless child?

"A pony, a pony!" Lark waged war with her seat belt, and Zoë had to get out of the car, open the back door, undo the latch and hurriedly get out of the way as her daughter flew off the back seat and raced toward the pony like a whirling dervish in pop-beads.

The pony was actually black, but his sleek coat did have a purple tint in the late-afternoon light. He shook his mane, and the fittings of his halter made a happy jangle. Always the protector, Brad pulled the lead taut as Lark approached. Zoë closed the car doors and observed the excited reunion of one small child, her gentle giant of a godfather, and the introduction of one purple-black pony. Lark patted the pony's broad forehead. He whiffled in return. She laughed in pure delight, and the deal was done. Not even five minutes into the vacation and she was already having the best time of her life. Zoë inhaled deeply, breathing in the sweet, fresh outdoor scents, breathing out the tension of all the getting-ready-to-go-on-vacation-for-two-weeks preparations. She owed Brad a thank-you for persuading her to come.

"Welcome to Lazy Daisy Acres," Brad said as she made a leisurely approach. "Meet Purple, the pony."

"Hello, Purple, the pony," she said. "Hello, Farmer Kenneally. Where's your straw hat?"

"Polka Dot has it." He grimaced. "*Had* it, I should say. I imagine she's eaten most of it by now. And that's my second hat in two days."

"Polka Dot being...?"

"The other pony."

"Oh, of course. The *other* pony."

"You 'member, Mom," Lark said, patting Purple vigorously and bonding as fast as any little girl and pony could. "Uncle Brad said he'd get two ponies. A purple one and and a poke-it dot one. Where's Poke-It Dot, Uncle Brad?" Before Brad had a chance to answer, before he could wave loosely toward the green pasture, Lark's thoughts were clearly spinning with even more exciting possibilities. "Did you get a puppy, Uncle Brad? You said you'd get a puppy. Did you get a puppy, too?"

"In the—" his gesture toward the barn's dark interior spun her into action, and she was gone before he finished the sentence "—barn."

Zoë's gaze followed the lightning bolts of pink that flashed from the heels of Lark's shoes, and she listened for the initial squeal of utter delight, before turning to Brad. "Two ponies and a puppy. My, my, you have been busy."

"There's a little mare in the pasture for you, too. I know I said I'd get you a horse with stripes, but since I was pretty sure you wouldn't want a zebra, I hope you'll settle for a dappled gray."

"You got a horse...for me?"

"I promised," he said with a shrug, "and you know I always keep my promises."

His most admirable, albeit often irritating, trait. "In that case, please promise me that you will not, under any circumstances, let Lark persuade you that this puppy needs to go home with her." He answered with a grin, and she knew she might as well concede the issue then and there—although she felt it was only fair to pretend she would take a great deal of convincing. Relenting too early in the game would simply result in two weeks of coercion to take the pony home, too.

"Isn't this place great?" Brad looked around, his brown eyes glinting with satisfaction. "I've been here a grand total of four days, and already it feels so familiar I'm sure I must have lived here in another life."

"That would have been pre-NFL, I imagine."

"Either that or I saw this farm once on some long-ago Sunday drive and memorized the setting."

"It's a little out of the way for a Sunday drive, considering you grew up in Texas."

"Factor in my parents, who thought a Sunday drive was the shortest distance between our house and any major sporting event, and there's no question I must have lived here in a previous life. Maybe when I was Johnny Appleseed." His smile held a tug of shyness, like a boy with a secret. "There are two apple trees out by the pond."

"Oh, boy. Apple pie for dessert…providing, of course, that we can find a recipe in *Pie Baking for Dummies.*"

"We'll have plenty of time to get our hands on a good recipe. It'll be autumn before the fruit is ripe, and since the best pies are made from the crispiest, freshest apples, we have a few months to go before they're at their peak. Looks like it'll be a good crop, too. The trees are healthy, and I've already netted both of them to keep the birds from taking their share first. So keep your fingers crossed for a mouth-watering pie in a few months."

She patted the pony, running her fingers through his wiry mane. "I'm impressed, Brad. You've obviously been studying up on apples and apple trees. Either that, or I'm going to have to give some serious consideration to that Johnny Appleseed theory."

She laughed, expecting him to join in, but unbelievably, he seemed embarrassed by her teasing. Or maybe he was embarrassed at not knowing all there was to know about fruit trees simply by virtue of being born male. Maybe, just the idea of having been caught out in actually *studying* the subject embarrassed him. It was hard to imagine Brad as having any interest at all in a place like this. He was the quintessential male, hunting for the thrill of the chase, gathering only enough trappings of domesticity to impress the female of the species. But here he stood, rather unimpressively adorned in bibbed overalls, holding the reins of a pony that was less than half his size, and trying to discuss apples as if he had more than a passing acquaintance with them in their native habitat. "I wish Tim could be here to see you now," she said, because she didn't know what else to say.

"Me, too." Brad scratched Purple on the ear, and the pony stamped a foot, indicating either approval or a desire to go back to the pasture. "He'd be laughing his head off over this, wouldn't he?"

"He would have loved seeing you in those overalls, that's for sure." Another laugh tickled her throat. "*I'm* going to love seeing you with the mule. Where is Elmer, by the way?"

"Anyplace he damn well wants to be." Brad's expression turned glum for an instant. "There's a reason the phrase 'stubborn as a mule' is so deeply ingrained in the English language. Elmer and I have already come to an understanding. He does whatever he wants, and I let him."

The tickle blossomed into delighted laughter, and the peace of Lazy Daisy Acres began to settle into her very bones. She was glad to be here, despite the surreal quality of seeing Brad in this pastoral setting, despite the mosquito of a thought that kept zipping in and out of her reverie. A thought that landed with a sudden and zesty sting. *Wait a minute. Lazy Daisy Acres? Lazy Daisy Acres?* As in *Daisy Rose Knows...Acres?* That was too obvious a connection to be coincidence.

Wasn't it? She opened her mouth to ask the question, but her daughter's full-blown giggles erupted from inside the shadowy barn before the first word could form.

"Mommy, look!" Lark waddled out of the barn, her arms full of wiggly pups—one blond, one brown, one black.

"Three?" Zoë's gaze swiveled to Brad, who shrugged with no discernible degree of compunction.

"Choosing just one seemed somehow sort of selfish," he explained. "They're still so little, you know, and I thought they might get lonely on this big place, without a brother or sister to play with."

Zoë sighed, wishing his heart had been a bit tougher this time around, knowing Lark would have a hissy fit when it came time to leave any one of the pups behind. "I suppose I should be glad there were only three in the litter."

"Maybe three is all she could carry." His smile turned teasing as he stepped out to give Lark a hand. Lifting two of them from her grasp, he kept the blond puppy for himself and plopped the brown one into Zoë's unsuspecting arms. The puppy was warm and baby-soft and smelled sweetly of milk and Puppy Chow.

"Hello, puppy," Zoë whispered, smiling at the pink tongue that tried so hard to reach her, loving the mewling sounds he made low in his puppy throat. "Hello."

"What are their names, Uncle Brad?"

"I've been calling them Tweedles, Dee and Dum," he said, pointing out the corresponding pup as he said each name. "But you can change that, if you want."

Lark held the black puppy in front of her and narrowed her eyes, consideringly. "Nope. I like Tweedles."

"Wait a minute," Zoë said, examining the sweet, brown face as the puppy made a determined effort to deliver a sloppy kiss. "I don't think I like calling a puppy Dum. It could cause self-esteem issues."

"When he's old enough, we'll tell him he was named after a porcupine." Brad stroked the yellow head of the puppy in his arms. "That may not make him feel better about himself, but it'll give him something to think about, for sure. Besides, I'm betting that once you get better acquainted with little Dum, you won't worry so much about his self-image. He's the ring leader of this motley crew."

Lark sighed happily, her hug full of energetic puppy. "This is the best present you ever got me, Uncle Brad."

"I'm glad you like the puppies, Larky Lou."

"I do. I like the puppies. And Purple, the pony. And Poke-It Dot. And the puppies and…and the *whole* farm. I've always wanted to live on a farm—and now, I am!" Tweedles licked her chin, and she giggled. "Can he sleep with me, Mom? When can I ride Purple and Poke-It Dot, Uncle Brad? And where's the cow? Did you get Mom a pony, too? You said you would. A big one, 'cause she's a lot taller'n me. Are you gonna milk the cow, Uncle Brad? I've never seen piggy goats, Uncle Brad. Where are the piggy goats? When can I see them, Uncle Brad? Will you show 'em to me, now? Huh, Uncle Brad?"

His smile deepened as the torrent of words rushed him like an entire backfield in motion, all intent on tackling him. "It's getting dark, so we'll do all those things tomorrow. I'm going to put Purple in the pasture, while you and your mom put the puppies back into their pen in the barn. Then we'll go in and have supper. Okay with you, Zoë?''

"Supper sounds good," she said, wondering what was so different about him—besides the overalls and the rural setting. "I brought groceries from home, so we're all set with pizza fixings."

"No pizza." He handed the blond puppy back to Lark, and turned the pony in a tight circle. "At least, not tonight. We're having real food. It's ready and waiting in the oven."

Zoë knew she looked impressed and more than just a bit surprised. Probably because she was. "You *cooked?*"

He moved toward the barn, but not before she saw again that look of embarrassment, like a boy caught leaving a scraggly bouquet of dandelions on the porch as a gift for his mom. "I had it catered," he said over his shoulder.

But, somehow, she didn't believe him.

SITTING IN THE MIDDLE of the mattress on the big iron bedstead in the middle of the bedroom, upstairs in the old frame house, Zoë knew something was out of whack. She wasn't sure what, but she recognized that some things about the farm—and Brad—didn't fit. It could have been the meal he'd set out with a telling touch of ownership, as if he'd been planning it for months, as if he'd shopped, chopped, diced and fixed with her tastes and preferences in mind, as if her opinion of it—and him—mattered. It could have been the house itself and all the furniture and household items the owners had left behind as part of the deal. She'd handled a lot of house sales in the past few years and not once had the owners "thrown in" things like cro-

cheted doilies, a pantry full of home-canned vegetables
and fruits, shelves of books, a basket of knitting yarn,
just to mention a few of the items Brad had inherited
along with the deed.

When she commented on the abundance—almost as
if the owners meant to come back—Brad had assured
her the Renfroes simply left so much behind because
they could take so little to their new home. She'd
wanted to point out that they couldn't have much use
for a Corvette at the retirement home, either, but decided that sounded critical. And she didn't want Brad
to think she wasn't happy for him, because she was.
She was happy to be here with him, too.

The gardens he'd shown her after supper had looked
well cared for, but she'd spied a few spots that needed
weeding, a rosebush practically begging to have the
dead leaves cut away, and about a thousand other aro-
matic plants she just wanted to examine up close and
personally. Lark had staked her claim to the bedroom
closest to the top of the stairs, which Zoë interpreted
as her desire to have the easiest bedroom to sneak puppies into and out of. Sure enough, there had been a
bedtime standoff over how many warm bodies could
fit in one bed. Brad had put a stop to the argument by
hauling in a large cardboard box and cautioning Lark
that the puppies had to stay in it—for their own safety.
He knew, to a T, what to say to win her agreement,
and, the last time Zoë had tiptoed in to check, all three
puppies and Lark were sound asleep in their respective
beds.

She should be feeling gloriously contented and relaxed. She was on vacation for the first time in ages.
The quiet—which was, in fact, not quiet at all—was
soothing. The darkness was spectacular, illuminated

only by a huge buttercup of a moon and millions of twinkling stars flung like clusters of baby's breath across a sky as black as a bottomless sea. City street lamps should have a curfew, she thought. At least on star-studded nights like this one. Ditto to neon and all other urban lighting. Civilization didn't realize what it was missing. She, herself, had forgotten until now what a lovely time evening could be. No doubt about it. The farm was a perfect setting for her brief hiatus from daily responsibilities.

But something bugged her about the house and Brad's behavior. Something she should have been able to identify, but couldn't quite put her finger on. *Lazy Daisy Acres.* It had to be that. Had to be the connection to the mysterious Daisy Rose. Had to be the reason Brad had sought out this strange farm and, in the twinkling of an eye, bought it and given it a name. A name, for Pete's sake. Lazy *Daisy* Acres. Forty acres and a mule. The place, the naming of it—everything went against all she knew of Brad Kenneally…and she knew a considerable amount. His living here, wearing overalls, cooking real food—cooking well, at that—none of it fit with the man she thought—no, was *certain*—she knew extremely well. Something was wrong with this picture.

Grabbing her chenille robe, Zoë left the bedroom and tiptoed downstairs to find him. He wasn't in the living room, with its worn, tapestried couch and curtains. Nor in the clean, cheery, cozy little kitchen that smelled of gingerbread and a lemon-scented cleanser, either. Then she heard a low *creak* outside and went to the door.

He was on the wraparound porch, sitting in the porch swing, pushing against the porch floor with his booted foot, rocking in a slow back and forth, back and forth motion. "Hi," he said, when the screen door opened with a comforting *squeak.* "Want to rock?"

She joined him in the swing, tucking one foot under her and drawing the robe down over her bare legs. Somewhere, in the distance, she heard a car horn and knew their isolation was mostly an illusion. But out here, with the moon as bright as a sunflower, and Brad so very close—almost unsettlingly close—beside her, the rest of the world seemed very far away. "Who is Daisy Rose?" she asked, and he stopped swinging.

"What?"

"Daisy Rose," she repeated. "The columnist. The one you led your boss to believe was me. Remember her?"

"Mmm-hmm," he said, and set the swing in motion again. "What about her?"

"I was just wondering who she is and what she has to do with your buying this farm."

"What makes you think she had anything at all to do with it?"

"Oh, I don't know, maybe…Lazy *Daisy* Acres?"

"Mmm," he murmured noncommittally.

"That isn't an answer, Brad."

"It's not a subject I'm particularly eager to talk about."

"Because…?"

He sighed, a telling sign in itself. "Because, Daisy Rose is…well, because just hearing you say her name makes me dizzy."

Zoë felt a twist of surprise, a squeeze of anxiety, as she pieced together what she already knew with what he'd said and wasn't saying, and arrived at the obvious conclusion. Brad had finally met his kismet, finally tripped heart over head, finally fallen in love…with an obscure, shy columnist, the mere sound of whose name made him dizzy, and whose identity, for whatever reason, he was keeping to himself. *Daisy Rose,* a.k.a....?

Who was she? Brad had met her through the newspaper office, of course. But why the secrecy now? And how had some shy country lass managed to snag the heartstrings of Brad "No Commitment" Kenneally, a man who generally avoided any woman with an I.Q. larger than her bust size, a man who thrived on being the protector of females who were perfectly capable of independent thought, but who never encouraged a relationship with any woman who might actually *need* him to protect her? "So, am I right about her being the reason you suddenly want to live on a farm?"

He considered that as the swing rocked gently, the chains posing a low *cla-chink* of a question, the wood responding with a creaky sigh. "Daisy Rose is part of the reason," he admitted with conspicuous reluctance. "Most of the reason, I guess you could say."

Zoë had an impulse to grab the front of his shirt and demand a detailed explanation of how, when and where he'd met this Daisy person, why he couldn't just call her by her everyday name, and just what made her different from all the other women he'd dated and discarded. But in her heart, Zoë already knew. Brad was in love. Dizzy with love. Probably forever and always, considering he'd just traded in his Corvette to buy forty acres, which he'd promptly christened in her honor, and considering the fact that he was bending over backward to protect her secret. Whatever it was.

"So," she began, unsure if she really wanted an answer, but unable to stop herself from asking, "are you going to marry her?"

His startled glance fell on her and skittered away. "What makes you ask that?"

"Just putting two and two together."

But his smile—the small, self-conscious curve of his smile—gave him away. He *was* in love. She could tell. What she couldn't figure out was why the idea didn't make her incredibly, utterly happy. She'd be free. He'd have someone other than her and Lark to fuss over. He'd be so busy protecting his shy little Daisy that Zoë would finally be able to breathe without his trying to tell her how to do it more efficiently. She'd always thought the solution to her problems with Brad would be for him to get married, for another woman to enter the picture and keep him on a short leash, safely out of her, Zoë's, hair. Suddenly, she didn't like the idea very much. In fact, she didn't like the idea at all. "Well, are you?" She pushed for his answer, told herself there was no good reason for him to keep his love anonymous. At least, not from her. "Are you planning on getting married? Is that why you bought this place?"

"Would you believe me if I told you I've just always had a yen to live on a farm like this?"

She didn't have to think that one over. "No. No, I wouldn't believe you. Come on, Brad. You can tell me. What's the matter with her?"

"Who?"

"Daisy Rose. What's wrong with her?"

"Nothing's 'wrong' with her."

"So why are you being so secretive? Is she already married? Is that the reason you're trying to protect her? Is that why you asked me to impersonate her?" Zoë frowned. "Isn't that sort of risky? I mean, Mr. Ames could easily find out who she is just by pulling her contract.''

"She doesn't have a contract. Well, not exactly, anyway. And she wants to remain anonymous. It's a...personal choice.''

"You can tell *me* who she is, though, can't you?''

"No.''

"Can't or won't?''

"Both.''

Zoë sighed, frustrated and agitated because she did not like the way she was feeling, did not like his having this particular secret. "Then tell me this much. She's the one, right? You're in love with her.''

Again, he offered up that odd little smile. "I'm very fond of her, if that's what you're asking.''

She didn't know what she was asking. She did not know why she was suddenly so restless, so breathless, so *intent* on hearing his answer. She *knew* the answer. Had known it almost the first minute he'd mentioned her name. *Daisy Rose,* he'd said in a voice laced with tender understatement. *Daisy...who had no one except him to stand up for her.* Zoë kicked her foot out from beneath the chenille robe and gave the swing a decent push. "It's none of my business,'' she said decisively. "Just like it's not any of your business whom I go out with, it's none of mine whom you choose to name your farm after.''

"Not exactly the same thing.''

"Oh, yes, it is.''

"No, it isn't. Lazy Daisy Acres is a good name for a farm. Macaroni Acres doesn't have the same ring to it.''

"You just don't like Newton.''

"Guilty as charged.''

"Well, then, I don't think much of your Daisy Rose, either."

"I never expected you would."

What could she say to that? Why would she say anything? It was none of her business. But the idea that she might wind up married to someone *he* didn't like and he might end up married to someone *she* didn't like did not sit well. She wanted Brad to get a life of his own, had wanted that for years. Centuries, it felt like. But she'd never imagined he wouldn't somehow, always be in her life, that he would have secrets he couldn't trust her with. Tim wouldn't have wanted them to drift apart. It had been so important to him, there at the end, that she and Brad stayed with him, together. His wife and his best friend. They'd spent many nights camped, one on each side of his bed, playing Crazy Eights or Five-Card Stud, or just idly turning over cards. They'd spent hours talking to him, talking to each other, sitting in a weighty silence. She'd resented Brad's presence and yet clung to it. She'd needed his steadfast support and yet hated that she did. She'd wanted him to go and yet dreaded the moments he was gone.

And now...? Well, now, she wasn't going to sit silently by while a wordy little mouse of a columnist broke his heart. "Sorry, I didn't mean to be so pushy," she said. "I'm sure you have your reasons for protecting her identity, and I won't ask any more questions."

His smile was quick and deliciously charming. "Can I get that in writing and notarized?"

She playfully punched his arm. "It's not like you haven't been asking me those same kinds of questions for months."

"I've never once asked if you were in love...and I won't, either. That's personal."

"Oh, but whether or not I've received a proposal of marriage, isn't?"

"Marriage involves a whole slew of people, not just the two who choose to enter into it."

"Like you, with me and Tim?"

He took her hand in his, affectionately, easily, the way he'd done a thousand times before...only this time the sudden heat racing across her skin, the blood pounding in her veins, the stark and utter awareness of him coursing through every nerve in her body was different. New. A startling and stunning deviation from the norm. "I got so lucky when Tim married you—" And she was somehow surprised she could hear at all over the thudding beat of her heart and the riotous voices in her head. *Are you crazy...crazy...crazy? This is Brad...Brad...Brad...!* "Not only did you make my friend incredibly happy," he went on. "You let me be Lark's godfather and gave me a perfect excuse to ask you all sorts of impertinent questions."

She had to get her hand back. She had to get control of herself. She had to stop trembling before he realized something was very much amiss. What had he just said? What did he expect her to say in reply? Would her voice shake with this strange new awareness? Would he know the minute she opened her mouth that something had changed between them? No. Nothing had changed. Nothing except the setting. It was strange...and she felt strange...and she'd just leave her hand where it was for another minute...or so. Until everything returned to normal. She'd breathe in, breathe out, breathe in again, and get her raging reaction under control. She'd sort out the reason for the phenomenon later. For now, she'd take her time—there was never a rush with Brad. She'd think of something to say. Something sensible. Something not remotely concerning the tingling sensation that was, at this very second, zinging over her like the sting of a hot shower.

"You're holding my hand," she said, needlessly pointing out the obvious and drawing attention to exactly what she wanted to ignore.

He looked at his hand encircling hers, looked at her, smiled that same delicious smile. "It's to keep you from thumping me on the arm when you can't think of a good comeback line."

"I thought it was because you like being impertinent."

"Me? You're the one asking all the questions."

She pulled her hand away, casually, as if it weren't as hot as bacon sizzling in a skillet, as if it had nothing to do with him. Which it didn't. Not really. "For someone who's asking *all* the questions, I'm certainly not getting any satisfaction. You haven't given me a single answer worth having."

He shifted in the swing, turned more toward her, crossed his arms low across his chest and asked with maddening amusement, "What was it you wanted to know?"

And just like that, he was familiar again. Tim's friend and hers, contained within the boundaries of long friendship. A known factor. Nothing strange or new at all. She laughed, almost giddy with relief—except the laugh sounded odd in her ears, strained and restless and searching.

"I want to know about the woman in your life. I want to know about Daisy Rose. But it's obvious you're not going to talk, so I think I'll just go to bed and try to sleep in this deafening silence.'' She got up, abruptly, setting the swing off balance so that he had to catch hold of the chain to compensate. She had startled even herself with the stampeding impulse to get off this porch and away from him. "Good night, Brad.''

"'Night, Zo. When you hear the rooster sound the alarm in the morning, that'll be for me, so you can roll over and go back to sleep.''

"Rooster?'' She repeated. "There's a rooster?''

"Yep. We lack no amenities here on Lazy Daisy Acres.''

"What time does your, er, alarm usually sound?''

"It varies, but sometime around four-thirty, five.''

Her eyebrows went up. "And you actually get up at that ungodly hour?''

He shrugged. "Somebody's got to milk the cow.''

"Okay,'' she said. "Who are you really? And what have you done with Brad?''

"Maybe this *is* the real me.''

She laughed, because the idea seemed so implausible. "I'm more inclined to think I'm only dreaming this whole conversation, and that tomorrow when I tell you about it—sometime around ten or eleven a.m.— we'll laugh at how bizarre it was.'' Of course, she'd leave out the part about her strange physical reaction to his touch. No point in mentioning that part of her unorthodox dream. No point in remembering it at all. Shaking her head to try to dispel the image from her thoughts, she walked to the screen door and opened it.

"Good night, Zoë,'' he said again, and just the words—the soft, deep flow of his voice—sent a quiver down her spine. Oh, dear. *Oh, dear, oh, dear, oh, dear*.

"Brad?'' she said softly, not knowing what else to

say, not knowing what question to ask, not knowing if those moments of awareness had been illusion or impending disaster. "Do you ever...?"

"Yes," he said in reply. "I think about Tim all the time."

Which didn't answer her question.

Chapter Six

...but take heart, Friend Neighbor, fertilizing doesn't have to be all dirty work. Making your own compost is easy and fun! All right, so perhaps that is a *small* manipulation of the truth, but if you follow the simple steps below (composted...oops! I meant *composed* by my dear Hubby Bee), I think you'll agree that a compost pile can be quite a simple project to begin, involving only a small amount of basic construction and a true commitment to recycling the abundance with which Mother Earth has blessed us....

Lark looked up from pouring syrup on her pancake as her mother shuffled into the kitchen. "Hi, Mom," she said from where she sat on a chair stacked with a phone book and a big, fat cushion. "Guess what? Me and Uncle Brad picked eggs and made you some pancakes! And I'm 'most all done and then Uncle Brad's gonna take me to see the cow...." She turned to her godfather, who was busy cooking more pancakes. "What's her name, Uncle Brad?"

"Homogenized," he said, giving one of the pancakes a flip. "But we call her Homee, for short."

"Homee," Lark continued as her mother shaded her eyes against the sunlight coming through the window and sank into a chair. "And then Uncle Brad said I could ride Purple and Poke-It Dot—*both* of 'em! And then I get to see the piggy goats, only Uncle Brad says I can't get too close 'cause sometimes they're kind of...of..." She turned to him again. "What did you say 'bout the piggy goats, Uncle Brad? I can't know."

"I said sometimes Curly and Moe play rough, and you should not go into their pen unless I'm with you."

"Oh," she said, remembering. "An' guess what, Mom. Uncle Brad got you a straw hat, too, so you won't get freckles. And he got me one, too, and he has one, too. Don't you, Uncle Brad?"

"Sure do." He looked over at Mom. "Pancake?"

She looked back with a frown. "What time is it, anyway?"

"After six, sleepyhead."

Mom made a face at him, then turned to Lark. "How long have you been awake, Little Miss Bright Eyes?"

"The puppies woked me up," she answered, in case she hadn't been s'posed to get up early. "Uncle Brad and me put 'em back in the barn and fed 'em their b'kfst, too."

Mom pulled the sleeves of her robe down over her hands on the table and eyed Lark's plate. "Is there a pancake under all that syrup?"

Lark nodded, feeling happy, happy, happy. "Uncle Brad let me pour it myself."

"I can see that. Need some help cutting it up?"

"I can do it." And to prove it, she dipped her spoon into the pancake and came up with a drippy bite. "See?"

"Mmm."

"Ready or not, your breakfast is served." Uncle Brad slid a plate of pancakes under Mom's nose, right in front of her folded arms.

"Yum," she said, although it didn't sound like she really meant it. "Did you make this, Laura Kate?"

Lark licked syrup off the spoon and her fingers, and shook her head. "Uncle Brad made it, Mom." Grownups were so silly sometimes. "He made the pancakes with the eggs we picked, didn't you, Uncle Brad?"

"Righto, my fine egg-picking assistant. We marched out to the henhouse and told the chickens to hand over the goods."

She giggled and spooned up more syrup. "There's a bunch of chickens, Mom, and some are speckled and some are not and some are red and some are black and some are white. You'll like 'em."

Mom kept frowning at the pancake, not pouring syrup on it or anything. "How many chickens?"

"A dozen or so," Uncle Brad said. "Plus a couple of extra Rhode Island Reds. The flock is pretty much evenly divided among the various breeds. Blue Andalusians, Silver-Spangled Hamburgs, three different varieties of Bantams, and the Reds. Very colorful group of chickens we have here at Lazy Daisy Acres."

Mom frowned at him. "You've been studying about different kinds of *chickens?*"

He shrugged and turned toward the window, and Lark looked from him to her mom and back again. "All the chickens got names, too, Mom," she said, grabbing the chance to talk again. "Me and Uncle Brad named 'em while we were pickin' eggs."

"It's good that all the chickens have names," Mom said, pinching off a piece of pancake. "It'd be terrible for a chicken not to have a *name*, wouldn't it?" She put the pancake bite into her mouth and smiled at Lark. Then her eyes got wide and so did her smile. She looked at Uncle Brad again. "Did you make these from scratch, Brad? They're wonderful."

"He made 'em from *eggs.*" Lark wished her mother would pay more attention before she hurt Uncle Brad's feelings. "He made 'em from the eggs we picked—I already tol' you that. Put syrup on your pancake, Mom. It tastes lots better with syrup."

Mom poured a tiny, itsy-bitsy bit of syrup on her plate and reached for her fork. "You, Farmer Kenneally," she said, "have been hiding your light under a bushel basket and an apron under those overalls. Either that or you've been studying cookbooks along with chickens and apple trees. Don't you think I won't expect a full explanation later—as well as breakfast in bed for the rest of my vacation."

Lark saw Uncle Brad's smile before he turned around to flip another pancake. It made her feel good that Mom liked his pancakes that he had made from the eggs she helped pick. She happily scooped up more syrup and licked it off the bottom of the spoon. "Sonchie says breakfast in bed means your parents are having sex—"

Mom's fork clattered against her plate. Uncle Brad's pancake landed on the floor with a smushy *plop!* Both of them frowned at her.

"That is *not* what that means," Mom said first.

"Breakfast in bed means having breakfast while sitting in bed, and that's *all* it means." Uncle Brad picked the pancake up off the floor and tossed it in the sink. He wiped up the goo that was left over with a paper towel, and then he looked real hard at Mom. "Zoë, you have to move out of that neighborhood. It is not a good place for an impressionable child.''

''And I suppose you think she couldn't have the exact same experience out here in Cowville?''

''Much less chance of it, that's for sure.''

Mom answered right back, but Lark didn't listen, because she was busy thinking. And what she was thinking was that maybe she and Mom could move here with Uncle Brad and not just stay for a v'cation. And what else she was thinking was that she wouldn't care if Sonchie didn't live across the street if she could have puppies and ponies and piggy goats as her friends. And what else she was thinking was that Mom might not know what a good idea it was. ''Mom…'' she said. ''Mom…?''

''Just a minute, Lark. The adults are talking,'' Mom said before she went back to talking to Uncle Brad.

Waiting for her turn to talk, Lark dipped her finger into the syrup and stuck it in her mouth. She liked Uncle Brad 'cause he let her do stuff like pour her own syrup, and he put a pillow on top of the phone book so she could reach the table better but still sit on something soft, and she 'specially liked him 'cause he bought three whole puppies 'stead of one, and 'cause he let her name the chickens and pick the eggs, and he was going to let her ride the ponies…just as soon as he and Mom stopped arguing.

''Okay, okay,'' he was saying. ''It's none of my business where you decide to live, but I just don't think she ought to have an eight-year-old Casanova telling her about *breakfast in bed*.''

''Your opinion is duly noted. Now can we talk about something more interesting? Like who showed you how to make pancakes like this?'' Mom forked a bite of pancake and thrust it into her mouth.

Lark figured this was her chance. "Mom," she said, "let's move here with Uncle Brad. Isn't that a good idea?"

Her mother choked, coughed, grabbed for her glass of milk and drank most of it before she patted her mouth all over with a bright green napkin. "Lark, we've talked about this before. Only people who are married live together in one house."

Lark didn't see that as a problem. "Then you and Uncle Brad can get married and we can all of us live here together. Isn't *that* a good idea, Uncle Brad?"

"A charming idea, Larka my heart, but marriage is a little more complicated than that."

"No, it isn't," she said stubbornly. "Mom wouldn't have to have breakfast in bed every single day, Uncle Brad. Sometimes you could have it, too."

"Lark," Mom said. "Your Uncle Brad and I are friends. We both loved your daddy. We both love you. We both like to spend time with you. But we are not getting married and we are not going to talk about it anymore. Understand?"

Lark looked down at her pancake and decided she wouldn't say she understood, because she didn't. She loved Uncle Brad and she loved her mom and they all had the best time when they were together—except she didn't always get to talk when she wanted. But if they'd just get married, she and Mom could stay on the farm with Uncle Brad and she'd get to ride the ponies whenever she wanted to and she'd have a real daddy like other girls did and Uncle Brad would be the *best* daddy in the whole world, and it was, too, a good idea. No matter what a silly grown-up thought.

"After I eat this last pancake," Uncle Brad said, as he pulled back a chair, sat at the table, and reached for the syrup, "it'll be time for all you cowgirls to ride your ponies, so finish up your breakfasts so we can have some fun."

Lark forgot she was mad and laughed at his joke. "I'm not a *cow* girl," she said.

"Oh, that's right." Uncle Brad poured lots of syrup on his pancakes, which was another reason Lark loved him so much. "You're a radish. I remember."

"I'm a *girl* girl."

"Does that make me a godfather's uncle?"

"No. You're a silly."

"Me?" He looked surprised. "No, I'm Johnny Appleseed." He looked at Mom, who was almost finished with her pancake, and even without enough syrup, she'd eaten it 'most all up. "Did I mention we might be having company today?"

"Company?" Mom repeated.

Lark's heart sank. She knew what that meant. "Noodle Roni can't ride my pony even if he is comp'ny! He's too big."

"Lark," her mother scolded. "Mr. Rooney is *not* coming to visit us, and I want you to stop calling him that awful nickname right now."

"Okay," Lark agreed, ready to forgive and forget as long as he wasn't the company that was coming on her v'cation. "I won't call him Noodle Roni anymore. But you should tell Uncle Brad not to call him that, too."

Mom wet her napkin in her glass of water, and Lark knew what was coming next. She scrunched up her mouth and tried to turn her head, but Mom caught her chin and started scrubbing—too hard.

"Ow!" Lark wrinkled her face in response. "Don't be so rough, Mommy."

"Sorry." She rubbed more softly, but not much, as she asked Uncle Brad, "So, who's the company? Are you springing the mysterious woman behind Daisy Rose Knows on us as a surprise?"

"Not exactly." He took a big bite of pancake and then a big swallow of milk before he got up and carried his plate to the sink. "More like a couple of people from *Home and Hearth Magazine.*"

Mom stopped rubbing at the sticky syrup around Lark's puckered mouth. "Why are they coming here?"

"They're hoping to capture a slice of life here on Lazy Daisy Acres." He winked at Lark. "Ready to ride old Purple and Poke-It Dot, kiddo?"

"Yeah!" Lark jumped from her chair so fast that it fell over with a clatter, and she had to hop over the pillow and the phone book to get to the door ahead of him. "Let's go!"

"Brad," Mom said in a warning voice that Lark understood very well. If he stopped now, she might never get to ride the ponies. So she grabbed her godfather's hand and tried her best to drag him outside before Mom could make him stay. "I think you'd better tell me what this is all about."

Lark tugged hard, and he took another couple of steps toward the back door.

"It's sort of complicated," he said. "But mainly, it's that Mr. Ames likes you and he likes the Daisy Rose Knows column, and he just kind of came up with the idea of putting it all together in a spread for his pet publication, *Home and Hearth Magazine.* It's not really such a big deal. It's a relatively new magazine, and I doubt more than, oh, say, nine-hundred thousand people will even see the feature. Oh, and he said to tell you not to worry. They'll just airbrush those freckles right out of the pictures.''

''Wait a minute,'' Mom said, pushing up from the table. ''Wait just a big fat minute.''

Lark planted her feet and pulled harder. ''Come on, Uncle Brad. Hurry....''

''You'd be doing me a big favor, Zo.''

''I'd be saving Daisy Rose Knows's nose, you mean—and at the cost of my freckles!''

Lark felt him give over to her tugging, and she scurried back, pushing open the screen door with her backside, making way for him to step onto the porch.

He grabbed a hat from the hat rack, pushed it flat on her head, then grabbed a hat for his head, too, before he walked out and let the screen door slam shut, separating them from the kitchen. ''Think of it as a noble cause, Zoë,'' he said through the screen.

''I'm thinking of it as *fraud*.''

''Oh, no. It's much more like being hired to play a role you're perfect for. You'll be great. Ames already loves you, and it's only for a day...or so. Then, I promise, it's breakfast in bed for the rest of your vacation.''

''Brad?'' Mom said in her do-not-run-away-from-me-young-lady! voice. ''Brad...!''

But Uncle Brad swung Lark up onto his shoulders, ducked low under the porch as he jogged down the steps, and headed for the barn.

''Run, Uncle Brad, run!'' Lark yelled.

And he took off at a gallop.

She laughed and hugged his neck, and was glad Mom was still in her robe in the house and that Uncle Brad was taking her to ride the ponies. ''You're the best godfather in the whole wide world,'' she told him.

"Hold on to that thought, Larky Malarkey," he said. "You may be called upon to testify. Now, which pony should I saddle first?"

Lark thought about it. "Poke-It Dot," she decided. "Then Purple. Then Poke-It Dot, again."

He laughed, and jogged the rest of the way to the barn.

"WE NEED TO TALK." Zoë came up beside Brad while he was trotting Purple the pony partway up the dirt driveway and then back to the barn, a distance of perhaps fifteen yards and at least fifteen giggles. Lark was straddling the small leather saddle that straddled the fat, black pony like an oversize belt buckle. She had a fistful of reins and mane clutched within her grip of the saddle horn, and the brim of her hat drooped across her forehead like a long, drawn-out sigh. "Lookitme, Mom," she said in a jostling, jogging, bounce of a voice. "I'm ridin' Purple."

"So I see," Zoë answered, truly glad to see her daughter having such a grand time. Even if Brad had finagled this whole vacation for his own devious purposes. Even if he was using her to protect his precious Daisy Rose. Even if she had stayed awake most of the night convincing herself she'd imagined those few moments of attraction on the porch. "I am *not* going to pretend to be your…your…someone I'm not," she informed Brad in a low—and firm—aside. "So you can govern yourself accordingly."

He lifted an eyebrow, turned, and trotted the pony back up the drive. When he reached her again, not even breathing hard from the exertion, he said, "Okay," turned the pony and trotted off on another loop.

Okay? She declared herself to be above deception,

took a stand for principle, spent a half-hour applying cover stick to her freckles and choosing the right outfit to wear when she informed him that what he chose to do to protect his girlfriend wasn't any of her business, but that she wasn't going to help him do it…and he said *okay?*

"What does that mean?" she asked on his next trip around.

He shrugged. "It means 'okay.' You don't want to be Daisy Rose, and that's okay with me. To tell the truth, I'm sort of relieved you feel that way."

"Well, I should hope so," she said, but he was off again, and she was left with the unsettled feeling that she'd just passed up a great opportunity to see what it was like to be the woman who'd tamed Brad's wild heart. Not that she wanted to know what that was like…well, all right, so maybe she did. Maybe she'd like him to look at her as more than a friend. Maybe she'd like to know how it felt to be held passionately in his embrace, to feel his lips on hers in a wild and reckless kiss. Maybe she'd like to know the touch of his hands in the heat of a long, dark night. Maybe she'd like to touch him freely…like a woman touches the man she loves.

Maybe she was losing her mind. Or not fully awake yet. She and Brad were friends, nothing more.

So, okay, she was somewhat curious about his new love interest. She'd seen him through a lot of meaningless relationships, it was only natural her interest would be piqued when he fell flat on his tight end over a woman, especially one who was too shy to acknowledge her own accomplishments. "You'll get your butt in a sling trying to deceive your employer like that," she said on his next pass, keeping her voice low and masked by Lark's calls of "Watch me, Mommy! Watch me!"

"It's okay. I can always get another job," he said.

"You're going to lose your job over this?"

He shrugged and turned for another jog, granting Lark's giggly request to "Go faster, Uncle Brad! Faster! Faster!"

Zoë frowned after them. She didn't want him to get fired. Brad had lived like a maniac before Tim's diagnosis. He'd worked harder than he'd played, and he'd played harder than anyone else she knew. Physical stress was nothing compared to the expectations he laid out for himself. He wasn't happy unless the pressure was on and rising—whether the name of the game was football, career or just plain living. He'd gone straight from the accolades of high school to the high expectations of a winning college team to the higher expectations of professional sports. And he'd given all he had and more. When the injury had occurred, it had only ended one aspect of his competition with life. He immediately dove into a high-level recruiting career, brokering athletes like there was no tomorrow, socializing like a pro, traveling so far, so fast that he might as well have resided in a suitcase. Tim had tried to warn him that a candle burned at both ends burns badly, but to Zoë's knowledge, he'd never taken advice particularly well.

Then, suddenly, Tim was sick, and everything that had been significant became trivial and unimportant. To her. To Brad. He quit his job to be with Tim, to help with Lark, to be with Zoë through the long days and longer nights. He'd said he didn't miss the rat race, said he never really had the heart for it, anyway. But she'd known he was only saying what he knew she needed to hear, protecting her from worrying over him.

She could not have managed without him, she knew that. But once Tim was gone, there had been no further need of the sacrifice. She had to make her own way in life and learn to depend on herself. She'd urged him—as lightheartedly as possible—to renew his old contacts and pick up the threads of his old life, and that's what she'd expected him to do. But he'd surprised her by taking the job with Ames Publications. It was laid-back, as low key as his other job had been frenetic—stationary and predictable, instead of transient and exciting. Joplin was a nice-size town, but hardly a hub of urban culture. She'd predicted he wouldn't last a month, but five years later, here he was on Lazy Daisy Acres, a captivating sparkle in his eyes, a quickness wrapped into his smile, wearing overalls, and seeming to have nothing more pressing to do than lead a pony up and down the drive to delight her daughter.

It was true he'd promised Tim that he would never take life for granted again. Zoë had been in the room and heard him say it, had heard, too, his promise to always and forever protect Tim's girls from harm. But she hadn't expected it to translate into milking cows and studying apple trees. She hadn't thought it would mean finding out the difference between a plain old chicken and the Foghorn Leghorn variety.

She hadn't thought he'd ever fall in love, either. Not for real. Certainly not for always.

"I'll just turn the magazine crew away," he said, slowing the pony to a walk on the next loop so that Zoë could fall into step beside him. "I'll tell them Daisy Rose has gone off to the Amazon to save boa constrictors, or something noble like that."

"I'm ready to ride Poke-It Dot again," Lark announced, swinging her leg over the saddle and waiting, like the Princess of Lazy Daisy Acres, for her humble servant to lift her to the ground.

"Can't you persuade her to give them an interview?" Zoë asked. "Even a couple of hours might satisfy Mr. Ames, and save your job."

He grinned as he swung Lark off the pony's back. "Are you worried about me, Zo?"

"No," she said. She was worried about where she'd misplaced her normal good sense. She couldn't seem to keep her eyes off him, couldn't stop watching his every move, couldn't help noticing the way his large hands caught Lark and lifted her so gently that she might have been made of spun sugar. She was paying close attention to the way the muscles of his arms flexed with each movement, too, heeding with overwrought intensity the way he seemed so *at home* with himself here on this ramshackle farm. She was shockingly aware of just how physically attractive he was and, oh, so conscious of how her whole being was on alert and newly alive in his presence. Oh, she was worried, all right...but not about him. "I'm sure you'll think of a way to explain why Daisy Rose isn't where she's supposed to be," she offered. "Even though I do think it's unfair of her to put you in the uncomfortable position of having to lie to protect her true identity."

"Maybe I put myself in that position."

"Any woman worth her salt wouldn't let a man lose his job over her." A second thought occurred to her. "Does she even know you could lose your job over this?"

"Oh, yeah. We've discussed it at some length."

"And she still refuses to step forward and accept the responsibility?"

His unexpected rumble of laughter tumbled over her with a mysterious and nubby-soft pleasure. "Yes," he said. "She does." He unfastened the girth and lifted the saddle off the little black pony, who sighed in pony relief. "And so, in the spirit of gallantry, I've decided to step up to the plate and take the consequences like a man. Come hell, high water, or the unemployment line."

She hesitated, realizing that, of course, he'd defend his lady even if she was in the wrong, even if it meant he'd be the one to sacrifice. It was probably a genetic trait, passed down from the original male, and finding a true chest-thumping he-man descendant in Brad. He'd lose his job rather than do the unthinkable and *not* protect a woman he'd vowed to protect. And darn it all, she found herself in the awkward position of being proud of him for it.

Even worse, she wanted to plant herself beside him and stand firm against the marauding world. Protecting an obscure newspaper columnist from having her face plastered across the pages of a magazine was not earth-shattering drama. Maybe Daisy Rose had a solid, sympathetic reason for hiding behind Brad's capable hands. Maybe there was a family situation that could implode under the brunt of exposure. Maybe she was disfigured or had a horrible, debilitating disease. Maybe she'd suffer tremendous embarrassment or even humiliation by being revealed to the public. Maybe authors all over the world hid behind the faces of someone who'd been hired to portray them. Maybe it *was* nothing more than playing a role—and Zoë had once had a flair for the dramatic. "You're positive there's nothing illegal about this charade?" she asked, resigned to her fate.

He looked at her, an expression of hesitation, amusement and utter wonder forming across the angles of his face. "You'd do that for me?"

"Well, I certainly wouldn't do it for *her*."

His smile revived that dangerous swirl of awareness and released a flood of contradictions inside her. *This is crazy,* she tried to tell her quickening heart, but somehow, she knew it was no longer listening. "I can't let you do it, Zoë. Much as I'd like to. It wouldn't be right."

"Yes, well, I'm not asking for your permission. I'm offering to help you, of my own free will, because besides this being the first time I ever recall your asking for my help, I'm glad to finally do something so that you'll wind up owing me for a change."

"You don't need to do it, Zo."

"Brad…yes, I do."

The curve of his lips tightened a little. "I promise if this gets too crazy, I'll put a stop to it. No matter what the consequences to me…or Daisy Rose."

"I never doubted it for a minute, Farmer Kenneally."

His gaze was a thank-you, a caress, and she shivered in the warm morning air. "Do you think it would now be possible to fill me in on who, exactly, I'm supposed to be? Maybe you could let me read some of the Daisy Rose Knows columns. It's going to be very embarrassing if I don't have an inkling of what I've written."

"It'd be less embarrassing all around if none of it had been written in the first place."

"But then, Lark and I wouldn't be here on vacation, would we?"

He had the good grace to wince, and for a minute she thought he was going to say something else, something of import, but then he turned to respond to the persistent tugging of Lark's hand on the loop of his overalls. "Okay, Polka Dot Pony," he addressed the brown-and-white spotted pony tethered near the pasture gate. "You're next on Miss Lark's agenda."

"Saddle her up, Uncle Brad! I'm ready to ride Poke-It Dot." Lark hopped impatiently from one foot to the other, the safety feature of her shoes sparking pink lightning with every hop, her haphazard hairstyle bouncing under the weight of a barrette surplus. It was a hairstyle only a mother—or a godfather—could love. "I've been waitin' and waitin' for you to saddle her, Uncle Brad. You should saddle Mom's pony, too. Then you can trot us both at the same time."

"Hold your horses, there, Larkarama. I'm movin' as quick as I can."

"I'll ride with you another time," Zoë said, although her thoughts were anywhere but on pony activities. She couldn't believe she'd just agreed to put her freckles on display in a magazine that (conservatively) nine-hundred thousand people might see. Wait, no freckles. The magazine would make them magically disappear. Maybe they'd increase her bust size while they were at it, push up her cheek bones, whiten her teeth. Maybe she wouldn't look like Zoë Martin, when all was said and done. Maybe she'd become—in the glossy pages of *Home and Hearth*—a genuine Daisy Rose.

She must be insane. Either that, or she was mere putty in Brad's hands. And while the first possibility was more likely, she realized with soft surprise that the second was far more appealing.

BRAD KNEW he should be shot for a traitor and hung for a horse thief. He had no business even breathing the same air as Zoë Martin, but just when he'd made up his mind to swallow his pride, disappoint the readers and confess the sins of his imagination, she up and volunteered—*volunteered*—to play the part. He should have told the truth then and there, should never have let her believe she was saving his job and his unfortunate love interest into the bargain. How she'd come up with the idea that he planned to marry Daisy Rose, he'd probably never figure out. But she was surprising him a lot lately. Offering to help, agreeing to spend two weeks on the farm, wearing dresses...

He watched her now, as she sat playing with Lark and the puppies in a nest of hay, her red dress pooled around her legs in folds of vivid color, her hair dark and loose about her face. He wasn't going to let anyone touch her hair. Or her freckles, for that matter. She was perfect, just the way she sat. If anything, she was prettier than he'd ever imagined Daisy Rose. Prettier, actually, than she'd ever seemed before. Oh, he'd always thought she was a beautiful woman, had told Tim time and again he was lucky Zoë had ever even looked twice at his ugly mug. Tim had always laughed and replied that the only reason he hung around with Brad was so Zoë could compare ugly to *really* ugly. They'd had a great deal of fun over that. Those had been good times. Some of the best times of his life. Zoë might have kept him at a distance in some ways, but the experiences they'd shared bound them in ways even Tim couldn't have predicted. And Tim had so liked to predict how things would work out.

But Tim was gone, and suddenly, out of the blue, Brad had taken Zoë's hand, felt it tremble, and seen everything in a new light. A softer, warmer and different light. And in it, she seemed lovelier than all of his daydreams put together. She looked sexy and sweet, alluring and...desirable. There was the kicker.

Last night, on the porch, when he'd felt that slight tremor in her hand, he'd wondered if she were nervous or cold or simply excited at the change of scene. But he'd wanted it to be something else entirely. Something shockingly elemental—and he'd recognized his own immediate and unacceptable response for what it was. Desire. Pure, hot, explicit and illicit desire. She was his friend, Lark's mother, Tim's wife, and those were all solid, legitimate reasons that he—her friend, Lark's godfather, Tim's trusted friend—should not feel anything akin to desire for her. It was wrong. Unthinkable.

Well, obviously not that, because he'd been thinking of almost nothing else since last night. Not that he'd do anything about it. Of course, he wouldn't. Couldn't. That would be a betrayal of his promise to Tim, a slap in the face to his own principles. He'd get past this feeling. He would. And he'd do it without Zoë ever knowing that at this moment, he wanted to kiss her, undress her, caress her...more than he wanted to keep on breathing.

"Uncle Brad!" Lark commanded. "Look! Tweedles is bitin' Mom's hair!"

The puppy nipped and pawed at a strand of Zoë's hair, and she responded with a husky, delightful laugh that tightened around Brad's heart and across his body, leaving a lingering sadness.

Sadness? Brad shook off the feeling, telling himself it was simply a by-product of wishing that Tim could be here to witness the scene with him. It was not—

Brad wouldn't allow it to be—that he had to deny himself something he wanted so badly.

Maybe he was reading this all wrong. Maybe what he was feeling had more to do with wanting to protect Zoë from the Noodle than anything else. After all, he'd had high hopes that this little vacation would give her the perspective she'd been missing. He'd imagined evening talks on the porch where he would gently point out Newton's failings as a human being, and where she'd gratefully acknowledge her blind spots as a woman. He'd been confident of his ability to improve her objectivity, turn her focus toward someone more acceptable. And he had not—no way—been thinking that that someone might be him.

Even the thought scared him. Excited him, too. No. Wrong. This was a blip on the radar of his long friendship with Zoë, a moment out of time, a segue into a new phase of their lives. It was *not* a plunge from the cliffs of sanity into emotional disaster. He wouldn't allow that to happen. He couldn't. He'd promised Tim.

"Look, Uncle Brad! Dee and Dum are licking me all over!" Lark rolled in the nest of straw and the puppies romped after her. Zoë commenced tickling Lark with one hand as the pup in her arms kept up his struggle to connect his puppy tongue with her chin.

It was a scene right out of a Daisy Rose Knows column, yet to be written. Not that it would ever appear in print. It was just a moment that would live long in his memory. Long after Daisy Rose had been forgotten. Long after Lark was grown and tickling a child of her own.

"Is that a car?" Zoë looked up from the frolicking, caught him watching her, blushed under his gaze, and still directed his attention to the sound of tires on the driveway outside. "Is that them?"

"We could get lucky," he said. "It could be somebody who's lost and just wants to ask directions."

"HOW THE DEVIL did you ever find this place?" Granite Ames stepped out of the black sedan and began asking questions before the dust in the driveway had settled. "A little off the beaten track even for you, isn't it, Kenneally? Where is she? Where's my little Daisy Rose?"

Okay. He couldn't do this. Brad could not let Zoë pretend to be his alter ego, not when it meant putting up with his short chauvinist of an employer. "Look, sir. I tried to tell you this before, but Daisy Rose does not ex—"

"Here, Mr. Ames." Finger-combing the straw from her hair, Zoë walked from the shadowy interior of the barn, followed by three roly-poly puppies and a tousled Lark, who was smashing her straw hat down low on her head. Zoë offered up a national treasure of a smile to the newcomers, self-consciously tugged her red jumper into place, and looked every inch the walking, talking country girl. And in just a few words, she snatched the moment of truth right out from under Brad. "Welcome to Lazy Daisy Acres," she said, and gave Ames yet another of her high-voltage smiles.

The man took it full force and never even blinked. "Well, well, well," he said, grasping her hand with both of his. "You look even better than I recall, my dear. Have you done something special to your hair?"

She laughed, either by chance or design, with just the right note of discomfiture to charm the old lecher right down to the soles of his flat feet. "I added some hay to the hairstyle. Like it?"

He looked at her from several different angles. "You'll do, missy," he said agreeably. "You'll do better'n lemonade on a hot day—which this one is, isn't it?" He loosened his tie as he glanced at the barn, the house and the rangy mule ambling across the patch of yard at the side of the house. "Give me the nickel tour, Kenneally. No time to see everything. I only came out to make sure you followed my instructions and to get an idea of what-all's gonna be required to get this job done properly. These fellas—" He indicated Lloyd, who, along with two lanky, long-haired young men, had gotten out of the paneled van that was now parked beside the sedan. The trio was looking around as if they'd just landed in an alien world and were expecting to be attacked any moment by giant insects. "—are here to take care of the preliminaries. Let 'em wander around at large, taking pictures 'til they run out of film. I told Lloyd he could be in charge of this phase of the project—not that he's got a clue what to do. But I thought he ought to feel like he's a part of this whole shebang, especially since I'm giving you a few days away from the office. Know what I mean?" Ames nodded, pleased with his insight into employer-employee relationships. "Sometime next week, the crew from the magazine will descend upon you and they'll be staying several days. Don't worry, you don't have to put 'em up. They've got a mobile unit and won't cause too much trouble. Now, I warn you, Carson, the photographer, is a bit of a jackass, and the art director is a real prima donna, but they're the best in the business. And I'm sparing no expense to get this job done right. The public is gonna fall in love with our Daisy at first sight. They won't be able to help themselves." He winked at Zoë, then looked down at the puppy pulling at his shoelaces. "Daughter Lark?" he said. "Is that a hair ball nipping at my pants leg? Or is it just an old barn rat?''

"Don't you know puppies when you see 'em?'' Lark asked indignantly. "That's Dum, and this is Tweedles and Dee."

"Dumb, is it? Now there's a fit name for a pup."

"Uncle Brad thought of it."

"Figures. Takes one to know one, I reckon." Abruptly, Ames's attention jerked to Brad. "What else have you got on this farm, Kenneally? Besides these pups and that mule? Any pigs? What about lambs? I want this to look authentic, you understand."

"One cow, several chickens, two pygmy goats, two ponies, the mule, a stout little mare and three puppies."

"What about corn, peas...pumpkins? Got any of those?"

"Too early for corn. We do have some handsome green bean plants, though, and the tomatoes are just coming on. Will those do?"

Ames frowned. "Not as colorful as I had in mind, but if that's all we've got, that's what we'll shoot." He motioned to Lloyd and the Bobbsey twins, who were standing back with hands thrust in their hip pockets, still gawking at the place. "Lloyd? You know what to do. Jimmy? Jack? This is Daisy Rose, Daughter Kate and Hubby Bee. Let's get this show on the road."

Brad felt Zoë's gaze on him, felt a red-hot spike of embarrassment as she mouthed the question, *Hubby B?*

Where *were* those Mack trucks when a fellow really needed one? "It's a long story," he whispered, then walked over to help the men unload the van with what he hoped was a purposeful air—and not the sheer cowardice which it, in fact, was.

Chapter Seven

So be forewarned, Friend Neighbor, unexpected company can foster the necessity that spurs creativity. The lovely chest now residing in our guest bedroom might still be languishing in the attic if not for the advent of an unanticipated, but welcome visit. Of course, Hubby Bee deserves the credit for finding Gran's old cottage cabinet with its faded rose stenciling, cleaning and restoring the piece, and hauling it to the spare room. But it was Daughter Kate's idea to copy the same rosebud pattern in a stenciling around the windows of the bedroom I'd already painted a tranquil ocean blue. And so it is that Lazy Daisy Acres came to have a 'Rose by the Sea' room. (Picture plus tried-and-true tips on creating your own stencil patterns below.) If you're ever in the neighborhood, stop by and we'll show you 'round....

Hubby B?

Zoë watched Brad scurry away like a mouse with its tail on fire to join the men gathered at the back of the van. *Hubby?* She must have heard wrong. But when she asked her memory for an instant replay, it came back the same: *Daisy Rose. Daughter Kate. Hubby B.* What other little tidbits—no, make that huge *chunks*—of information was he withholding? And how did he expect her to help him when she had to find out the details of this charade in a hit-or-miss and extremely confusing, fashion?

"You must scare the bejeezus outta that boy," Mr. Ames said, his gaze lingering on Brad, as well.

"Me?" Zoë let out an uncomfortable laugh. "I think you're the intimidating factor."

Ames disagreed with a jovial shake of his head. "Nope. For all his bluster, Kenneally doesn't give a penny's worth of chewing gum for my opinion of him. Got to be you that has him rattled."

"Maybe it's the situation," Zoë suggested, thinking perhaps Granite Ames knew more than he let on.

"Could be," Ames replied, not giving much away in either direction. "He's got himself in something of a pickle, it seems, but truth is it works like a four-leaf clover for me. I'm turning his 'situation' into a gold mine, or my name's not plastered on street signs all over Texas!" Ames bent and removed Dum's teeth from his pants cuff before lifting the puppy and dropping him into the curve of one beefy arm. "Since Kenneally's forgotten about me, you can give me the tour, Zoë Rose. Daughter Lark, you mind if I carry this Dum pup around with me on a tour of the farm? No? Good. I'll bring him back to you safe and sound, although he may be missing a few of his baby teeth. Only kidding, kiddo. I'll take good care of him, I swear. Now, Zoë, walk fast and show me all there is to see on this Lazy Daisy farm in the next ten minutes. If you can do it in five, I'll kiss a freckle on your nose."

If that wasn't incentive enough to walk slow, Zoë didn't know what was. She supposed there was no harm in taking Brad's boss on a ten-minute tour, although she could have turned him in a circle and pretty much shown him everything she herself had seen up to this point. The gardens were behind the house. The pond, too. So she set off toward the back, relenting and bending down to pick up the black puppy bounding beside her like a short, round grasshopper in his efforts to keep up. "Lark," she said over her shoulder. "Either come with me or stay where Uncle Brad can keep an eye on you."

Lark raced after the blond pup, and since they were heading toward the van and Brad, Zoë took that as her decision, and continued on with Ames. "This is the house," she said, indicating it with a tepid wave. "That's the barn. Pasture runs from that fence line way over there, along this field, back to that stand of trees, turns and cuts across here. There's a pond, with ducks and frogs and maybe even fish. The vegetable garden is here, the flower and herb gardens on that side." She paused, wondering what he was, in fact, looking to find. "Is that the kind of tour you had in mind? Or did you want to see something else?"

His smile was nice, not trollish at all. "I want to see what kind of pig-in-a-poke I'm buying into, and while I did tell Brad to get you a farm, what I'm investing my dollars and business sense in is the author of Daisy Rose Knows."

"I thought men in your position hired other people to keep them informed about pigs in pokes and—you *told* Brad to buy this place?"

"Hell, yes. Can't turn you into a national icon without the proper setting. You created Lazy Daisy Acres.

I merely told Brad to get you one. Well, I didn't exactly say *buy* one, but I did tell him to find a farm and get you on it. Typical of that boy to think small. If it was me who was smitten with you, I'd have bought up an entire county and given it to you as a wedding present.''

"Wedding present?" Zoë tried not to stammer, though her heart had given a flutter. Smitten? Brad smitten with *her?* "I think you have the wrong idea, Mr. Ames. Brad and I are friends. Just friends.''

"That a fact? So you're not in love with him? Don't want to marry him? Is that it?"

"No. No, I...." In love? With *Brad?* She didn't think so. Sure, lately she'd had some oddly sensual thoughts about him, and some unsettling responses to his physical presence. Last night, in fact, when she'd been thinking about him in ways she'd never thought about him before, in ways she'd never thought of any man—not even Tim—before. But that was fantasy, pure and simple. A momentary imagining. The result of being a female whose sex life consisted of abstinence, abstinence and more abstinence. "Brad is in love with someone else,'' she said.

"Daisy Rose,'' he supplied, as if it were the obvious answer in a crossword puzzle.

His quick, definitive reply nearly knocked the stuffing out of Zoë. If Ames, in all his self-absorbed planning, had picked up on that possibility, as well, then it must be true. She should be glad to have the confirmation, glad to know she wasn't imagining things. But she didn't feel glad at all. Her heart sank like a stone to her toes. "Yes,'' she said, braving a smile. "He's in love with the infamous Daisy Rose.''

"Soon to be the world-famous Daisy Rose.'' Ames

eyed her speculatively. "And what a coincidence. She's you."

"No, she's not." The instant the denial tripped off her tongue, Zoë's heart jumped to her throat in a panic. Only a few minutes into the masquerade, and she'd let the cat out of the bag. "I mean, I'm not *really* her. She's...well, not *real*." Saying more could only make things worse, so she stopped after one last, lame "Not in a *real* sense, I mean."

"Kenneally may act dumb, but he's not stupid." Ames grappled with the wiggly antics of Dum, shifting the little guy from the crook of one arm to the other and trying to keep the puppy from climbing up his barrel chest and licking his chin. "He'll figure out Daisy Rose *is* you, sooner or later. And just so we're clear on this from the start, I don't give a damn who you are, just so long as you understand that any time you're representing Ames Publications, you *are* the Daisy Rose everybody loves like she's their favorite kissin' cousin."

"I don't know if I can handle everything you have in mind, Mr. Ames. Being the author of a small-town newspaper column is one thing. Setting out to become a 'national icon' is something else altogether. Brad never mentioned any of this to me, never asked how I felt about doing it, never even told me there would be a magazine shoot until this morning at breakfast." She was going to pin somebody down on these details, if it was the last thing she did today. "I'm not sure he would have told me even that much if he'd thought he could get away without it."

"You don't seem like a shy gal to me. Have you got a problem with being rich and famous?"

She considered the question, not believing this

scheme had half a chance of succeeding on a small scale, much less on the scale Ames apparently had in mind. "What if I said yes?"

"I'd convince you the right answer is no." He was suddenly so focused on her that he let the pup get a good tongue-swipe across his chin and had to wipe puppy slobber away with the back of his hand. "I'm a persistent man, Zoë Rose. And I get what I set out to get. You don't want to go along for the ride, you just say the word, and I'll have Kenneally round up somebody else to play the part. I own the newspapers and I own the Daisy Rose Knows column. Daisy Rose is the commodity I'm interested in selling, no matter who winds up as the star. I'm here to tell you, Kenneally wants you in the role. He wants it maybe more than I do. So here's my deal with you. Off this farm, out of the public eye, you can be whoever and whatever you please. You can dress up like John Wayne or pick your teeth with tree bark, for all I care. But when you're on my time, when you're representing my interests, you look like Daisy Rose, you talk like Daisy Rose, by damn, you *are* Daisy Rose. You do that, and I'll put you on the fast flight to fortune and fame. But I expect you to do your part. Otherwise, I move on to Plan B."

"What's Plan B?"

"I'll put Kenneally in a dress and put his big nose on the cover of *Home and Hearth.*" Ames winked at her. "That'd jump-start our little Daisy Rose's career and how. Wouldn't it?"

He laughed a big, bawdy laugh, and Zoë couldn't help but smile at the man's heavy-handed method of amusing himself at Brad's expense. "He wouldn't be caught dead in a dress, much less on a magazine cover.

Brad's probably the most *male* male in Missouri. Maybe in the entire country.''

Ames set the puppy on the ground and bent to examine the green tomatoes plumping, but not yet red, on the vine. "He does have an image to maintain, that's for certain. What do you think, Zoë Rose? How long before I can pick one of these and have it with my supper?''

"I don't know," she said. "Why don't you try telling that little green tomato to turn red and ripe, and see if you get what you set out to get?''

He laughed. "I like sassy women. My wife's a world-class sasser. That's half the reason I married her.''

"You're married?" Zoë was embarrassed at the way the question popped out and at her astonished tone, but Ames didn't seem to notice. He just smiled with unexpected tenderness.

"Best twenty-seven years of my life. Her name's Grace and she's the most graceful thing about me. She doesn't travel well, though, so I make my travel fast and efficient, and get home to her.''

"I was married," Zoë said impulsively. "He died.''

Ames looked up and his eyes held genuine sympathy. "Can't imagine anything tougher than that.''

"It was bad, but it was also a long time ago. He and Brad were best friends since kindergarten.''

Ames continued to touch the tomatoes, weighing their potential, perhaps, in the palm of his hand. "Well, that explains it, then.''

"What?''

"Why you scare him the way you do." He straightened and, as his gaze strayed past her shoulder, his forehead creased in a frown. "Hey!" he yelled. "Hey, you! Get away from that."

Zoë turned to see Elmer, his ears tilted forward, tail swishing lazily, teeth bared as he calmly munched on rose petals. "Go away," she said. "Get. Shoo." Gathering the folds of her loose-fitting jumper, she snapped the fabric, hoping to scare the mule. He was extremely under-impressed, and leisurely nabbed another rosebud. Zoë was incensed. This was her garden. She'd been planning for two weeks how she'd tend it, had indulged her sense of smell in the fragrant petals just last night, had had visions of gathering a bouquet of the very buds the dumb mule had just chomped into oblivion. She advanced and flapped the jumper fabric again. "Get out of the garden, Elmer. Get out, *now*."

The two puppies sensed fun in Zoë's snappy efforts, and joined in the game by bounding like terriers to *yip* and *yap* at each other and occasionally at the mule's fetlocks. They were never, of course, quite brave enough to actually get near a hoof. Not that Elmer would have bothered to lift his foot. That might have diverted his attention from the roses, and he was nothing if not focused on his entree. He paid no attention to the dogs and even less to Zoë's attempts to shoo him away. For all practical purposes the animal was rooted to the spot.

"Elmer!" she yelled, her voice climbing in frustration. "Get! Get out of my garden! Leave those roses alone!"

Drawn by the staccato barking of his litter-mates, the third puppy raced around the corner of the house and dashed over to join the fray. Lark followed a moment later, chasing the pup. Brad made the corner a moment after that, chasing Lark. He, however, paused to assess the situation, which caused Jimmy, Lloyd and Jack, who were hot on his heels, to stack up behind him like the Three Stooges hitting a wall.

Ames stood back and laughed—a big belly-shaker of a laugh—amid the shouting, yapping, flapping, and Lark's shrill giggles when Brad scooped her up like a loose ball and tucked her under his arm in a football carry. "Grab his ear, Zoë," he yelled above the noise. "And whisper to him. It's the only way to get Elmer to listen."

She stopped flapping and snapping and waving to look at Brad, thinking she must have heard him wrong. "What?"

"Whisper," Brad repeated loudly. "Whisper in his ear, and he'll move."

She looked from Brad to the munching mule and back again. *"Whisper?"*

"Yes, whisper!"

Zoë turned back to Elmer, looked from his scroungy ear to the tip of rose petal still protruding from his rubbery lips. "Whisper," she repeated, thinking it made more sense to grab his ear and give it a good twist. But what the heck did she know about mules? Feeling like the butt of a joke, she reached out, pulled the mule's ear toward her as she balanced on the balls of her feet, and whispered, "Move your bony behind before I move it for you, understand?"

And, wonder of wonders, he moved. Reluctantly, slowly, certainly without enthusiasm—but he moved. Zoë glanced at Brad with new respect as, her hand just touching Elmer's ear, she walked the mule away from the roses. "It worked," she said with a soft laugh. "It really worked."

Brad grinned and shrugged lightly. "Don't get over-confident. You're still a good ways from the pasture gate."

"We'll get there, won't we, Elmer," she whispered again into his fuzzy ear. He smelled musky, dusty, and faintly of grass, and his ear twitched at the warmth of her breath. But best of all, he plodded like an obedient companion beside her.

"Want me to take him from here?" Brad turned Lark in an underarm flip and set her feet on the ground, ready to relieve Zoë of her old, gray charge.

"No, I'll do it." Zoë thought she deserved to be the one who put Elmer behind bars. "It's the least I can do in memory of the roses he chomped."

Brad smiled his pride in her and a liquid warmth of pleasure flowed through her as she led the mule past the row of men watching in hushed astonishment. "I'll get the gate for you," Brad said. "But watch him. He has tricks you do not want to see."

Striding ahead of her, Brad reached the metal gate leading into the pasture and swung it wide.

"Don't pull his ear, Mom!" Lark yelled from the sidelines, always a champion of the underdog. "He's just a mule."

"Did you hear that, Elmer?" Zoë whispered to the animal, who did seem to like the soft sounds of her voice. "You're just a mule, and from now on you stay in the pasture and out of my garden or I'm going to *yell* in your ear, understand?" She walked him through the opening, gave his ear a rub, then scratched behind it. "If you're a good boy, I'll bring you a treat every day for the next two weeks. But it won't be roses. I don't care how much you like them."

The mule made no indication that he cared one way or the other, but as Zoë walked back through the open-

ing and Brad closed the pasture gate with a *ca-thunk,*
Elmer turned his head, yawned, and made a rude noise
that couldn't possibly have been the razzberry it so
closely resembled.

Startled, Zoë gave a little jump and looked back at
the mule, just as Lark's giggles trilled out across the
yard. "He *thfffted* you, Mom. He *thfffted* you!" She
giggled harder, buoyed by the deep rumble of bass and
baritone laughs joining in, all of which were quickly
overshadowed by Ames's own huge guffaws. He
laughed and laughed and laughed, then wiped his eyes
with the back of his hand and said, "I'd give a thousand dollars to the man who caught that on film."

Jimmy and Jack looked with identical dismay at their
empty hands.

"What am I paying the two of you to do?" Ames
demanded gruffly. "Stand there like a dadgum fence
post with your finger up your...nose? And you call
yourselves professionals. Not a camera to be had between you!" He glared at them. "Well, what are you
waitin' for? A swift kick in the rear? Move!"

They moved. Even Lloyd—guilty by association—
dashed at a race-walk around the corner of the house
as if a giant boot wasn't far behind him. The puppies
spied moving targets and raced after them. Lark
whooped like a banshee and took off after the dogs.
Ames bustled over to meet Zoë and walk her back
across the yard. He tucked her hand in the crook of his
arm and patted it approvingly. "Gardener, philosopher
and mule skinner," he declared with a broad smile.
"Oh, yes, ma'am, you are my Daisy Rose."

Zoë laughed, a trifle uneasy, but a little bit pleased
with the attention. But as her gaze locked with Brad's,
as he gave her a conspiratorial wink, she felt a shift, a

tickle of awareness, a curious connect-the-dots kind of knowing. How had Brad—urban, sports-minded, fast car fanatic, a macho fan of loose women, and all around *guy* guy—known that to move a mule one should whisper in his ear? It wasn't exactly the sort of folklore floating around men's locker rooms. It wasn't the kind of cultural myth likely to be picked up along with a degree from the University of Texas. She'd certainly never heard anything like it before, and she'd grown up in a rural Arkansas town.

Of course, it could have been invented on the spot— a ruse to keep four males from rushing in and creating more havoc than help. He might not have known or even expected that it would work. He could have been as surprised as everyone else that it had. But somehow, Zoë sensed that none of the above was the correct answer to the question she couldn't quite form in her thoughts. The right question would foster the correct answer—and both lay mysteriously in the hands of another woman.

Hubby B. Daughter Kate. It all came back to one…*Daisy Rose.*

Zoë listened to Granite Ames talk about photographers and art directors and the best way to deal with them. She heard him say he was leaving and would return later in the week. She watched Brad check the rosebush for damage, observed the tender care he took when turning over a single leaf, watched as he examined the underside by running his thumb delicately, carefully, and with obvious knowledge, across it.

And she was suddenly and completely determined to get her hands on a newspaper. Whoever and wherever Daisy Rose might be, the best place to find her was going to be in her own words, in black and white…in Daisy Rose Knows.

IF IT HADN'T BEEN for Daisy Rose Knows and the *click-click-click* of thirty-five millimeter film being exposed at a rate of six frames per second everywhere he turned, Brad would have been in hog heaven. He'd wanted to be on Lazy Daisy Acres since the first moment he'd typed the words on the computer screen. He'd invented a home similar to, if not exactly like, this one. In his mind, he'd planted flowers, vegetables, herbs and fruit trees. He'd soothed the squeak of a rusty hinge with a homemade fix and furnished the rooms in antiques he'd refinished himself. He'd tended chickens, gathered eggs, fed and milked cows, and taken care of animals, large and small. And even if his imagination had never conjured anything close to the mulish detail that was Elmer, life on a few acres of unpaved earth had been Brad's favorite daydream for years. That was even before Tim's illness gave Brad the kick in the pants he needed to realize he was working as hard as he could to please everyone except himself. And long before he understood how very quickly life could pass him by, how brief was the opportunity to be happy.

And now he was here, surrounded with the details he'd dreamed up. Maybe not in the exact order he'd dreamed them, maybe not even true to his original concept. But it was an honest interpretation. It was his chance to mesh a secret yearning with a real-life challenge, an opportunity to apply the knowledge he'd acquired in pursuit of those daydreams, a shot at—as Tim would have described it—hearing the music in the meatloaf. He liked his job with Ames Publications. He even, honestly, enjoyed being the anonymous author of a chatty column about life on a fictitious farm. Was it wrong to want to taste an experimental bite of that fantasy, to see what it might be like to live in those daydreams? At least for as long as it took to grow tired of sitting in the porch swing in the evenings, feeling weary, perhaps, but at peace with the world and with himself.

Brad waited as the camera guys snapped off a dozen pictures of the downstairs bathroom before moving into the kitchen. Ames had left a long time before, taking Lloyd with him. Lark had protested the need for, but quickly succumbed to, an afternoon nap. Zoë had announced she was going to locate the nearest town and the closest supermarket. He supposed she'd forgotten something essential and deemed it better to get it now than need it later. So that left him to escort Jimmy and Jack around the property, playing tackle for the two long-haired cameramen as they snooped and nosed around and *click-clicked* into every nook and cranny of his life, collecting preliminary data for someone else who'd come in and do it all over again.

Okay, so it was more Daisy Rose's life than his, more pretense than fact. But he didn't like it for her any better than he did for himself. Hers was a private personality; she was someone more comfortable in a garden than in public, someone with fewer grand ambitions than quiet intentions. Ames was crazy to think Daisy Rose could ever be competition for somebody like Martha Stewart.

Ames was crazy? That was the pot calling the kettle black, now wasn't it? Brad stepped aside as Jack aimed his camera lens at the rows of home-canned fruits and vegetables in the pantry. He'd looked forward to these two weeks with Zoë and Lark, had had plans for their time together and had blindly ignored the farce he'd set in motion. He had to tell Zoë the truth, had to give her the chance to tell him he was an idiot to have believed for one second that he could pass her off as the author of Daisy Rose Knows.

The fact that he had done exactly that, twice now, was due more to fluke than finesse. He'd seen the flash of irritation in Zoë's eyes, knew she was aware that he had yet to tell her the truth. The truth that would disappoint so many people. Besides, if he tried to tell the truth, chances were no one would believe him. *You couldn't write your way into a paper bag, much less out of one,* they'd say. Well, he'd written himself into this one, hadn't he? Maybe sending Daisy Rose to the Amazon hadn't been such a bad idea.

"What's in here?" Jimmy asked, letting his camera dangle from the strap around his neck while he picked up a jar and held it up to the light. "Pickled pigs' feet?"

Jack laughed, pulled out a spent roll of film and dropped in a new canister. Brad took the jar from Jimmy's hand and stacked it back with the others. "Pigs' feet don't look a whole lot like canned apples, which is what is in that jar," he said. He noted that the lid bore last year's date and the words, Apple Pie Filling. Hopefully Jimmy was better at taking pictures than he was at reading. "You boys finish up your camera tricks and leave me alone for a while, and maybe I'll make an apple pie for you to eat after your supper."

"You can make pie?" Jack glanced up from his camera with a look of surprise. "I thought you played professional ball for the Chiefs."

A familiar chagrin attacked Brad head-on. *Real* men didn't bake pies. *Real* men played football. "Yeah," he said. "But I had to major in *something* at college, and cooking was an easy *A*."

The two men exchanged glances, then Jimmy thrust out his chest, grinned uneasily and said, "You didn't major in cooking."

"No," Brad said. "I didn't. It was Interior Design."

Both men shifted uncomfortably, not quite in unison, but close. Then Jack narrowed his doubtful gaze, made his decision and called the bluff with a gruff chuckle. "You're quite a kidder, you know that, Kenneally? But you're workin' for one of Ames's papers, so you must have a degree in Journalism or Marketing or something like that."

Something manly. "You got me," he said with a halfhearted, but oh-so-manly shrug. "I took Journalism."

"Yeah, me, too." The relief was almost palpable in the younger males, and they laughed, nudging each other with an I-knew-it-had-to-be-a-joke elbow. Their reaction was typical, as familiar to Brad as the routine of shaving every morning. Men—*real* men—were more than a little suspicious around any male who cooked, cleaned, or even admitted he knew how. "Figured you were joshin' us," Jack said with a grin. "Figured a guy like you wouldn't waste his time making pies."

Brad would have liked to waste his time knocking their heads together, but considering the fact that he'd taken the macho and easy way out, he deserved a knot on his forehead every bit as much as they did. When would he ever find the courage to look another person in the eye and admit that he could not only make a great pie, but he could do it without a recipe? If he had the apples, he wouldn't even consider using Alphie

Renfroe's canned filling. If he didn't have to show these yahoos around every square inch of the farm, he could put together an entire meal, including appetizers, that would have them drooling all over their T-shirts. Not that *that* would be difficult. A little barbecue sauce, a slab of meat and ketchup would probably have their eyes glazing over with culinary glee.

But that, of course, would be acceptable. *Real* men could grill. *Real* men could cook up a plate of barbecued ribs with both hands tied behind their backs. It was apple pie, chocolate soufflé, salmon-shrimp crepes and spinach quiche that caused the step back, the wary expression, the uneasy humor. Okay, so he knew that wasn't entirely fair. He knew there were men—*real* men—who could and would talk recipes and oven temperatures, organic gardening and healthy pruning, interior decorating, and the delicate balance between restoring and refinishing an antique treasure. Brad realized his size was a factor—he looked like a man's man and was expected to act like one. He recognized that his short but notable career in football, both college and professional, lent credence to that theory. He also freely acknowledged that he'd done nothing to alter that macho image—had in fact, done all he could to promote it. But in his heart of hearts, he knew the problem was his own. It had everything to do with his upbringing and the expectations of his family and friends. Even Tim had never breached Brad's defenses. Even Zoë had never suspected he was interested in anything outside of chasing footballs, fast cars and wild women. Not that he wasn't all male. Not that he didn't genuinely enjoy sports, sports cars, and sporting a beautiful woman on his arm, or in his bed. It was simply that he felt torn between the facets of who he was and who he wanted to be. He was, he supposed, as much Daisy Rose as Hubby Bee.

The only way to bring the two parts of himself into one was to admit that aloud to someone else. But he couldn't tell his parents. Or his impressionable brothers. It was too late to tell Tim, and Granite Ames was hardly a desirable confidant. That left…Zoë. His heart skipped a beat with the thought, and he felt the sweat beading across his brow.

Because as much as he wanted to tell the truth, she was the one he least wanted to tell.

"MORE COFFEE, HON?" The waitress at Buckthorn's Main Street Diner refilled Zoë's cup without awaiting her reply. "You want somethin' else to eat, sugar? You've been sittin' in this booth for quite a spell now, with nothin' more substantial than that little side salad. Sure you wouldn't like a piece of carrot cake? House speciality."

Zoë shook her head, knowing the Main Street Diner probably didn't get too many people who lingered longer than the time it took to order up and eat up Saturday's blue-plate special. "No, thank you," she said, glancing at the woman's plastic name tag before offering her an appreciative smile. "I won't be too much longer, Maxine."

The waitress waved away any worry on that account with a blithe flip of her hand. "No need to hurry. It isn't like we've got customers stacked up waiting for a table this afternoon. You from out of town?"

"Tulsa. I'm visiting nearby."

"Oh. I've been through Tulsa many a time." Maxine nodded and tapped the newspaper spread out on the tabletop. "Readin' Daisy Rose Knows, I see. Y'all get that column in your Tulsa papers?"

Zoë shook her head. "This is the first time I've seen it."

"Well, it's good, I'll tell you that much. That column's the first thing I read when the *Bugle* comes out. Sometimes I read it half a dozen times." She hooked an elbow on the padded edge of the booth and cocked an eyebrow as she leaned in and lowered her voice. "Don't tell anyone I told you this, but nine times out of ten, if there's a recipe in that column, it'll be on our menu the very next week. It's called somethin' different, o' course, but folks who read the column know where the recipe come from. Good cleaning tips in there, too. I mean, I never've thought of adding sugar in with soap to wash grease and such off my hands. Makes it gritty, you know, and scuffs that dirt right off. And vinegar—I'll bet Daisy Rose has a hundred-and-one uses for a bottle of vinegar. Then, there's all those decorating ideas she has...." Maxine shook her head in wonder that there could be so many creative ideas in the universe. "Why, I followed her directions to make a canopy headboard for my bed and it turned out real nice, and not just a little romantic, too. Even Cheeve—that's my husband—thought so...if you know what I mean."

If Zoë hadn't known, the wink and clucking of the tongue would have clued her in. But she had known, because she'd spent the last two hours reading and re-reading all the back issues of the twice-weekly *Buckthorn Bugle* that she'd been able to carry from the newspaper office across the street. Four months' worth of newspapers equaled just shy of thirty-five Daisy Rose Knows columns, beginning with the piquant "Hi!

You probably don't know me, but I'm your neighbor down the road at Lazy Daisy Acres...." There were a few missing issues, once or twice when the column hadn't appeared in its normal front-page position, but she hadn't read far before she was as charmed as the rest of Daisy Rose's "Friend Readers."

And Zoë had not expected to be charmed. She'd approached the columns with real resistance, anticipating an insipid, silly, falsely countrified and condescending tone to run throughout the articles. She should have known that the love of Brad's life would be someone shy, sweet and silken-tongued. She shouldn't have been surprised that when he did finally fall in love, he'd fall for someone very special.

And Daisy Rose was certainly that. There was a novelty to the articles, a shy, let's-be-friends approach that somehow transformed the print into a genuine connection between the reader and the writer. It read like an easy conversation with a neighbor down the road. A friendly chat. The exchange of a recipe for a few minutes of time. A sharing of ideas: "This is how I tackled that problem and maybe it would work for you..."

"I'm enjoying the columns very much," she said to the waitress, who nodded in enthusiastic agreement. "Do you know the author?"

"You know, I'm just not sure. I thought once it might be Darlene Altmier. She lives on a place that sounds an awful lot like that Lazy Daisy Acres, and she does have the gift of gab, let me tell ya. But one day she come in here and accused me point-blank of bein' the one who wrote it. So that put the end to that idea. Even Bobby Dean—he's a reporter for the *Bugle*—said it's sent anonymous-like, and he doesn't know who the real Daisy Rose is.'' The woman shifted and leaned more of her weight against the side of the booth. ''I do think it's somebody from Buckthorn, though.''

Zoë smiled, encouraging confidences. ''Surely a woman with a strapping hunk of husband like Hubby Bee and a precocious little girl like Daughter Kate would stand out in a small town like this.''

''Oh, I don't think she used their *real* names.'' The waitress shook her head, then furrowed her brow at the possibility. ''Do you?''

''Probably not. That would sort of defeat the purpose of a pseudonym. Of course, she could have made them up entirely.'' Zoë knew that wasn't true—there were too many details in the columns to be coincidence. Brad had to be feeding the writer those details, coaching her through every column. How else could she have known? How else did she give it such a feel of truth?

Maxine disagreed by pursing her lips. ''Nope. Somewhere around here is that farm and those people. Maybe not exactly the same, but near 'nough that sometime, somebody's gonna recognize 'em. Although I'll tell you one thing, if it was me writing somethin' like that, I'd turn Cheeve into a hunka-hunka burnin' love, too. Who wants to read about a potbelly and a bald spot? Wouldn't it be funny if'n it turns out Hubby Bee's got a gut as big as Claremore and not ten minutes' worth of hair on his head?'' She laughed, fished an order pad from her apron pocket and peeled off the top ticket. ''Coffee and a side salad,'' she said, laying the ticket on the table next to the chipped, blue-and-white saucer. ''Sure I can't get you a piece of that carrot cake, hon?''

"No." Zoë thanked her with a smile. "I've got to return these newspapers and head for home."

"Goin' back to Tulsa this evenin'?"

"Head for the farm, I meant. I hope I can find my way. It's a little off the beaten path."

"What's the family's name? Maybe I can give you some directions."

"I don't know who owned it before. My friend only bought it a couple of weeks ago."

Her penciled-in eyebrows rose. "Well, only place I know of that's been up for sale is the Renfroe farm. That it?"

"Maybe. The name sounds somewhat familiar."

"That must be it. Nice little place 'bout twenty, twenty-five, miles from here. Funny thing, though. Every time they sell it, something peculiar happens a few weeks later and they wind up taking the place back. Why, from what I hear, they must have moved in and out of there half a dozen times." She tucked her pencil behind her ear. "You notice anything odd about the place? Does it seem okay to you?"

There were odd things about the farm, for sure, but Zoë wasn't having any luck figuring out what pestered her like a mosquito about Brad and Lazy Daisy Acres, much less the previous owners. However, she was suspicious about the Renfroes and all they'd left behind. And she would certainly be on the lookout for anything "peculiar." "It's a lovely farm." She made a face. "Well, except for the mule."

Maxine patted her pockets, then her hair, and finally withdrew the pencil from the nest of salt-and-pepper curls above her ear to point it at Zoë. "You take care now. And if'n you find out who our Daisy Rose is, you be sure and let me know, ya hear?"

"Same here." Zoë began to gather up the scattered pages, half tempted to tell Maxine to be on the lookout for a future edition of *Home and Hearth* magazine. But the front door opened and a family of five poured into the restaurant with a deluge of noise, so Maxine bustled over to get them seated.

Zoë stacked the newspapers, making an effort to put them back into the proper order. Her gaze kept picking up a word here and there in the columns, and she found herself wanting to reread them, wanting to be charmed all over again by the down-to-earth Daisy Rose. But pleasure was not the reason she'd originally wanted to read these columns. It certainly wasn't the reason she'd come to Buckthorn this afternoon. Somewhere in these newsprint pages was the clue she'd hoped to find. She'd missed it somehow, hadn't been able to ferret out the information she wanted, could not seem to read between the lines.

Brad had filtered so much information from his life—and hers—into these Daisy Rose stories that it was difficult to separate the reality from the fiction. He must have spent hours with Daisy Rose in order to create this fictional world that read like truth, that was, in so many ways, absolutely true. He must have laid out the whole idea for her to write up each and every time, then edited it with a fine-tooth comb. Twice weekly for at least four months, probably longer. That was a lot of effort to put into helping someone else. Someone too shy to accept a well-justified success.

Zoë sighed and slid from the booth. Brad might as well have written the column himself—

And there it was—like the last drop of punch that fills the punch bowl to overflowing and sends the liquid spilling down the sides. Impossible, improbable and unbelievable as it was, it was the only answer that made curiously simple sense. Brad *had* written these columns. From that first self-effacing "Hi, you probably don't know me, but...." to the more confident "...well, needless to tell you, Friend Neighbor, I spent that Sunday afternoon making a daisy-chain necklace for Daughter Kate...." Brad had crafted the words, the characters, the setting and the charm of Daisy Rose Knows. And without help from anyone else.

She didn't have a clue how the Brad she knew—or *thought* she knew, anyway—had learned about chocolate soufflés, organic methods of fertilizing a garden, and kitchen curtains. She couldn't even get her imagination around the idea that he would have any interest in all the tips and tidbits Daisy Rose had written about. He'd never, to her knowledge, admitted that he had any inclination to write anything other than a check. He'd never displayed more than a basic impulse toward tidiness, much less real housekeeping. As for decorating, his apartment certainly didn't reflect Daisy Rose's flair or her eye for color. Zoë would have staked a million dollars that in Brad's lifetime, he had never even tried to grow a leaf of ivy. Yet he was offering advice on how to start a compost pile...

She sank onto the vinyl-covered seat again and her gaze sought out the now-familiar byline one more time. This couldn't be—yet she knew it must be true. He was the author. And for all the years he'd been in her life, despite the emotional journey they had shared, she didn't really know him at all. She'd accepted him at face value, not looking deep enough to see the entire spectrum of colors in his personality. Had Tim known? Maybe. Probably. How could he not have known? How could she not? And how had she misjudged Brad so completely?

She should have realized the incongruity when he first asked her to stand in for Daisy Rose. Should have picked up on the possibility the minute she set foot on the farm, the very second she saw him in those overalls. Grabbing up the top newspaper, Zoë read through the column again, then shuffled the papers and read another…and another.

It was all there, the answer as clear as spring water, now that she knew the question to ask. Every column was packed full of clues that pointed straight as an arrow to Brad Kenneally. It was like suddenly discovering that the sky she'd always believed to be a nice shade of blue was really a rather spectacular orange. It was a grand twist at the end of a good book, the surprise *Gotcha!* in the last two minutes of a well-made movie.

Zoë wasn't certain what she should do with her new insight. But she did recognize, with equal parts stunned certainty and sure acceptance, that what bothered her most at discovering Brad's true identity was not the surprise, but the fact that her first, overriding emotion was a pure, sweet, wellspring of happiness that he was not in love with another woman.

Chapter Eight

So imagine my surprise, Friend Neighbor, when there under the dried and dying foliage of the much-maligned hydrangea bush I found a thriving colony of lemon balm. (Drying tips follow.) Daughter Kate and Hubby Bee had gone into town and there was no one to call to see this whimsical touch of Mother Nature's, so I share the mystery of it only with you. The plant should not have been so far from its relatives in the herb garden, and it should not have been growing, short and stocky, there in the dark, sweet shade of the dying hydrangea, but so it was. And this winter, at the first sign of a cold or on a day when the sky is gray and chilly, I will brew lemon balm tea and remember with grateful affection the gift of a small miracle from my garden....

Brad felt her eyes on him even when she wasn't in the room. He felt her watching even when she seemed completely absorbed in other things. He felt unsettled, uneasy and cautious in her presence, and he wasn't liking the change one little bit. Something was different

with Zoë, had been different since the episode with
Elmer, but damn if Brad could figure out what it was.

He had some very good ideas what it *wasn't,* and
could run through that list with alphabetical precision.
Eerie, imaginary and spooky, the feeling was not. Ditto
to bizarre, magical and weird. It was subtle, strange,
and nothing he could put his finger on. He didn't believe she was angry with him, although, Lord knew,
he'd never been particularly adept at correctly inter-
preting a woman's emotions before they just up and
smacked him in the face. He didn't think he'd done
anything to hurt her feelings, either, but that, too, was
an arena in which he'd never bet cold hard cash.
Women were hard to predict, and they could turn sensitive over the most innocuous comment…or lack of a
comment…or even a comment that wasn't what they'd
wanted to hear.

But something about Zoë had definitely changed,
and whatever it was caused a nervous little jump under
his skin every time she walked into a room, sat beside
him, across from him, or just walked on by. Every time
she smiled or touched her hair, or even when he caught
a lingering fragrance that signaled that she had been
where he was, his whole body went on alert, as if he
were trying to walk through an unfamiliar room in the
dark. There was a new awareness on her part that
hadn't been there before, which made him more aware
of her. And he had absolutely no idea what to do about
it.

If she'd been any other woman, he'd have chalked
it up to a simple, basic physical attraction, kissed her,
slept with her, perhaps, if she were agreeable, and then
gone about his business without dwelling on the what,
how, when and why of it. But this was Zoë, and the

mystery of it frustrated him. None of the answers he thought of seemed to fit—and he wanted an answer, despite the undoubtedly saner, wiser voices of reason in his head that warned him not to name this simmering, disturbing condition. There were any number of reasons—chief among them that women were basically beyond a man's understanding, anyway—to shrug his shoulders, put it down to female foibles and let it go. Not his concern. Not his worry. If she wanted him to know, by golly, she'd tell him when she was good and ready.

He told himself to forget about it, quit thinking about it, ignore it. He decided a dozen times or more that he would do exactly that, was even able to pretend for as long as five full minutes that he was under stress because of the magazine shoot and was simply imagining reactions in the people around him. But the awareness was there only with Zoë…and he could not forget it, stop thinking about it, or make it go away. And he certainly could not ignore it. The jump under the skin, the prickly sensation along the back of his neck, the sit-up-and-pay-attention tingle of his very male nerve endings every time he caught a glimpse of her bare leg or the curve from her throat to her shoulder, or the shape of her beneath the wispy float of her dress. What she wore, what she said, what she happened to be doing—none of that made any difference. Something had changed in the way she looked at him, and that something had changed how he looked at her, as well.

He didn't know what it was, and he was ninety-nine percent certain he did not want to know. But damn if that one niggling, leftover percent wasn't causing him a whale of a lot of doubts.

ZOË COULDN'T take her eyes off Brad. Well, of course, she didn't stare at him twenty-four hours a day, but she never stopped thinking about him. From morning to night to morning, he was on her mind. Whether he was in her sight or out of it. Where was he? What was he doing? What was he thinking? Was he Brad, the athlete? Or Brad, the writer? Was he a split personality or a man of unsuspected depths? Was he truly knowledgeable or just a know-it-all? How had he come to create Daisy Rose? And why? Was she his ideal woman, neatly contained within the thousand words or less of a newspaper column? Was he more the man Zoë had always known, or more closely akin to Daisy's Hubby Bee? Zoë had no answers, and so she thought and watched and watched and thought some more.

For three days after her trip to the *Buckthorn Bugle,* she watched Brad like television, attuned to the nuances of drama, comedy, and the breaking news of her shifting perspective. She watched him, aware that if what she suspected was, in fact, true, and that if what she was feeling was real, she would be risking the comfortable balance of their relationship by pursuing that truth. Yet, in just acknowledging that a different relationship was possible, the balance had already slipped out of her control. So for three days, she watched and listened and tried her best to figure out how she felt about him.

She'd never given the matter much thought before—the question had simply never arisen. He had come into her life through his relationship with Tim, and remained in her life, she believed, because of that friendship. When she'd married Tim, she'd accepted Brad as a member of her new family in the same way she would have accepted a close relative or a beloved pet.

Brad was a fixture in Tim's life and therefore he became a fixture in hers, a faithful companion who was with her through thick or thin, whether she wanted him or not. He was an entertaining playmate at times, a comforting presence at others, and, yes—quite often, in fact—an annoying pain in the butt and more hindrance than help.

But through the good times and the bad, her feelings for Brad and his feelings for her had been filtered through their love for Tim. Tim was their link and their interpretation of each other. Tim loved them both, and in doing so he bound them together and kept them separate. There were unwritten rules between a man's wife and his best friend. No one had pointed them out to Zoë. No one had needed to. Certainly, Brad had never needed any instruction on how he and Zoë should get along. She had accepted Brad because—and only because—he also loved Tim. Brad had accepted her for the same reason. Tim—and by extension, Lark—was all Brad and Zoë had in common. All they ever would have in common. Or so she had always believed.

But that did not explain why she had been threatened by, been positively *green* with jealousy over, his perceived relationship with a woman named Daisy Rose. None of it explained how she could feel so totally bewildered by this change in perspective. Tim would have confronted Brad, challenged his secret identity, and wound up laughing at the magnificent coup pulled off by a man who, above all else, he respected. Zoë respected Brad, too, but wasn't ready to confront him—didn't know if she ever wanted to do so. Daisy Rose wasn't her secret to confess. It wasn't her option to applaud the audacious way Brad had written himself into the small-town hearts of his readers, and she definitely did not want to be the one to disillusion those readers, either. Insisting Brad admit that it was he who wrote the column would accomplish more harm than good, as far as Zoë could see.

He was a man fiercely devoted to his image of himself, to his persona as a he-man, an athlete, a former football hero. She had met his family—the parents who saw him as the embodiment of their ambitions, the younger brothers who idolized his athletic accomplishments. She had been with him when a sports fan, who had followed his stellar career and mourned his injury, asked for an autograph. She had watched him over the years and she understood the battles that now must surely rage between the All-American athlete and the folksy-wise Daisy Rose. That Brad had published the column in the first place spoke volumes for his conflict, in her opinion. The fact that he'd kept writing it told her he enjoyed the relationship he'd built with his "Friend Neighbors," and she knew in her heart he'd never willingly let them down. Not that she would ever point that out to him. Not that he would be anything other than embarrassed if he found out she knew. Not that he'd let himself believe for a second that she admired him for declaring himself at war—even if he'd done it under a pseudonym.

But privately, he had to be pleased with all the interest in the column, and, conversely, he must be scared all the way down to his rock-hard abdominal muscles by the success of Daisy Rose Knows. He had to have mixed feelings about asking Zoë to take on the role…about asking for help at all. On the other hand, who else could have, or would have, been able to slip into the part? Brad could hardly deny that she and his fictitious columnist had a great deal in common. A turn of phrase, the obvious love for Daughter Kate, who could be none other than Lark, the subdued yearning to live in a house with a garden, and so many other clues. There was no doubt in Zoë's mind that Brad had watched her over the years and transferred some of what he'd observed into the character he'd created.

She was flattered by, intrigued with, and attracted to this glimpse into Brad's secret life, the secret way he must—or, at least, might—feel about her. She wanted to dive into him, discover who he really was, explore who she was with him, find out who they might be together.

And therein lay the change, the subtle switch in understanding that overwhelmed her with a fierce and fearful excitement. Was she in love, or only newly conscious that love was possible? Not just possible, but, oh, so suddenly desirable?

Brad might not share any of her emotions. That, too, was possible. Probable, even. He could not have failed to notice that from their very first meeting, she'd kept him at a distance. She'd always supposed it was a natural defense, her way of excluding him from the inner circle of her relationship with Tim and Lark. But suddenly she saw it as a more primal barrier against an attraction that could not have been allowed to grow— or even to exist. An attraction that of necessity had to remain unrecognized and unimaginable during her marriage. An attraction that had lain fallow in the months of Tim's illness, and been rendered dormant by the heartbreaking sorrow of their mutual grief. But now, five years later, as strange as it seemed, Zoë had come fully awake to the possibility—probability, even—of an emotion that had been growing in the shade of her sorrow. An attraction—dare she call it love?—that held more possibilities than she had ever allowed herself to imagine.

She was scared that he didn't feel the same.

And just as scared that he did.

So she watched him…and she wondered.

LARK WATCHED HER MOTHER and Uncle Brad so hard that it made her teeth hurt. There had to be a way to get them married. She liked the farm. She wanted to live on the farm. She wanted Uncle Brad and Mom to live on the farm with her. She didn't want to go back to Tulsa, but she did want to talk to Sonchie. He'd know what to do to get people married. He'd know how to make them see what a good idea it was. But she couldn't talk to Sonchie, so she'd figure it out by herself. She would.

Before the v'cation was over. Before Mom said it was time to go home. Lark would find somebody to help her make a wedding. Everybody liked weddings. Sonchie had said so when they were playin' honeymoon. He said that after a wedding people smooched and slept in the same bedroom and lived in the same house and had the same kids, too. Lark didn't know what smooching was and she didn't know how to have a wedding, except for one time she went to one and there was cake with lots of icing. And it was real good cake and *real* good icing. So if she could get Uncle Brad and Mom to eat cake and smooch, then maybe that was how they'd get married. All she had to do was make the cake and tell them to smooch and then they'd be married and they'd all live on Lazy Daisy Acres forever. Lark and Mom and Uncle Brad, and Tweedles, Dee and Dum, and Homee the Cow and Purple and

Poke-It Dot, and all the chickens, and the piggy goats, and even Elmer.

"I want cake," she announced at breakfast.

"What kind of cake?" Uncle Brad asked, pouring her a glass of orange juice.

"Wedding cake."

"Who's getting married?" Uncle Brad wanted to know.

"You and Mom," Lark told him.

Mom's bowl turned over all of a sudden, spilling cereal flakes and milk across the table, and then she jumped up so fast that her chair wobbled and fell over with a *ka-thunk!* Uncle Brad had a funny look on his face as he reached behind him to grab a dishcloth from the counter and laid it across the milk-and-cereal mess. Mom had a funny look on her face, too, but then she bent to pick up the chair and Lark couldn't see her expression anymore. Uncle Brad watched Mom with a frown for a minute, then he raised his eyebrows and turned to Lark. "Where did you get that idea?"

"I got it from thinkin'," she said proudly.

He glanced again at Mom, sort of like he was waiting for her to say somethin', but she was on her hands and knees on the floor, using her napkin to mop the milk puddle down there, and didn't say a word. So then he said, "I'm glad to know you're using your noggin for something more than a place to wear your hat, Larkaroo. But just because you think of an idea doesn't mean it can happen."

"This can happen. All you got to do is eat wedding cake and smooch Mom, and then we'll be married!"

"*Smooch Mom?* Did that Sonchie kid tell you this stuff?"

Lark shook her head vigorously. "I thinked it myself."

He rubbed his ear and then his chin. "Do you even know what *smooch* means?"

"I can't know, but you can do it, Uncle Brad. I'll help you. Smooch her, Uncle Brad! Smooch her *real* good!"

There was a loud *thump* on the underside of the table. "Ow," Mom said, pulling to her feet and rubbing her head. "I bumped my head."

Lark knew how to fix a bump. "Let Uncle Brad kiss it and make it all better, Mommy."

Mom got the funny look on her face again, and when Lark looked at Uncle Brad, he had it on his face, too. "It's okay," Mom said in a rush. "It doesn't hurt at all."

Uncle Brad didn't say anything; he just kept looking at Mom like she'd said something he didn't hear right. Lark took a drink of orange juice and set down the glass, careful always to hold it with both hands. "Don't you think gettin' married's a good idea, Uncle Brad? Don't you want me and Mom to live here with you? I think it's a real good idea. And we can eat wedding cake and smooch and then we'll be married and happy as warthogs!"

"Warthogs?" Zoë repeated. "Are warthogs happy?"

Lark nodded. "Sonchie said so."

"Well, if he said it, it must be true." Brad hoped that would put an end to this discussion. Wedding cake and smooches did not make for comfortable conversation around the breakfast table, that was certain. The subject played havoc with his appetite, too. And his imagination. If the morning light weren't dancing all over this cozy kitchen in vagrant, elusive sunspots, it would have been easy to believe Zoë had blushed like a bride for no reason other than Lark's innocent remedy for a bump on the head.

"Sonchie's real smart," Lark announced happily. "And I am, too. Sonchie says I have real good ideas—and I do, don't I, Uncle Brad?"

Brad knew this was shaky ground. Not because he hated to agree with anything that eight-year-old hoodlum said. And not because he didn't know how to answer Lark's unspoken question without hurting her innocent feelings. The thick feeling in his throat had less to do with Lark's attempts to live happily ever after on Lazy Daisy Acres than with Zoë's startled reaction to the idea. It had to do with her spilling the cereal and bumping her head. It had to do with the even more startling expression he'd glimpsed briefly on her face. Not once, but twice. It had to do with a sudden, nearly irresistible urge on his part to take his godchild's advice and give Zoë a "smooch." "Larkarena," he began, but had to stop to clear his throat before he could set the record straight. "Your mother and I are not getting married."

Lark raised her chin, and her blue eyes pinned him with a cool, take-no-prisoners regard. "Why not?"

"Because." Zoë suddenly found her voice as she carried the wet cloth to the sink and prepared to rinse it out.

Lark's regard swiveled to her mother. "Because why?"

"Because we're not. Now, finish your orange juice so we can get you dressed."

"How come?"

"Because you can't wear your pajamas all day."

"How come we can't get married?"

Brad wanted to jump in and salvage the discussion with a quick and witty diversionary comment, but all he could think about was Zoë's hair tumbling prettily about her shoulders, Zoë's hands wringing out the dishcloth, Zoë's bare foot worrying—up and down, up and down—over the calf of her supporting leg. "Laura Kate," she said. "Remember what I said about adult conversations and how children should not expect to be a part of them?"

Lark wasn't giving up that easily. "No, ma'am," she said. "I can't know that." She crossed her arms and pointed her determined little chin at the sky. "I want wedding cake!"

The *So there!* might have been silent, but it hung in the air like the smell of frying onions, and Brad knew he had to do something before the whole day became shadowed by a gloomy pout between mother and daughter. "After we feed the animals, Lark-o-Crocker, you and I will bake a cake. How about that?"

"What kind of cake?"

"Chocolate?"

"Nope. A wedding cake."

Obviously, there would be no negotiation on that point. "I suppose we can make it a wedding cake," he said slowly, wondering if Zoë's stillness was as tension-filled as it seemed. "Curly and Moe have been thinking about getting married. We'll just ask them if they want a wedding cake."

Lark's gaze swept from him to her mother and back again, and Brad saw distinct calculation going on in those baby blues. "We'll make a *real* wedding cake?" she asked. "With *real* icing?"

"Yep."

"A *wedding* cake?" Lark stressed her qualification and double-dog-dared him to back out of the deal. "You promise?"

"A wedding cake," he said. "I promise."

Zoë turned from the sink and leaned back against it. "A wedding cake for two goats?"

Her eyes met his and his knees practically buckled with the impact. And to think he'd been wondering if she could have been blushing. He was the one in danger of that. He was the one who felt as if his whole body were stuttering with anticipation and alarm. Something was going on here, all right. Something a little too familiar for comfort. He didn't want to think what he was thinking. He didn't want to feel what he was feeling. And he was damn sure he did not want to understand what was happening. He took a deep breath. "Do you have a better idea?"

There was a long pause, accompanied by a long look, before she pressed her lips together and shook her head. "Yes," she said. "I think I'll take Lark upstairs and get her dressed. Then maybe we'll go into Buckthorn and…and buy the stuff to make the cake."

Brad nodded, grabbed his hat and headed out the door, bent on a fast getaway. It was either that or he was going to find himself going along with Lark's instructions. *"Smooch her, Uncle Brad. Smooch her real good!"*

"WE NEED TO TALK."

Zoë looked up from weeding around the begonias, sat back on her heels and pushed up the brim of her hat. Brad's shadow loomed like a thundercloud above her, but his expression was more troubled than thunderous, his manner more nervous than perturbed. A tickle of awareness flip-flopped in her stomach. A dizzy spin of attraction forced her to look down, away from this man who was suddenly exciting her in ways she couldn't even begin to count. "Did you get the cake baked?" she asked.

"It's in the oven now. All four layers."

"Four? That sounds ambitious."

"I felt lucky to whittle her expectations down to just four. She has very strict ideas about wedding cakes."

"I don't know where she comes up with these ideas. I think she's only been to one wedding in her whole life."

"Well, it obviously made quite an impression. Either that, or the H-O-A-B-C kid has told her all he knows about the subject."

Zoë decided not to expand on that theory. "What's she doing now? Scouring the cookbooks for decorating ideas?"

"She's napping." He stooped down next to Zoë and pulled a particularly scraggly weed up by its roots, then tossed it aside. "I read the *Three Billy Goats Gruff* and *The Little Gingerbread Man* and had to faithfully promise about a thousand times that I would not, under any circumstances, ice the cake without her...before she finally gave up the battle and fell asleep."

Zoë worked in silence for a moment, awed by the excitement she felt at his nearness, confused at how quickly he'd gone from being an old friend to an unknown factor. "I'm surprised she managed to stay awake through two stories and even a hundred promises, considering how early she's been getting up every morning."

"She seems to be making up the difference with long naps every afternoon." His hands stilled, his wrists fell slack as he rested his arms on his large, tightly corded thighs. "She's got the idea that the three of us could live happily ever after here," he said, edging into the subject Zoë knew he'd come out to talk to her about. "She thinks if we eat the wedding cake, we'll be married. Simple as that."

"You left out the smooching."

"She doesn't even know what that means."

Zoë risked a glance at his face, but he looked out across the pasture, very carefully avoiding looking at her. "But you and I know what it means, don't we, Brad?"

His dark eyes came to hers, full of questions and genuinely puzzled. "You want to tell me what's going on with you, Zo? Because something sure as hell is out of whack around here."

She hadn't expected a direct question. A flippant remark, perhaps. A super-studly comment, maybe. Even an abrupt change of topic. But not honesty. How was she supposed to respond to that? "I don't have any idea what you're talking about," she lied.

"How about the way you jump every time I get within arm's reach of you? How about the way your expression turns guilty every time I glance in your direction? And how about the—the way you're looking at me right now? Like I'm Santa Claus checking up on whether you've been naughty or nice? How about that, Zoë? Does that give you any ideas?" He rose like a phoenix, and stood there looking down at her. "Well? Does it?"

Feeling unaccountably shy and as much afraid to speak her mind as afraid the chance might not come again, she dusted dirt from her gardening gloves, took them off and let them fall beside the begonias. Then she braced a palm on each knee and pushed upward. Brad's hand was on her bare arm, to steady her and protect her from falling, before she was a quarter of the way to her feet—and his shockingly sensual touch submarined her efforts, sent a fury of longing ricocheting from her skin to the very core of her body. She tried to conceal her trembling, hoped the straw hat hid the desire she knew had to be obvious in her face. But she had to see him, couldn't take her eyes off his, and simply gave up on keeping any more secrets.

"What?" His voice was rough, low and edgy. His grip on her arm was firm and enquiring. His whole body felt tensed and wary next to hers. "What is it, Zo? Is it the Noodle? Is that what this is all about? Is he the reason you're pulling this…this blushing bride routine?"

Zoë blinked. "N-Newton?"

"You've decided to marry him, haven't you?" Brad pressed for an answer as his fingers pressed into the flesh of her upper arm. Not hurtful, but demanding. Very demanding. "Tell me the truth, Zoë. If you've decided to accept that…that bumptious bag of bad breath, I think I have a right to know."

"A right, Brad? You have a *right* to know?"

"Yes, damn it. I promised Tim I'd take care of you, and letting you marry Rooney is a profanely poor way to do it."

Was he—could he possibly be—jealous? "So you're saying I need your permission to marry Newton?"

His lips tightened. "Be reasonable, Zoë. The Noodle is probably the worst possible choice you could make, and I can't just stand by and let you do it. Not without a fight."

That was about the most promising thing he'd said

so far, no matter what his reasoning. Feeling braver, she pulled off her hat and shook out her hair before she raised her chin defiantly. "And how are you going to fight me, Brad? With your bare hands? Or maybe with a—" she swallowed hard and issued the challenge "—a *smooch?*"

Any other self-proclaimed macho male would have kissed her then and there, without further provocation or invitation. Brad, on the other hand, looked as stunned as if she'd asked him to unzip her dress. Which, if things didn't improve, might be what she'd do next. Could she be that bold? He had scruples. He had principles. What if he thought of her as a sister? What if he only thought of her as Lark's mother, as Tim's widow? What if he didn't think about her at all? Maybe that's what this was about. Maybe that's *all* this was about.

Without any clear sense of moving toward him, Zoë threw her heart ahead of her, thrust her body against his, looped her arms around his neck, and pulled him into an awkward, unanticipated and graceless kiss. Her lips pressed to his; her breasts flattened and then embarrassingly peaked against his chest; her hands locked at his nape to keep him from pulling away. She wanted this kiss, damn it, and she was having it whether he liked it or not. She had to prove to herself that nothing more than friendship was possible...or prove to him that something more than friendship was.

It took several pulsating heartbeats before she realized he wasn't fighting her. It took a few more before she felt his hands slide from her arms to slowly encircle her waist. She'd thought he might push her away, but instead he was lifting her, repositioning her to fit more easily into his embrace. His lips on hers were gentle but insistent, and that first, searching taste of him made her giddy and gleeful and drunk with serious longing. He was kissing her. She was kissing him. With curiosity, yes, but also with a hunger, hesitant though it might be, that was equally and unequivocally matched.

When she felt him start to pull away, she parted her lips and swept the tip of her tongue across his with pure purpose and not-so-pure motive. He groaned, shuddered in response, and caught her closer to him, nearly knocking the breath out of her as he plunged into the kiss with an enthusiasm she hadn't anticipated. But how could she have foreseen this hot, frantic rush of passion that surged through her with the pounding, painful beat of a solo drum? How could she have predicted that it would feel so extraordinary, so very *right,* to be in Brad's arms, to be kissing him, to be kissed by him?

She wanted the feeling to go on and on for as long as there was breath in her body and a scent of sweet promise in the air, for as long as his warrior arms held her as if she were the harvest moon and he the velvet night. But abruptly Brad broke the spell, and, with his hands on her shoulders, he pushed her away and kept her there with arms that visibly trembled. "What was that about?" he demanded in a voice husky-thick with emotion. "What the *hell* was that about?"

She gathered her defenses, prepared herself for a swift and stunning rejection, hoped for a happy surprise, and offered a tiny, wistful start of a smile. "I…I think you just convinced me that I…don't want to marry Newton."

Brad's gaze was already locked with hers, and in the next few moments, nothing in his expression changed. A lingering frown battened down the corners of his mouth. Tension vibrated like cello strings in the space that separated him from her. Then his grip on her arms slackened, and he shook his head. "No," he said. "No, no, no, no, no, no, no. This isn't right. This isn't the way it's supposed to happen. I never meant to…. No. We can't do this, Zoë. *I* can't do this. I promised him I'd take care of you and Lark. I promised him I'd protect you."

"You have, Brad. For five years now—probably even before that—you have protected me, cared for me. And I'm grateful. More grateful than I can ever say." She inhaled deeply, drawing hope from the need to believe that she saw in his eyes. "But, Brad, what happened just now, what I felt—what I'm still feeling at this very second—has nothing at all to do with gratitude and everything to do with…possibilities."

His chest rose as he breathed in and held her in suspense, until slowly, slowly, he released the breath…and her. "You're Tim's *wife,* Zoë."

She understood then, as clearly as if Tim, himself, had whispered the understanding directly into her heart. Brad was stuck. Not with the promise he'd made, but with the idea that any alteration of it meant he'd fail. He might as well still be in that room with Tim's life fading away and his own unflinching faith that his promise could give meaning to a future without his best friend in it. For Brad, with his a-man-is-a-man-is-a-man indoctrination, disloyalty came in many forms and a hundred temptations. To step into the role of lover, husband, father would be to profit from his friend's death, and that was betrayal of the highest order. So he continued to play by the rules, to think of Zoë only and always as his best friend's wife. Untouchable and safely out of his reach. Even if he was the one who held her there.

She lifted her chin, ready to claim a future that Tim would have claimed for her if it had been within his power. And as an angel, who knew? Maybe he had plotted the whole thing. "Brad," she said softly, putting her hands over his, willing him to hear the words—spoken and not spoken—she had to say. "I'm not Tim's wife. I'm Tim's *widow*."

He knew that, of course. But he had yet to accept the truth of it. And as they stood there in a garden planted by other hands and other hearts, Zoë willed him to believe that far from betraying his promise to Tim, he had kept it, and continued to keep it, with honor.

A lifetime apart would not change that. A lifetime together wouldn't, either.

"Zoë," he said, the husky emotion in his voice turning rich with confusion and—dare she hope?—wonder. "Zoë, I...."

The smile bloomed on her lips and she stepped closer again. But just as she lifted her face to invite another kiss, the sound of a powerful engine and tires crunching gravel traveled down the drive to steal the moment. Brad's sigh indicated either frustration or relief. Zoë couldn't tell which.

"Guess the magazine crew has arrived," he said.

"Well, they have very bad timing." She looked past him in time to see a head pop up through the sunroof of a shiny, dark blue Suburban. Then a second head—startlingly like the first—popped up beside it.

"Brad! Hey, Brad!" The heads yelled, and then arms appeared through the opening, waving wildly. "We found you!"

"That's my dad's truck and those loony tunes are my brothers." Brad set Zoë firmly away from him as his tone and expression took on a startled, almost appalled nuance. "This isn't just bad timing, this is Disaster with a capital *D*."

Chapter Nine

Whoever coined the phrase *easy chair* never sat
in this one, Friend Neighbor! The springs were
sprung, the upholstery was full of holes, the legs
were shaky, and the cushion had lost its *cush*.
Hubby Bee took one look at the pathetic piece
and banished it as a hopeless case. But I wasn't
so persuaded and was determined to fulfill an old
promise to the big chair that held me faithfully
when I was not much bigger than Daughter Kate.
I won't insult your intelligence by saying it was
easy. I'll admit right here in black and white that
it was a challenging and often daunting task. But
as with any labor of love, believing is the first
requirement and action is the second. So with
more faith than forte, I set out to mend the easy
chair (before and after photos appear at left) and
if I do say so myself, the finished project turned
out better than even I had dared to hope....

"This is a surprise." Brad greeted his family with what
he hoped was a welcoming grin. "How did you find
me?"

His father laughed and clapped him on the shoulder

in a rough and familiar hello. "Were you trying to hide from us?"

"Lloyd told us where you were when we stopped by the office." Jonna Kenneally didn't offer even the clap on the shoulder, just gave her oldest son an assessing gaze and passing smile as greeting. "We're on our way to the summer All-Sports Challenge Camp at KU. Want to go along? Brush up on your coaching skills? Having a pro in attendance would give the kids quite a thrill, as I'm sure you know."

"Yeah, big bro." Chris slugged Brad on the arm. "Give everybody a thrill, would ya?"

Kellen slugged Brad on the other arm. "Seeing you in *overalls* is about as big a thrill as I can take. What are you doing in that getup? Getting a jump on Halloween?"

"Can't decide if I want to be a scarecrow or a pumpkin patch," he said, falling into the family pattern of using jokes as salutations. This branch of the Kenneallys was long on back slaps, shoulder slugs, and avoidance of meaningful interaction. Hugging or anything resembling a display of affection was awkward at best, and seldom, if ever, a part of any homecoming or visit—no matter how long it had been since family members had seen one another. "I can't believe you're all here."

"Imagine how we feel," his father said, tongue in cheek. "Finding you out here on Green Acres. Must be miles from the nearest gym."

"Where's my grandson?" The querulous voice belonged to Grandma Tildie, who hopped out of the Suburban like a flea off a Great Dane. If his parents and brothers were uncomfortable with hugs and kisses, Grandma Tildie more than made up for their lapse.

Less than half his size, she grabbed Brad and gave him a fiercely affectionate hug. "Why, Bradley, I do believe you've grown a foot since the last time I saw you," she said. "You're gonna have to quit that, too, 'cause I'm gettin' too old to knit you new underwear every Christmas."

Grandma Tildie was as bright as a new dime, but for as long as Brad could remember, she'd been about nine-and-a-half pennies short of making ten cents' worth of sense. Brad caught Zoë's approach from the corner of his eye and turned to draw her into the family circle, recalling, with a serious lack of pertinence, how hotly seductive her kiss had been. "Zoë?" He forced the memories off to the side and concentrated on this unexpected, rather astonishing, family visit. "You remember my family, don't you? Jonna and Larry Kenneally, Kel, Chris, and Grandma Tildie."

"Of course, I remember." Zoë offered her knockout smile to the group. "We've met a number of times."

"Twelve times," Grandma Tildie said firmly. "Once at Bradley's football game and once at the liquor store."

"Oh, Grandma," Chris teased her. "You've never been in a liquor store."

"I most certainly have not, young man. Liquor is the devil's workshop." She eyed Zoë suspiciously. "What were *you* doing in a liquor store?" Without waiting for a reply, she aimed her suspicions at Brad. "And what are you doing out here in the middle of nowhere? Who do you think you're foolin' in that union suit?"

"He's *working*, Mother Kenneally," Jonna said, stressing the verb. "Lloyd told us you were on an assignment this week, Brad. Something about one of your columnists and a magazine?''

Brad did not want to talk about that. What was the matter with Lloyd, that he spouted off private and personal information to family members, anyhow? ''Let's go in the house. It's pretty hot out here. Can you stay for supper?''

''As a matter of fact, we're staying overnight. If you've got the room, that is. We were only planning to spend a couple of hours with you on our way to Lawrence, but I called ahead and found out the Pre-Challenge Camp events were canceled at the last minute, so we have a little extra time on our hands.'' Larry motioned to the twins. ''Boys, get the bags, will you?''

Brad looked at Zoë, whose brows arched in sympathy. He felt the instant connection, the shared thoughts. *They're staying all night? I can't ask them to leave. There's room for them to stay, if everyone doubles up. It's just one night. They'll never have to know about Daisy Rose Knows. Tim's widow… widow…widow….*

Boy, did he wish his family hadn't arrived at the precise moment they had. He wished he could have kissed Zoë again. Then, just as suddenly, he wished the family had shown up sooner and prevented that first kiss from happening at all. It shouldn't have happened. It wasn't right. He needed time to think. He needed to stop going over and over the words Zoë had spoken. He needed to remind himself that what he was feeling was…. Was what? Wrong? It certainly hadn't felt wrong. But she was Tim's wife. *Widow.* And Tim had been gone a very long time. Did that make a difference? He couldn't get involved with Zoë. She was just a friend. She was his godchild's mother. She was his friend's wife. *Widow.* Tim's *widow.* He needed to think about that. He needed this reunion to end before it got started. He needed not to have to run interference between his family and his reasons for being a resident of Lazy Daisy Acres. He needed a vacation. A long vacation. Starting now, ending some long time from now.

"What's wrong with you, Bradley?" Grandma Tildie knotted her hands around his arm and stood, waiting for him to escort her into the house. "Rats in your belfry?"

"Bats, Grandma," Chris corrected. "Bats in his belfry."

"You hear what your brother said about you?" she challenged Brad, clearly hoping to start a fuss, which she could then referee. "You gonna let him get away with calling you a dingbat?"

"He meant it in the nicest way, Grandma." Brad patted her hand politely and started for the house, only to be halted in his tracks by the hum of an oversize motor. Moments later, not one but two large motor homes rumbled down the drive and pulled up beside the Suburban. Not thirty seconds behind them came Granite Ames's black sedan. Brad wondered why he hadn't had the foresight to buy a thousand acres, instead of just forty.

"You've got company," Grandma Tildie pointed out to him.

"Sure looks that way," he answered, and moved on toward the house, hoping against hope that he could get the family group inside before the professionals pulled out their cameras. "Could be tourists. Somebody's always getting lost on this road and pulling in to ask for directions."

"Well, it's a good thing." That was Grandma's point of view. "Otherwise, they'd be wanderin' around lost in my neighborhood."

"I'll see if I can find out what they…uh, want." Zoë lightly touched Brad's arm, offering her help before he had to ask for it, and then strolled slowly over to greet, and momentarily deter, the new arrivals. He loved her for that. *Loved?* Well, sure. Like a friend. A good friend. His good friend's widow. *Widow.* It was suddenly easier to remember that since she'd kissed him. Okay, so he'd kissed her, too. Even if she had started it, he could have said no. Right or wrong, he was as guilty as she.

Right or wrong? Was it really a question of that? Of guilt? And did he have to decide that now, when the only sure thing in his mind was that the Kenneally family had the worst timing in the world?

LARK YAWNED, sat up in her bed, and checked to make sure all her necklaces were in the pouch she always put them in when she had to take a nap. One by one, she took the pretties out of the pouch, admired them, touched them and slipped them carefully over her head or wrapped them around and around her arms. Mom or Uncle Brad would fix her ponytail later and put all the barrettes back in her hair, but she could do all the jewe'ry by herself. She picked it out by herself and put it on by herself 'cause she was a big girl. She'd helped Uncle Brad make the wedding cake.

The cake! Scooting to the edge of the bed, she slipped off the mattress and reached back to get the pouch, clasping it, and the hair barrettes still inside, tightly in her hand. It was then that she heard the voices outside. Somebody was talkin' and somebody else was talkin' back. And it didn't sound like Mom and it didn't sound like Uncle Brad and it didn't sound like somebody she knew. Hurrying to the window, she stood on tiptoe, but wasn't tall enough to see, so she dragged the rocking chair over, climbed carefully up on the seat, and pushed the seat back against the window glass. She could see real good. She could see a blue truck, a black car and two big, white buses. There were people, too, moving around, and shiny stuff laying all over the yard, and even propped up in front of the barn.

Her eyes widened with excitement. "The wedding," she whispered aloud. "They came to the wedding."

It was going to happen after all. Even though Uncle Brad had said it couldn't. Even though Mom had said it wouldn't. They were gettin' married and she'd baked the cake and now they could live on the farm forever and ever. Lark and Mom and Uncle Brad. She should go see if the cake was done. Quick like a bunny, she jumped from her perch and raced out of the bedroom.

Zoë saw Lark gallop down the stairs and rush past the front room on her way to the kitchen. She raised her eyebrows but continued to feign interest in the conversation—civilized argument, actually—between Carson, the photographer, and Annelle, the art director.

"I'm telling you the room's too small." Carson seemed to enjoy hearing the sound of his own voice, because he kept repeating the same complaints over and over. "The whole house couldn't hold enough flash equipment to light up this room. It's dark. It's tiny. It's not going to work. I told you that when we saw the preliminary shots and I'm telling you now. It's not going to work."

"It will work," Annelle said in tones too patient to be anything except impatient. "Because you get paid

the big bucks to make it work. Now I want photos of
this room with her—'' she pointed accusingly at Zoë
''—in it. I want photos with her, the kid and the husband in this dark and tiny room. So quit griping about
it and do what you have to do.''

"You're not going to like the result." That was his
parting shot.

"If I don't, it'll be my responsibility, and I'll do
what I have to do. Now, will you get out of my face?''

He stalked over to scowl at the books in the tiny
bookcase—darkly bound books, every last one of them.

Annelle celebrated her victory by awarding Zoë a
tight smile and an encompassing glance. "Is this the
kind of…thing…you wear all the time?"

Zoë looked down at the trendy *au natural* linen overalls with the bib pocket front and shapely drawstring
back, signature metal clips and real brass buttons, and
at the not-exactly-crisp, but certainly still clean, white
cotton T-top underneath. Other than a little dirt on both
knees, she thought the outfit looked remarkably comfortable and Daisy-Rose-like. "This is a farm," she
pointed out gently.

The art director sighed. "It certainly is." She ran a
critical gaze from just under Zoë's chin to her open-
toed *huaraches*—which Zoë badly wanted to point out
were made of genuine leather. "I realize we have to
work with what we have," Annelle continued, using
her hands to emphasize that this particular project
would require far more work than most, "but do you
have anything that's more at-home-in-the-country and
less where's-the-wheelbarrow?"

"A dress?" Zoë suggested, not wanting to create
any more difficulty for Brad than was already afoot
within his household. "Would a dress be better?"

"Possibly." Obviously, Annelle didn't want to commit herself until she actually saw the dress. "If not...." Leaving her stout doubts to hang like dried peppers, she turned from Zoë to other, perhaps more preventable, calamities.

"Are you through with me now?" Zoë asked, her attention already straying toward the kitchen, where a good twenty minutes earlier, she'd left Brad encircled by curious relatives and one very talkative boss. "I have chores to do."

Annelle's grimace came before her minute hint of interest. "What kind of...chores?"

Zoë couldn't resist. "Oh, I'll probably change the oil in the tractor, clean out the chicken coop, exercise the orneriness out of the mule, fertilize the cucumbers...those kinds of chores."

The art director—who'd traveled all the way from New York City to twenty-three miles outside Buckthorn, Missouri, in one day, just to do what had to be done—smiled easily at Zoë. "Don't forget your wheelbarrow."

Zoë laughed, feeling better than she had any right to feel. She was impersonating a woman made up of words made up by a man who was doing his best not to let anyone know he could write a cohesive sentence. Or bake a cake. She wondered what else Brad knew how to do that he took pains to keep secret from the world. She wondered mainly, though, what he was secretly thinking about their kiss in the garden. *She* could hardly think about anything else. Despite the invasion of the magazine people. Despite the overnight ambush by the Kenneally clan. Despite the not-particularly-flattering interview just conducted by the prima donna art director and the Grand Pooh-bah of photographers.

She wished them all a million miles away. At least until she and Brad had a chance to talk.

All right, so talking wasn't entirely what she had in mind. What was wrong with that? She was an adult. So was he. And it had been a long time since she had....

No reason to go there now. The house was full enough without adding a sexually frustrated female to the mix. Hitching up her overalls because both Annelle and Carson were watching, Zoë waved and headed out of the room toward the kitchen, where gleeful conversation buzzed. It stopped dead the minute she walked in, and every eye in the room turned in her direction.

"Hello," she said, wondering if she'd be better off to stand her ground or run for cover. "Any coffee left?"

"Hi, Mom." Lark beamed from Grandma Tildie's spacious lap. "We were talking 'bout ya."

"We certainly were, Zoë Rose." Granite Ames gave her a candid wink and shared an oddly conspiratorial grin with the others at the table. "Were you blushing like a *bride?*"

Brad's chair scraped noisily across the floor. "I'll make more coffee," he said. "Want a sandwich? A piece of cake?"

"Uncle Brad! She can't eat the wedding cake now. It's not got icing on it!" Lark was all scolding smile. "It has to have icing on it," she told the family circle. "Lots and lots of icing."

Still no shift in attention, Zoë noticed. Would it be more helpful to ignore the wedding cake issue or explain it? She looked to Brad for clues. Nil. Okay, there were enough issues already being ignored in this house.

"Curly and Moe needed a wedding cake," she said with a ready laugh. "They're getting married."

"Curly and Moe? Aren't those the goats?" One of Brad's brothers grinned broadly. "Which one are you, Brad? Curly? Or Moe?"

The coffee canister hit the floor with a clatter and rolled under the table. "Lucky the lid was on, huh?" Brad said lightly, then ducked down to retrieve it.

"Nervous as a bridegroom," Grandma Tildie said, and everyone laughed.

Everyone except Zoë. "Bridegroom?"

Brad popped up with the canister in hand. "Don't get upset," he said. "I wasn't going to tell them until you were here, but Larkarena, there, jumped the gun, blasted in here asking about the wedding cake, and just flat-out let the cat out of the bag."

Zoë frowned. "Tell them…what?"

He came around the table to take her arm and draw her firmly into the room in a rather proprietary manner. "You know what," he said in an animated mumble, accompanied by an expression of bright-eyed and barely disguised panic. "About the wedding. About…us."

"Us?" Zoë's brain raced through the possibilities. Us…as in Hubby Bee and Daisy Rose Knows? Or us…as in…? She couldn't think of any variation on *us* that worked well with the word *wedding*. "*Us?*" she repeated more forcefully.

He patted her hand awkwardly. "I know we agreed not to tell anyone until after the fact, but well, now everybody knows."

"Congratulations," someone said—one of the boys, perhaps. Then Brad's father was pushing back his chair and standing up to…well, *not* hug her. He didn't seem to know if he should shake her hand or give her shoulder a congratulatory bop. He smiled inanely, said, "Welcome to the family," and sat back down. Brad's mother stayed seated, but offered a reasonably warm regard. "I can't tell you, Zoë, how thrilled I'll be to finally have another woman in the family. Plus a granddaughter. You and I should have a talk about signing Lark up for soccer this fall. She's old enough. In fact, she's missed a year of playing already, but Brad will help her catch up to the skill level of the other team members."

Zoë took the coffee canister from Brad's grasp, unsure whether she just needed something to get a grip on or whether she was going to eat the coffee beans right out of the can. She didn't need the caffeine, because a jolt of adrenaline was pumping through her veins, but chewing a hole in the aluminum can might prove soothing. "I can't believe you told them," she said tightly, giving him a look that would have had him shaking if he wasn't so obviously already quaking in his boots. "It was supposed to be our secret."

"I told 'em, Mom," Lark announced proudly. "You said it's not nice to keep secrets and so I told 'em all about the wedding and all about the wedding cake and all about me and Uncle Brad cookin' the cake and all about you and Uncle Brad smoochin' and havin' breakfast in bed and...and everything."

The twins elbowed each other, grinning and behaving like adolescent boys, which they were. "I'd like to see a wedding cake *Brad* made," one of them said to the other, intending, of course, for the whole table to hear. "It'll probably look like the Leaning Tower of Pisa."

"And taste like it, too." Another elbow, double guffaws of laughter, lenient smiles from the responsible adults.

"He made a *good* cake," Lark pronounced firmly, not about to let anyone tease about her wedding cake. "And I helped, too! And it tastes real good and we're gonna put icing on it and Mom and Uncle Brad are going to eat it and smooch and then we'll be married." She sighed, replete with happy plans. "Isn't that right, Mr. Ames?"

"Right as rain, young lady." Ames beamed on the happy couple. "I told Brad the first time I met you, Zoë, that you were gonna marry him, by hook or by crook. I can sense these things in a woman. My Grace says I'm sensitive to that—" and here he added an impressive wiggle of his caterpillar eyebrows "—*thang called love.*"

Under different circumstances, Zoë would have laughed at that cockamamy statement. But she was just a little too choked up. Instead of pinching the heck out of Brad's arm, which she wanted to do, she squeezed the coffee can so hard that her thumb made an indentation in the metal. "Well..." she said, not knowing how Brad thought he could cover up this misunderstanding. "It's, uh, great...that everyone knows and we don't have to keep *that* secret anymore."

"I told them you'd be relieved." Ames was off and running again. "I'll admit I was having a qualm or two myself about this magazine spread. Wouldn't be good publicity for our Daisy Rose to get caught with her, uh, pants down...so to speak." He chuckled at his glibness. "Although, there's nothing like a scandal to turn a nobody into a celebrity. 'Course, that's neither here nor there since we're not having the scandal. No, indeedy. We're having a wedding and sewing you two up good and proper. I've already called into Joplin and arranged for the minister, the music and everything. The wedding'll take place tomorrow noon, all right and tight. No need to thank me. The sooner the deed is done, the sooner we can get Daisy Rose on the cover of *Home and Hearth Magazine*. Right? Right! I'll have Carson take some pictures after the ceremony—hell, we may even use one or two in the spread. We don't have to say *when* they were taken, now do we? So, Zoë Rose, now that it's all planned out for you, aren't you glad Daughter Lark let that wedding cat out of the bag?''

As if he thought she might be having trouble standing against the torrential rain of information, Brad slipped an arm around her shoulders in support. ''Oh, we're just as glad as glad can be, aren't we, Zo?''

Zoë was too stunned to offer more than a weak ''But.... But we don't even have a phone.''

''Modern technology,'' Ames said, holding up his palm-size cell phone. ''Slices through complications like a hot knife through butter.''

She turned a rueful gaze on Brad. ''You should get yourself one of those.''

His answer was a sickly smile.

Ames held the phone out to her. ''Want to call somebody?''

Yes, actually. She wanted to call 9-1-1 and get somebody out here to help her pound the nonsense out of Brad. ''No,'' she said brightly. ''Can't think of anybody who's not already here.''

''No family you want to invite to the wedding?'' Jonna asked.

''No.'' *Absolutely* not. ''There's not even a cousin close enough to get here by tomorrow.''

"I can send my jet for them," Ames offered. "Just say who and where we need to pick 'em up."

"No," Zoë said again, liking the feel of the word on her tongue. "There's no one I want to invite."

"If you change your mind, you just say so, you hear me?"

"What?" Grandma Tildie stopped nodding and snapped out of her ten-second nap. "Who says I'm hard of hearing?"

Lark slipped off Grandma's lap and danced over to her mother, tossing imaginary rose petals. "Watch me, Mom. I'm practicin' to be a flower girl in the wedding! And me and Uncle Brad are gonna dec'rate the wedding cake, too."

The twins elbowed each other again. "You're gonna *decorate* the cake you baked, Brad? Oops! Don't forget to wear your *apron*." They giggled like girls and Brad's dad frowned first at the twins, then at his eldest son. "Do you even know which side of a cake to frost?"

"'Course he does!" Grandma Tildie slapped the table. "Why, I taught that boy everything there is to know about goats!"

"Who said anything about goats?" Ames demanded. "We're talking about a wedding."

"We are?" Grandma pursed her mouth. "Well, that's lucky."

Brad's mother agreed with a nod. "It is lucky the sports camp coincided with Brad's wedding, isn't it?"

Zoë looked up at Brad and tried not to think about how comforting his arm felt around her shoulders, tried not to feel a twinge of sympathy for him, tried not to dwell on the disaster he'd just dumped in her lap. He caught her gaze and momentarily tightened his hand in an encouraging squeeze. Then he cleared his throat, and Zoë knew he was about to confess his crimes and misdemeanors and clear up the whole mess. After all, he was a man of honor and a devout protector of innocent women.

"If you'll let me use that cell phone, Mr. Ames," he said, "I'll order pizza."

"PIZZA! PIZZA!" Lark bounced to the kitchen door in answer to a loud knock. "The pizza's here!"

Zoë followed her to the door, thinking there was no way anyone could have made a pizza, much less delivered it, in the relatively few minutes since Brad had completed the call. But everyone else was here.

Everyone, that is, except Newton Rooney.

"Zoë," Newton said, looking frazzled and frustrated on the other side of the screen door. "I thought I'd never find you. How Kenneally convinced you this backwater was a vacation spot, I don't know, but take heart—I've come to rescue you."

Lark made a face and abruptly turned back to the congenial and rowdy family grouping around the kitchen table. "It's Noodle Roni," she announced.

"Newton?" Zoë was too surprised to see him to insist her daughter come back and offer a more polite greeting. The truth was, Zoë had all but forgotten he existed during the past few days. Her job seemed like part of another lifetime. "What are you doing here? How did you find me?"

"Not easily, that's for sure," he said. "I made a copy of the directions Kenneally gave you, but once I got off the highway, they were pretty hard to follow. Luckily, I stopped for gas at the last little town, and some guy there was able to point me down the right road.'' He frowned. ''Are you going to invite me in?''

''Um…sure,'' she said. But when she glanced over her shoulder, she caught Brad's belligerent gaze and changed her mind. The kitchen was crowded as it was. No point in subjecting Newton to the entire Kenneally crew. She stepped out onto the porch and pulled the kitchen door firmly shut behind her. ''We can talk better out here,'' she said. ''It's a bit crowded in there. Brad's family, you know.''

''They travel in style.'' He glanced at the travel trailers. ''Must be a bunch of them.''

''It's not entirely family.'' She realized she was nervous, realized too that it had more to do with what Brad might be thinking than with Newton's unexpected arrival. ''What are you doing here?''

''I told you. I've come to rescue you.'' He offered a fawning smile in reply and took her hands, as if he had a right to them.

Zoë pulled away from his touch, because she was suddenly sure he didn't. ''I can't believe you went to all the trouble to come.''

''You didn't have a phone, Zoë. I didn't really have any other choice.''

''You could have…not come,'' she suggested, wishing he hadn't. ''It is my vacation, you know…and I did tell you I'd be gone for the whole two weeks.''

''You told me, but I figured you'd be back in two days. Let's be honest, Zoë. You're not cut out for life on a farm, especially not this scrubby Green Acres. Besides, I've found a house for us and I want you to come back with me and take a look at it. It's in The Glens—that exclusive, gated area near the country club where houses almost never go up for sale. Anyway, the couple's divorcing, and we can buy the place for a song. It's perfect for us. All the homes are very upscale and the residents are all top-level professional peo—''

"Newton, you came all the way from Tulsa to tell me about a house?''

"Not just a house, Zoë. The perfect house. We can buy it now and make a small fortune if we want to sell in a few years—trust me.''

She didn't. Trust him, that is. Not because he didn't know a lot about real estate. But because she didn't want a house in The Glens. Or anywhere else with Newton. It was a revelation. A small one, compared to the discoveries she'd made about Brad during the past few days, but enlightening nonetheless. It was unsettling to recall that less than a month ago she'd been dating this man, but that since coming to the farm, she hadn't given him a thought. In fact, if he hadn't come knocking at the door of Lazy Daisy Acres tonight, she was absolutely certain she would have finished out her vacation without remembering he was in the world. How could she ever have thought she might marry him? "I'm not interested in buying a house in The Glens, Newton.''

His brows drew together in a frown. "You haven't even seen it yet, Zoë. I'm telling you, it's perfect. More house than we could normally afford and a great investment for our future. Get your things and come back with me. I've already made an appointment to see the house tomorrow.''

"I'm sorry you made the trip out for nothing.'' She felt uneasy with him now—as if he were robbing Daisy Rose's back porch of its charm just by standing on it. "But it could have waited until I was back in the office.''

"I just told you, we have an appointment to see it in the morning."

"I'm on vacation, Newton."

"Here?" He laughed. "Give me a break. Kenneally can't expect you to stay longer than you already have."

"I like it here, and I'm not going back to see a house."

"This isn't the time to demonstrate your independent nature, Zoë. We're going to need to make an offer right away. The house won't last twenty-four hours. I'm telling you, it's a steal, and even though we haven't officially talked about marriage, you know that's been my intention all along. This will push the timetable forward, maybe, but—"

"Newton, I'm not going to marry you. I thought once that maybe...." She let the sentence trail away, not wanting to hurt him, but relieved to be speaking the truth. "It's not going to happen. Not now and not later, and especially not because you've found the 'perfect' house."

"Well, of course not just because of the house, Zoë. You know how much I admire you. We're great together. We like the same—"

"No, Newton. I'm really sorry I didn't realize it sooner, but I don't love you and I don't want to marry you."

His frown tightened. "I'll tell you what, Zoë. I'll go ahead and make an offer on the house myself, and let you think about this for a while. You don't have to decide right now. I know you never think very clearly when Kenneally's around, so I can give you a little more time to realize what a great deal this is for—"

The kitchen door opened with a jerk, and Brad stood

in the doorway, smiling at them through the screen. "Everyone's asking for Zoë," he said.

"Do you mind?" Newton scowled. "This is a private conversation."

"This is a private residence, but you came knocking on my door, anyway."

"I came for Zoë."

Brad's gaze flicked to Zoë's face, returned to Newton's with a noncommittal expression. "She's on vacation."

"I *know* that. I'm here to rescue her from this milk-maid's nightmare."

"Careful there, Noodle Roni. You're gonna hurt my feelings."

Newton held out his hand to Zoë. "You can't be having a good time, Zoë. This place isn't exactly The Ritz. I haven't been inside yet, but I'm sure it wouldn't even get a one-star rating in the *Hillbilly Hotel Guide*."

"Now, look, Noodle, I've been very generous with my welcome up until now, but you're beginning to get on my very hospitable nerves."

Zoë knew she had to nip this confrontation right here, right now, so she took Newton by the elbow and hustled him away from the porch—and Brad. "Thanks for the offer of rescue, Newton," she said. "But I actually like being out here in the back of beyond. I enjoy the country and I like this farm and I'm in no hurry to leave it."

"You're going to regret this, Zoë," he said as they reached the driver's side of his late-model Volvo. "And it'll be too late when you get back to the office. The house in The Glens will be long gone, and don't think I'm going to be waiting for you with open arms.

It's not like you're the only woman in the world, you know.''

"Not for you, anyway." She wanted nothing more than to open the car door and shove him in. "But luckily for me, I have other options."

"You mean Kenneally?" A gruff, derisive chuckle came through his nose. "Don't make me laugh."

"Thanks for taking the time to find me," she said, waiting until he slid onto the car seat before pushing the door firmly shut behind him. "I'll see you in the office when my vacation is over."

"If that's your attitude, maybe you shouldn't come back to work."

"Are you firing me?"

He looked momentarily as if he'd like to, then apparently thought better of it. "No, but you may find it uncomfortable working with me after this. I'm not going to sit on my thumbs waiting for you to come to your senses, Zoë. I will be dating other women. Women who can appreciate what I have to offer."

"I encourage you to do just that," she said sweetly. "And don't worry about me. If it should become uncomfortable for me at the office, I'll resign. Thomas Terry has been trying to get me to come to work for his real estate agency for months. Now, take a right when you get to the top of the driveway, and stay on the dirt road for about four miles until you come to Highway 12, then turn left and head straight for Buckthorn. If you see a sign for Chicktown, you're lost and you should probably stop and get directions from somebody."

He frowned, staring at her as if she'd lost all sense. "I'll find my way to the highway, Zoë, don't worry."

She wasn't worried in the least. "'By, Newton."

"Goodbye, Zoë."

The screen door slammed, and a couple of seconds later Brad was standing behind Zoë. "Take a left at the top of the drive," he said to Newton, as friendly as if the two of them were neighbors, "and a right at the first intersection you come to. It may look like just another fork in the road, but stay left and you'll be at the highway entrance in twenty, thirty miles."

"Zoë told me to turn right."

Brad put his hands possessively on her shoulders, and the heat was so instantly riveting that Zoë felt as if she'd been struck by lightning. "Are you going to take directions from a *milkmaid?*" Brad asked.

Newton gunned the motor. "The two of you deserve each other." With that, he threw the gear into Reverse and backed up the driveway as if he were in a life-or-death race.

Brad's hands remained clasped loosely, protectively, seductively on Zoë's shoulders. "He'll probably never find his way off these back roads."

"Well, I did tell him to…get lost."

"Ah," Brad said, his voice a purr of satisfaction. "Poor man. Sentenced to a lifetime of wandering through endless farmlands and dirt roads. That's what he gets for being a noodle, I guess."

Zoë watched the Volvo disappear up the driveway and heard the throaty hum of the engine fade and disappear into the deepening evening. "I can't believe you ever let me date such a macaroni."

"Me? I've been trying to get you to wake up and smell the pasta ever since you met that guy."

"Hmm," she said. "Isn't that interesting? Just before Newton got here, I thought you were trying to force-feed me wedding cake."

"Oh, that...." He stuck his hands into the hip pockets of his overalls. "I guess I need to straighten out—"

"Hey, Brad!" one of the twins yelled from the porch. "Me and Kel are getting up a football game with some of the magazine crew. We want you to play...unless you'd rather *decorate a cake*."

Zoë knew—even before Brad's shoulders went back in unconscious acceptance of the challenge—that he would not only play ball, but decorate the silly wedding cake, too.

With a sigh, she decided she might as well help. "Got room on your team for a milkmaid?"

Chapter Ten

When looking for that perfect recipe for a cool summer delight, seek out the fruits of the season. Mix together blackberries, blueberries, peaches, a few leftover strawberries from spring (remember when we froze them whole for just such an occasion?), and whatever other fresh fruits you may have on hand to create a naturally sweet dessert. Tossed with lemon and poppyseed dressing (recipe below) they'll make a sweet addition to any picnic table. It's easy, quick, colorful, and tastes divine—and you can take Hubby Bee's word on that! I blush to admit it, but he does say the only things tastier than my Summer Fruit Salad are the kisses we share in the midst of a hot summer's night....

Zoë slipped out of bed, leaving Lark sound asleep and oblivious to light, noise or movement. That was definitely a selling point for the farm—sleep was easy to come by and good to the last drop. Even Lark, sleep-fighter extraordinaire, didn't last long once the sun was down. Zoë had slept better since arriving at Lazy Daisy Acres than she had her whole life. But she wasn't sleeping tonight. Partly because her muscles ached from the football game that had lasted until it was too dark to see the football. Partly because she had a few things to settle with Brad.

Moving like a shadow, she eased open the door and paused to listen. In the room behind her, Lark's breathing was whisper-deep, blending with the intermingled purling noises made by the puppies dreaming puppy dreams in their box by the bed. Beyond the bedroom door were the slumberous sounds of an old house, the creaks and groans that testified to the weathering of many a storm. The house was packed tonight, not a bedroom unoccupied, everyone sharing either a bed or a bathroom, sometimes both. Zoë had given up her bed to Grandma and settled in with Lark. Brad's parents were in his room, and he'd moved to the spare room at the end of the hall. The twins were downstairs in sleeping bags on the living room floor. Outside, the magazine crew were sleeping—or not sleeping—in their home office/travel trailers on wheels.

The whole evening had flown past without a single chance for private conversation. Grandma Tildie had given continual pep talks from the sidelines. The art director and photographer had taken out their frustrations on each other in a few illegal tackles. All the Kenneallys had played the game with a competitive streak, buoyed by some rival coaching between Larry and Jonna. In between plays, Brad's parents had talked to him incessantly, it seemed, about the triumphs and personal joys of coaching. Granite Ames had left as the teams were forming, claiming a pressing engagement and vowing to return with the minister and whoever or whatever else it took to have a decent wedding.

The wedding was the main reason Zoë wasn't sleeping peacefully next to her daughter. It was the reason she slipped soundlessly into the hall and pulled the bedroom door closed behind her. It was the reason she was on her way to Brad's room like a nymph on a midsummer eve. Okay, so a nymph probably wouldn't be going there to talk. But she was. They had to talk. Alone, and without interruptions. He couldn't seriously think there was going to be a wedding tomorrow. Certainly, *she* wasn't participating in one. And she knew he wasn't, either. She was surprised that he could even say the word without stuttering. Why he'd allowed the charade to get this far out of hand, she couldn't imagine. But he was going to tell her—just as soon as she traversed this dark hallway and found his bedroom door.

From downstairs drifted an unintelligible noise recognizable as music only because of the rhythmic beat of the bass. The teenagers, whether asleep or still awake, were listening to their music of the night. Behind bedroom door number two, Grandma Tildie snored like a rocket. There was no noise at all from the room Brad's parents were in, although Zoë wouldn't have been surprised to hear the sound of calisthenics coming from behind that door—and not bedroom calisthenics, either. The real thing. Serious calisthenics. Jumping jacks, push-ups, handstands, chin-ups. But no. Not so much as a minute's worth of heavy breathing. Just the total quiet of competitive sleepers.

She tiptoed on and stopped at the door to the spare room, the one Daisy Rose had named in her column the Rose by the Sea. Of course, this room hadn't yet been painted ocean blue or adorned with a rose stencil around the window, but there was a beautiful cottage cabinet inside—and possibilities. Lots of possibilities. Without thinking, she raised her hand and knocked, her staccato tapping echoing back down the hallway like a machine gun.

The door jerked open too fast to make a squeak, and Brad frowned at her from the darkness. "Zoë! What are you trying to do? Alert the media?"

With a guilty glance over her shoulder, she dashed past him and whispered hoarsely, "Close the door! Close the door!"

He did, then leaned back against it. "Subtle, Zo," he said. "Very subtle."

"Shh." She pressed a finger to her lips, listening for sounds of alarm in the house, any sound at all. When she was satisfied the bedroom police weren't hot on her tail, she relaxed a little and eyed him in the dark, realizing too late that he was—*gulp*—naked. "What are you wearing?" she asked, even though it was perfectly obvious.

"What I always wear to pace the floor. Or sleep. Whichever comes first."

She kept her gaze angled away from—well, from anything below his chin. "I can't sleep, either. What are we going to do?"

"We could try a back massage," he suggested. "That could prove relaxing."

"Or not." That much, at least, should be obvious. "We should talk."

"I've been talking for the past hour."

"Well, now I'm here to listen."

"Really? I sort of had the idea you were here to tell me what I have to do to untangle this mess."

She gave a noncommittal shrug. The truth was, she didn't know what he ought to do. She didn't know why she thought they could have a serious discussion in his bedroom in the dark. Well, if it had been pitch black, maybe conversation wouldn't have seemed so unappealing. But there was a dappled moonlight spilling through the lace curtains, and there were easily defined shapes. A chest. A bed. A woman. A man.

Oh, she should not have come to his room. Not tonight. Not after kissing him as she had in the garden. Not after her blatant effort to force him into admitting there was no reason they *shouldn't* be in a bedroom…together. That, in fact, it might turn out to be a very good idea. She was mortified, suddenly, by her actions. What was she doing? Brad entertained women in his bedroom as often as a football star sacked the quarterback—and with about as much forethought. Seduction was a way of life for him, and she'd had the perfect excuse to prevent him from trying his techniques on her. Until she'd insisted he stop thinking of her as Tim's wife and begin thinking of her as his lonely widow. Until she'd begun thinking of him as a sexy, sensitive, single guy with unexpected charms. "I'd better go," she said. "I don't know why I came."

"To talk, Zo. You came to talk about how the hell I let you get sucked into this situation and why I didn't step forward like a man and stop it."

She blinked. "That seems a little harsh."

"Yes, well, I'm feeling like Elmer's next of kin at the moment." He walked into the adjoining, tiny half-bath, and came out a moment later wrapping a towel around his waist.

Zoë felt a response—sensual, physical and hotly sweet—stir deep within her. But she was not here for that. She was here to talk. Wasn't she? "I'm sure it's difficult to know what to do," she said. "The situation has gotten a little more complicated than we expected."

"*Complicated?* That's the understatement of the millennium. I could have stopped it, too. *Should* have stopped it. But my family would never—" He knotted the towel so hard, she heard the fabric tear. "Well, let's just say, their arrival threw me completely off balance. I think I could have handled the magazine crew and their patronizing views of life on a small, country farm. I can deal with Ames. But Dad, Mom, the twins, Grandma…they always have these expectations." He sighed and shook his head, obviously angry with himself.

The sympathy that had been building for him ever since the scene in the kitchen carried the day, and Zoë reached out to touch his arm. Sparks didn't fly, but she instantly felt their crackly fire ripple through her and knew that, regardless of what she'd told herself, she had not come to this bedroom to talk. "I understand," she whispered. "You couldn't just blurt out your secret identity." *Oh, no.* She had not meant to say that. "I mean…your secrets."

He stopped working the towel knot and went perfectly still—unless, of course, she counted the thrumming tension that snapped suddenly taut between them. "*What* secret identity?"

Zoë gulped, her heart in her throat, knees shaking. There was no way she could wait for him to entrust her with the truth now. For better or worse, she had to admit she already knew. "You know. The secret identity where I'm not really Daisy Rose and…you really are."

He sucked in a shallow breath, and for a moment all she could hear was the telltale pounding of her own

heart. If he denied it…? Well, she'd go quietly back
to bed and let him worry about how to extricate the
two of them from this nutty charade. But if he didn't—
Well, then that would be a different ball game altogether.

"You think I'm…?" He stopped, swallowed hard,
and looked down at his forearm where her hand rested
in silent entreaty. "Just how did you arrive at that ridiculous conclusion?"

She wasn't backing down. This was too important.
"Well, once I really thought about it, it was the only
explanation that made any sense. Plus, I read the columns."

"It *doesn't* make sense and—" He broke off
abruptly. "You read the columns?"

"Mmm-hmm."

A brief, but bitter battle raged in his eyes, and then,
with a sigh, he asked hopefully, "Did you like them?"

Her whole body relaxed, and a wide, relieved smile
came straight from her heart. "Very much…Daisy
Rose."

His expression was a grimace, but there was pride
in it, too. "So the jig is up, huh? I should have known
you'd figure it out sooner or later."

"Don't give me that. You never expected anyone
could figure you for a nice guy with a real talent for
words."

He perked up. "Talent?"

"Talent." She reassured him with the one solid
word, and let her hand slide from his arm—not because
she didn't want to touch him, but because she couldn't
think too clearly while doing it. "I spent last Saturday
afternoon in a restaurant across from the *Buckthorn*

Bugle, reading every Daisy Rose Knows the newspaper would let me borrow.''

''So how did you…when did you know it was me?''

''Not until I'd read through all the columns once, looking for clues about who this mysterious woman in your life might be. I started out as curious about her as a cat with a paper sack and, I'll admit, not just a wee bit jealous.''

Surprise entered his expression. ''You were jealous of Daisy Rose?''

''You've never been secretive about a woman in your life before, Brad. Not with me. And you seemed so…seriously protective. More protective even than you've been of me…and, well, I just really wanted to know who she was.''

''And from there, you jumped straight to the theory that I must have made her up?''

''No. But as I was getting ready to return the newspapers—feeling pretty frustrated, I might add—I had a passing thought that you might as well be writing the column since you obviously had provided most of the details for it. And…that's when I knew.''

''The devil's always in those details, isn't he? Darn, I should've remembered that.''

''Just how much light have you been hiding under the expansive apron of Daisy Rose Knows anyway?''

His gaze turned coy. ''I can't think what you're talking about, Zo.''

''Well, for one thing, whispering in a mule's ear just never seemed like the sort of trivia you'd know.''

''You'd be surprised at all the trivial information I have stored up here.'' He tapped his temple, and the towel slipped. Grabbing for the ends, he barely managed to keep himself covered. "Unfortunately, none of it is a good substitute for a safety pin."

"I could go get one from my room," she offered.

"Grandma Tildie is in your room. And it seems a bit redundant to make a special trip for a safety pin since, once you're out of the room, I won't need one anymore."

"Oh." Suddenly nervous, Zoë rubbed one foot across the other, her thumb and forefinger pinching at the hem of her cotton nightshirt. "I didn't think to put on a robe."

"Not quite the same thing...and I've seen you without a robe on before."

"Well, I've seen you naked before."

"When?"

"That time the three of us were supposed to be studying for the English Lit final and we went skinny dipping instead. Oh, and there was another time, too."

"When?"

"Just now."

"That doesn't count. You were pounding on the door."

"Well, I haven't had much practice sneaking into a man's bedroom."

"I'm glad to hear it."

"Oh, like that's some big surprise to you. Every time a man came within three feet of me, asking for a date, you were right there playing the role of bodyguard."

"No need to thank me," he said, grinning. "I know I've done a damn fine job of protecting you from the riffraff." His grin faded and the trouble returned to his gaze. "Well, until lately, anyway."

"You can stop worrying about Newton, Brad," she said on a sigh. "I'm not going to marry him."

"I wasn't thinking about him…this time." He rolled the top edge of the towel between his fingers, unrolled it again. "I was thinking about this afternoon in the garden."

"Oh." She stopped breathing…started again. "Oh."

"We, uh, never finished that conversation."

"Oh," she said again, then, "I guess, we could do it now."

"I guess so," he agreed. "As long as you don't mind discussing delicate matters with a man who hides behind a woman's good name."

"If it weren't for Daisy Rose, there probably wouldn't be a delicate matter to discuss."

His eyebrows rose. "She changed your mind about me, did she?"

"Let's just say, she helped me see you in a new light."

"I hope it's not a glorious techni-pink-colored light."

"Are all men as defensive about their masculinity as you are?"

"Probably. I'm just more honest about it."

"Honest. Right. I'll keep that in mind tomorrow at the wedding."

He winced. "I'll put a stop to that, Zoë. If Ames wasn't always in such a hurry to leave, I'd already have set him straight about that. I wish Lark wasn't so happy about the prospect, though."

Zoë shrugged. "We'll give her the whole cake, and she'll be happy. It's not as if her life will be ruined because we don't get married tomorrow."

"Or ever."

She turned away from him and faced the window. Stars twinkled encouragement and the moon glowed like hope. "'Ever' is a long time, Brad. Let's just leave it at tomorrow and see what happens, okay?"

He put his hands on her shoulders, a friend's hands offering support for a moment of truth. "I've known you a long time, Zo. But you're going to have to spell this one out for me. Slowly. Very slowly."

Okay. She could do that. She'd already done it a dozen times in her mind. Turning back to face him, she stayed within the parameters he'd set as she sucked in a fortifying breath. "I think I might have...fallen in love with you."

In the twilight, she couldn't see the expression in his eyes, but something in his stillness communicated an acceptance she understood. Love wasn't what either of them had ever expected to feel, but somehow they were both aware now that the possibility had always been there. "Wh—" He cleared his throat. "When?"

"Just now. Or maybe when we kissed today. Or maybe when I read the column about the lemon balm in the garden. Or it could have been the whispering in the mule's ear incident. Or possibly it was when you let it slip that you can bake an apple pie. But honestly?" She gave a delicate shrug. "It's probably been happening for a very long time."

He lifted his hand, brushed his fingers across her cheek. "Are you sure this isn't just a little too convenient?"

Along with being barely able to breathe, none of this felt "convenient" at all. "No, Brad. This is *not* a matter of convenience."

"Well, I've always been around, and I love Lark more than life itself, and it's been five years since...."

"Tim died. You can say that. He's gone, and no matter how we felt about him, he's not coming back.

It's just you and me and whatever we want to make of the future. Whether we're together or apart, Tim is no longer in this picture."

"But, Zoë, I promised him—"

She shushed him with her finger against his lips. "Tell me to leave, if you want. Tell me you don't reciprocate my feelings and never will. Tell me I'm not your type. Tell me you can't come up with even a cheap fantasy about me. But do not stand there and invoke Tim's name and your promise to him like it's some sacred justification for not taking me to your bed."

If the tension had felt taut and uneasy before, it was nothing to the way it sucked all the energy from the room now and held it prisoner in the square foot of space between his chest and hers, his gaze and hers...the past that was theirs together and the future that was still up for grabs.

Then he cupped her face in his big hands and lowered his head. She came up on tiptoe to meet him...and the first touch of his lips to hers seared her with need and desire and truth. Whatever the reason she and Brad had kept the barrier of Tim's memory between them all these years, it was gone now for good. She had loved her husband. Brad had loved his friend. But Tim was banished from this moment, from the bed they might soon share, from their present, from whatever emotions were just coming to light within them.

Zoë hadn't planned this. Brad certainly seemed taken by surprise. But for all that, the kiss was perfect, quickly becoming deep and wet and shockingly passionate. His mouth angled across hers, devouring her with desire that was heady and new. Her tongue sought his in a purposeful challenge. Whatever control he'd had to exercise vanished now in the onslaught of discovery. Sensual, stimulating, purely sexual discovery. He knew her so well. Her likes, her dislikes, her smiles, her frowns, her tones of voice, her body language. She knew all about him, too. And yet, they knew nothing of each other. Not in this arena. Not where the only language was touch and the only dialect, passion.

He drew the kiss into a stroking, tasting, sucking, nibbling retreat, leaving her gasping for more. Then he swung her easily, like a featherweight, into his arms and carried her to the bed. There were no words as he laid her there and followed her down. Just his eyes, shadowed by night and unexpected emotion, revealed in shades of moonlit wonder and desire. And then his lips were on her throat, the lobe of her ear, the soft hollow below. And his hands…

Ribbons of tingling response fluttered with each contact of skin on skin. Her breasts peaked with invitation and pouted with envy when his hand slipped beneath the nightshirt to splay warmth and anticipation across the planes of her stomach. Her lips hungered for his kiss, but as his lips were quite pleasurably buried in the valleys of her neck and shoulder, she turned hers to exploring the texture of him, set her tongue the task of tasting him, let the man-scent of him fill her with longing. Shivers danced from every point of contact, from every soft suckling, from the caress of every fingertip, to gather in a collective and building tension. It pulled at her breasts and pooled in hot, wet invitation between her thighs.

Zoë knew her body was out of the loop of sensual knowledge. It had been a very long time since she'd lain with a man. But she hadn't expected the need to be so great, the excitement so complete, the urgency so tremulous and untested. She'd yearned for the touch of a man, the feel of a hard body around and within her softer one. And yet she hadn't sought to satisfy the craving before, had told herself she'd know when the time was right, when the right man came along.

Well, the time was now and the right man had been there all along, as trapped within the past as she, as blind to possibility as she, avoiding the look, the words, the touch that would have marked the end of a beautiful friendship and the beginning of so much more. Zoë promised herself that later—much later—she and Brad would talk about all the moments when their tide might have turned, would revisit memories both sorrowful and sweet, would wonder at the parallel paths of their lives, and speak in awed whispers of this night. For now, all she wanted was this magnificent and silent communication.

When he shifted his weight, she took advantage and wiggled out of the nightshirt. The towel was long since gone, somewhere on the floor or crumpled into the sheets. Moonlight spilled like silk across their naked bodies, draping them in a glistening, pearly luster. His hand moved lower...and so did hers. Touch exploded to new delights, skin turned damp and hot. His mouth opened over hers, drawing her breath into him, breathing his into her. Then his lips left her, limp and needy, to minister the same painful pleasure to her aching breasts. His fingers stroked her into quivering frenzy, and she tugged at him, urged him to fill the needy place within her.

When he stopped and raised himself above her, she quivered with sensations more akin to great thirst than mere anticipation. He didn't make the moves she expected, however, but huskily whispered her name. "Zoë?"

"Brad," she whispered back in an equally husky encouragement.

"Zo."

She squeezed her eyes tightly shut. "Please tell me you don't want to talk now."

"I don't want to talk now."

"Good. Don't."

"Have to. Unless you have a pocket in that nightshirt with a packet of latex protection in it."

"Protection," she repeated, drooping head to toe with disappointment. "It's been so long, I forgot about that. But we don't have to worry—"

"Yes," he interrupted. "We do. Look, this probably isn't a good idea, anyway. There are people all over this house. My parents are in the next room, Lark is just down the hall. There are people with cameras only a few yards from the front door. And we are adults—responsible adults."

She frowned. "Lark wouldn't wake up if we danced the mambo beside her bed. I don't know how soundly your parents sleep, and honestly don't care. As for the media, trust me, this room is too small and dark to produce good photographs. And stopping to consider the consequences *does* make us responsible adults. Now, where do you keep the condoms?"

"At my apartment in Joplin?"

"No, really."

"Yes, really."

"You must have at least one in the house somewhere."

He rolled onto his side beside her. "I must, huh? What is this—a test of male readiness?"

"No, but...." She shifted onto her side to face him, head propped miserably on her fist. "Well, you are something of a...swinging single guy."

"That was before Daisy Rose came along and turned me into the *un*prepared Hubby Bee." He leaned in to kiss her nose, then, as if he couldn't help himself, her lips.

"Mmm," she said, following his lips to gain another tender kiss. "So you're sure there's no way we can...?"

"There are other ways to pleasure each other, Zoë."

"My body is pretty set on having the full experience of your 'hunka-hunka burnin' love.'"

"What?"

"That would be your secret identity as Hubby Bee, the studly." She coiled her fingertips into the curly hairs on his chest. "Are you *positive* there isn't a single condom on Lazy Daisy Acres?"

"I suppose I could go out to the trailer and ask Carson if he has a spare. Or maybe Dad—now there's an idea, huh?" He rolled onto his back with a groan, and she sat up with new purpose, grabbed her nightshirt and hopped off the bed.

"Zoë?" His whisper was hoarse and warning. "You're not going to—"

She leaned back in, planted a hearty kiss on his lips and headed for the door. "If I'm not back in ten minutes, the cover story is that I walk in my sleep. Got it?"

"No!" He grabbed for her, but she slipped away and tiptoed quickly to the door, where she waved a jaunty "bye" before heading out on her quest.

TEN MINUTES was too long to maintain the euphoria her desire for him had created, and as the seconds slipped by, recrimination set in. Five more minutes and he was deep into an anxious soul-search. Lying on the bed, the towel draped across his loins, an arm covering his eyes, Brad tried to keep from thinking about what had just *not* happened. He hoped to heaven she'd come back with a condom, hoped to hell she wouldn't. To say she'd "surprised" him was like saying Elmer was a "little" stubborn. And there was no context, no nice, neat box into which he could fit this sudden shift in perspective. Zoë had found him out, but instead of finding it laughable, ludicrous or bizarre, she'd set out to seduce him.

Okay, so maybe that was a bit simplistic. But holy moly, what was he doing taking her up on this offer? Love. She'd talked of being in love like it was something she'd been thinking about long and hard, like it was something that had already happened, like it was their destiny. Was it possible the two of them might…? That she…? That he…?

No. How could love happen without both of them knowing it, committing to it, inviting it in as a welcomed guest? Bottom line was, he had never done anything to deserve a woman like Zoë. Never would. She was so far above his touch, it wasn't even funny. Tim had been perfect for her. They had been perfect together. Brad had been happy just watching them smile at each other. So what had she been doing in Brad's bed? Why was there a lingering warmth on the pillow next to him? Why did his sheets smell of her hair and his fingers of her sex? Why did his body still ache with desire for her? Why was he fighting so hard to say yes, when he knew in his heart the answer had to be no?

The door opened, squeaking softly as it swung

closed again, and she was there. He saw the shadowy swing of hair about her shoulders, smelled the fragrance of honeysuckle that clung to her skin, heard the *pad, pad, pad* of her feet on the floor, felt the bed dip, heard the springs creak, as she slipped in beside him.

"Got it," she whispered.

"Zoë," he said, determined to put temptation behind him before she touched him and he lost his resolve to restore the status quo—which was the right thing, the best thing, for a bodyguard to do. "Zoë, I...."

"Shh." Her kiss amazed and delighted him—no matter how hard he tried to tell himself otherwise. She was naked, too, her skin silky against his rougher texture, warm where he was cool. Okay, so he didn't deserve this miracle and had no hope that tomorrow she'd still believe he did. He couldn't send her away—not even to keep his promise.

Closing his arms around her, he held her tight, drowning in her intimate attention, in the stolen pleasures of not thinking about what was right, but only about what was right now. Taking charge of the embrace, he kissed his way to her ear, pushed aside the wealth of silky hair, and whispered, "I do not, under any circumstances, want to know where you found that."

Her laugh was throaty and low, a caress of breath against his cheek. "I stole them from one of the twins' billfolds."

He grimaced. "I wish you hadn't told me that. Wait a minute. You stole more than one?"

"I know it was optimistic of me, but...well, life is short. Besides, I didn't want to have to go back after more later."

Oh, yes, he could love this woman. Did love her.

And considering they were lying naked in his bed, and had not one, but several, condoms, it was apparent he wasn't going to do a damn thing to save them both from tomorrow's regret. He had broken his promise tonight, crossed a bridge he had never meant to cross, and now, there was nothing left to do but leave it burning. "To hell with friendship," he said and kissed her roughly, rolling her onto her back and following her over, using his hands to memorize every curve, every angle.

"Please, Brad," she whispered, sounding desperate and demanding against his mouth. "Love me. Love me now."

He gave himself up to her then, retracing the sensual paths he'd explored once already tonight, remembering the sweet spots that made her gasp and breathe out his name. "Brad," she said in seductive murmurs. "Brad."

She whispered his name over and over in ragged sighs, careful to be private, but still recklessly imprudent when he touched her there…and there….

"Shh," he said. "Shh." Soothing her, quieting her, loving her as she'd requested, loving her as his own heart and soul demanded—purely, powerfully, passionately. Only at the last, in the final moments when climax shattered what remained of his control, did he call out her name in tender and bittersweet surrender.

"Zoë," he called. "Zoë."

Chapter Eleven

So consider the mysteries of mustard, Friend Neighbor. Is it a seed? A plant of pungent salad greens? A spicy relish for our hot dogs? A flavorful spread for our sandwich? A symbol of abundance contained within the single tiny grain from which it grew? It can be all of these and more, but as I cut the young and tender leaves in anticipation of having a dish of greens for supper, I can't help but smile at the mustard plant's simple needs...sunlight, rain, warm rich earth, and the occasional song from the wrens, who frequent the branches of a nearby birch tree. The recipe for Lazy Daisy Apple Pie printed below has nothing at all to do with mustard...unless you have faith (as I do) that the simple joys of tomorrow are sown within the seeds of today....

Brad awakened slowly, aware of Zoë's warmth spooned against him, mesmerized by the even rhythm of her heartbeat, the soft puffs of her breathing. He couldn't remember the last time he'd spent the night with a woman, but he knew the memory of these few early morning moments would be relived again and again over the course of his years. There was a sweetness to the day that hadn't been present yesterday. A dawning hope that had never been in his heart before. Last night had been...delicious.

He didn't move, just breathed in and out...in...out, loving the woman in his arms, memorizing the feel of her skin, the scent of her hair. In a minute, he'd kiss her and rouse her to the reality that her bed was down the hall and that she should not linger too long. In a minute, he'd get up, get dressed, make coffee, go out to the barn. In a minute, he'd begin pretending that nothing had happened, nothing had changed, that a broken promise wasn't eating a hole in his heart.

The smell of coffee wafted up from downstairs to tickle his nose. The faraway *clank* of a pot being put on the stove stirred a faint recognition. The low rumble of voices somewhere in the house roused him. The sound of footsteps on the stairs completed the journey into full and frantic consciousness. A blink, a glance at the daylight, bright and bonny, beyond the bedroom window, brought him sitting up in bed.

Zoë mumbled and rolled onto her back, her arm stretching up to shield her eyes as she blinked herself awake. Seeing him, she smiled sleepily. "Hi, you," she said, and despite the disaster he feared was approaching, he wanted nothing more than to slide back down beside her and make love to her until night blanketed them in darkness all over again.

"Hi, you," he said, hoping no one was acting as hall monitor and checking who came out from behind what door. "We overslept."

"We did?" She yawned prettily. "I thought you were going to wake me up early so I could go back to...." Her eyes opened wider. "Is Lark already awake?"

"I don't know, but it's a good bet that if she's not already, she will be any minute now."

Zoë tossed back the covers, shivered at the chill of exposure and swung her feet over the edge of the mattress. "I'll slip out and— Do you know where my nightshirt is?"

Brad wasn't listening. Well, not to her, anyway. There was a commotion rising out in the hallway, a clatter of sounds, a collective murmur of voices, and, unless he was mistaken, all of the noise was converging just beyond his bedroom door. "Get under the covers, Zo."

"What?" She barely gave him a glance. "I can't find my nightshirt."

"That's why you need to get back under the covers *now*."

The sounds finally made an impression on her, too, and she brought her gaze to his in questioning alarm. "Who could be making all that noise?" she asked. But she pulled her feet back up on the mattress and drew the covers up to her chin, covering him in the process, as well.

Not a second later, a chipper knock—*rap, rap, rap*—shook the door in its frame. Brad just had time to wonder why last night, of all nights, he'd forgotten to set the alarm clock, before the knob—he was installing locks on these doors today!—turned. The door cracked open and the hinges squeaked as first Lark's, then Grandma Tildie's, heads popped into view. "They're awake," Lark whispered over her shoulder to someone out of sight, then she turned a sunny smile on her mother and godfather. "G'morning," she said, pushing the door fully open to admit herself, Grandma and Granite Ames, who was carrying a rosewood tray. "We brought you breakfast in bed," Lark announced. "'Cause today we're gettin' married!"

"It's chow time," Grandma Tildie said.

"Breakfast was Lark's idea," Ames said, setting the tray across Brad's lap with an arch look at the four bare arms draped tightly across the chest-high sheet. "Normally, we wouldn't bust in on you like this, but this picture shoot is all about Daisy Rose and Hubby Bee in their natural setting, now isn't it? So, once we figured out the two of you had to be in here together, well, heck, why not get some photos of you having breakfast in bed?" Turning, Ames motioned toward the doorway where Carson, Annelle and the crew stood ready. A moment later, the bedroom was teeming with workers and well on its way to becoming a camera set with light poles, lights, silver metal reflectors and deflectors, and all manner of electrical cords and gadgets.

Ames beamed like a proud papa. "Now, this is gonna take a while to get set up, so you both just relax. And don't you go worrying about how you look, Zoë Rose. Annelle will get the makeup and hair situation squared away before Carson even aims the camera at you. Hmm, you may have to shave, Brad." He looked to Annelle for confirmation. "What do you think? Oh, right, we're looking for reality here, so never mind about the shave. Can they eat the breakfast, Carson, or do you want the food in the picture?"

Carson shook his head, indicating either that he didn't care if they ate the food or that the room was too small and dark for good photographs.

"Hey," Brad said, finding his voice in the well of

embarrassment that ran clear to the soles of his feet. "Hey, get these people out of here!"

"Now, now...." Ames sat at the foot of the bed and watched the hurrying and scurrying with obvious satisfaction. "I know this is something of an intrusion, but you did agree to let *Home and Hearth* do the story."

"I didn't agree to anything like this. Get them out of here."

"You should read the small print on the documents you sign," Ames said, not the slightest bit perturbed by Brad's furious glower. Lights came on, flooding the room with an obnoxious glare, and Brad and Zoë raised hands simultaneously to shield their eyes. Ames pulled a pair of sunglasses from his shirt pocket and slipped them on. "Bright in here, isn't it?"

"Which bedroom is this?" Annelle sorted a stack of paper, obviously looking for the pertinent information. "Is this the master bedroom or the Rose by the Sea spare?"

"It's the Rose by the Sea," someone answered. "That's the cottage cabinet over there."

Annelle's glance found the chest, returned to check the paper again. "The room's got to be blue. Ocean blue with rose stencils around the window that match the cabinet."

"I'll take care of it in the lab." Carson snapped a back onto the camera and advanced the film. "Adding color is easy. Adding rose decorations is easy." He rolled his eyes in Zoë's direction. "But doing something with her hair is beyond even my abilities."

"Hey," Zoë protested.

"I'll handle that." Annelle looked around a light

pole into the hallway and yelled out, "Makeup! Stylist!"

Ames's grin got as big as Texas, his pleasure in the hubbub crystal clear. "See? I told you she'd make sure you looked good."

"I do my own hair," Grandma said, arms folded across her ample chest. "Wash it in mustard and vinegar twice a week."

Lark suddenly stopped playing hopscotch among the electrical cords and eyed her mother and godfather with focused curiosity. "Hi, Mom. Hi, Uncle Brad. How come you're not wearing clothes? Are you havin' sex? 'Cause Sonchie says that's what breakfast in bed really means and he says you have to take off all your clothes to do it, and he's a very smart boy. What's the matter? Don't you like your pancakes? I can getcha more syrup if you want it."

Helpless to do anything of real value at the moment, Brad scowled at Zoë. "No more arguments. You're moving out of that neighborhood."

"I'm moving out of this one first." She crossed her arms above her breasts, partly to help hold up the sheets, and partly because she was furious. "I don't see how you could let this happen."

"Me?" He exercised significant effort to keep his voice low and strictly for her ears. Not that shouting could be heard over the noise in the room, anyway. "If you hadn't spent the night in here, we wouldn't be stuck in this bed right now. I tried to tell you that what happened last night shouldn't have happened, that it wasn't a good idea."

Her gaze snapped to his. "*What?* So this is *my* fault? Is that what you're saying?"

"Shh," he said under his breath. "Don't complicate this by bringing the whole crew into our argument."

"Oh, I hadn't thought of that," she said, her tone rising with her frustration. "We certainly wouldn't want to *complicate* this situation, would we?"

"Getting angry with me isn't going to help, you know."

"No, I can see that. Apparently, expecting you to do *anything* is clearly out of the question."

"I don't know what you think I can do." He lowered his voice even further. "I'm as naked under this sheet as you are."

"Yes, but you're a man, and men like to walk around naked."

"I beg your pardon."

"Oh, just get up and get my nightshirt, so at least I can get out of here."

"If I get up, I'm taking the sheet with me."

She clutched the sheet as she would have a life preserver. "You touch an inch on my half, and you die."

Ames slid from the mattress to sidle closer. He leaned in and said, sounding amused, "Cool it, kiddies. You can slug it out later. But for right now...smile! You're on *Candid Camera.*"

THE SHUTTER CLICKED. The lights went off in a blinding flash. Carson and Annelle argued over the next shot. Somebody poufed Zoë's hair, and somebody else brushed powder across her nose. Then the first somebody returned to flatten the pouf and the somebody else dashed back in to whisk away stray dots of powder from the bodice of her blue dress. Annelle sent a critical gaze over the setup, changed her mind, directed a new shot, plopped Zoë down in the middle of it, and the whole process started all over again.

In the three hours since the photo shoot had begun with the bare essentials in the Rose by the Sea bedroom, Zoë had been moved a dozen times. She'd been photographed in every room of the farmhouse, in six different outfits—all of which merited a sad sigh from Annelle; six different hairstyles—none of which met with Carson's approval; and in poses no woman in her right mind would consider *casual,* much less conducive to the oft-repeated instruction *"Look like you love being a country girl!"*

Zoë had a tension headache, black spots in her vision from all the flashes, and was literally cooking under the heat of the lights. She'd been Daisy Rose in the kitchen, Daisy Rose on the sofa, Daisy Rose in the pantry, and Daisy Rose in the porch swing. And that, apparently, was only to be the beginning. Annelle referred to setups in the barn, the garden, and possibly by the pond.

Carson argued the sun was at the wrong angle for outdoor shots and insisted on working indoors where he could control the lighting. Annelle stressed the need to use their time efficiently, and Carson replied that if she'd wanted efficient instead of brilliant, she shouldn't have hired an artist. Ames wandered in and out, rocking on his heels as he watched the shoot and listened to the ongoing quarrel, winking at Zoë at every opportunity. From time to time she'd catch a glimpse of a Kenneally—none of them Brad—peering past a flash unit to see how things were progressing. Lark raced past a doorway every so often, in a hurry to get wherever she was going. At the center of so much attention, Zoë had never felt so much on the outside.

It was Brad's fault, really. He could have stopped this nonsense at any juncture, ended her performance as Daisy Rose with a single announcement. *I'm the author of Daisy Rose Knows,* he could have said, and everyone would have packed up and gone home. Story over. Truth told. The end. But he'd said nothing then and nothing since. He'd let the charade continue, while he did heaven knew what. And it was beginning to feel like a tug of war inside her over what she didn't want to have to do and what Brad was leaving it up to her to do.

After last night, she'd thought the future would unfold like a field of wildflowers, vivid with possibilities, shimmering with new awareness. She'd thought loving Brad, letting him feel her acceptance, would smooth the way for him, allow him to be himself—all of himself—regardless of who was watching. His parents were here, his brothers and his boss. How hard could it be to say, *Hey, I'm a writer. I'm also a whiz at baking pies and wedding cakes. I know a thing or two about gardening. I know how to move a mule and make a little girl giggle. I'm an ace in the kitchen and damn good at identifying a dozen different breeds of chickens. I like puppies, ponies and pink petunias, and if you have a problem with that, tell it to your therapist.* How hard could it be to face other people's expectations and stand up for the person you really wanted to be? Especially if you had the support of someone who loved you?

She could have done it for him in a heartbeat, could have made the announcement and given some direction as to what the response needed to be. But it wasn't her identity at stake or her choice to make. Of her own free will, she'd agreed to help Brad, and just because the situation had escalated into a circus wasn't reason enough to abandon him. She was angry with him, angry with herself, and angry that they simply couldn't be alone. A few days with him and she could have all those years of family indoctrination wiped out.

After all, he should have no regrets. He'd done what they'd expected of him, fulfilled their dreams for him, been the son they wanted. He'd excelled in sports and life. It was just that they only acknowledged the former, only bestowed merit to the achievements that could be measured in goals scored, games won. Brad was so afraid of being a disappointment that he'd buried his own dreams and convinced himself they were the wrong dreams to hold. He'd built an image of Olympic proportions and had tried to pretend it did not have feet of clay. His macho persona had evolved into a wall of protection as solid as any he'd ever erected on her behalf.

The time was right to shatter the wall and his fears of facing the world, and his family, without it. The opportunity was here, now, but it wouldn't last long and it might never come again. With all her heart, Zoë wanted him to step up and take responsibility for writing the columns. She wanted him to claim his identity as athlete, writer, gardener guy and all-around hero. Not to save her. But to save Daisy Rose and all she symbolized for his future.

"We're gonna need to wrap this up," Ames announced from the opening into the living room. "It's eleven-thirty and the minister's here. Zoë Rose, you'll want a few minutes to get that dust off your freckles, then it's 'Here comes the bride'...!" With a happy wiggle of his brows, he headed out, oblivious to Zoë's call for him to come back.

Okay, so maybe it was noble of her to want Brad to step forward and courageously declare himself a man of many talents, but she wasn't crazy. She might have fallen hard for the man she was just beginning to know, but no way was she ready to plunge into a last-minute marriage just to save his handsome face.

BRAD WATCHED from the shadows as Zoë was hustled up the stairs to the bedroom. He was the bridegroom and he wasn't supposed to see the bride. Someone or other had been telling him that all morning. But he wasn't the bridegroom. He was the bride*goof.* As if he could ever hope to marry Zoë. As if she would ever agree to marry him.

He'd been going over and over the possibilities in his head, trying to fit last night's miracle into today's wake-up call. Clearly, he should never have asked or expected her to take part in such a farce. Clearly, he was a coward for suggesting it. Clearly, he had to do something to save the day. But just as clearly, the only action that might do the trick required a sacrifice he wasn't at all sure he could make.

To get up in front of everyone—no way could he tell them individually—and announce that he wasn't the man they all believed him to be...well, that had every last milligram of testosterone in his body screaming out in protest. He had imagined the horror in his mother's eyes when he said that he had not only written a column called Daisy Rose Knows, but had actually enjoyed writing it. He could see the embarrassment his brothers would try to hide behind a wave of dumb jokes and awkward elbow nudges. He knew his dad would have to ask him several times just how sports and Daisy Rose were connected, in the effort to understand how his macho son had been turned to *the dark side*. And on top of all that, Ames would fire him on the spot. There had to be another way. A less revealing revelation. A way to protect his woman *and* his identity *and* still be Superman.

What he wouldn't give to be able to talk to Tim right now. Five minutes. That's all he'd need. Tim had always been able to see through situations to the sane and sensible solution. He had always found the right words to shift a problem into a new and obvious—*well, duh!*—perspective. "You know, Tim," he whispered. "If you are an angel…and I'm not saying you are or you're not…I could sure use a little heavenly interference about now. Just a little divine intervention. Doesn't have to be big. Any help at all will be appreciated."

Nothing.

But what had he expected? He'd betrayed Tim last night, claimed what wasn't his to claim, broken a promise he'd made in good faith, taken advantage of his position as friend and protector. It was more than arrogant to expect not just forgiveness, but an outright miracle.

Disgusted, Brad pushed away from the stairwell and ran smack into Grandma Tildie. "Well, that's a fine how-de-do," she said.

"Sorry, Grandma. I wasn't looking where I was going."

"That's for sure. You best dust off your overalls and get out there before that pretty gal changes her mind and takes off with the gardener guy."

"Thanks, Grandma, I'll do that." He made a move to pass her, but she reached out with a surprising grip and caught his arm.

"I've got a few words of advice for you, young man, and here they are. Ready?" She pinned him with a lucid pair of watery blue eyes. "Remember yesterday. Dream tomorrow. But live like crazy today." She let go of his arm. "Got it?"

He nodded his head, not sure who she thought she was talking to. "I got it, Grandma."

"Good," she said. "'Cause I'd hate to see you keep trying to live in the past."

Brad stood stock-still, watching her waddle off muttering to some unseen partner, and told himself he should not be thinking what he was thinking. Angels didn't deliver messages through dotty old women. On the other hand, it was the only thing she'd said in years that made absolute sense to him. Odds were that it was a freakish coincidence, a million-to-one shot that she'd echoed the words that, since Tim's death, he'd honestly tried to live by. *Remember yesterday. Dream tomorrow. Live like crazy today.*

So what on God's green earth was he afraid of? Losing an image he'd never been comfortable with? Losing a friendship that was no longer there to lose? Or losing a woman who knew his deepest, darkest secret...and loved him anyway?

He'd been looking at this sacrifice all wrong. It had already been made for him. Zoë had done it by pushing down the walls he'd built to protect himself. She'd already claimed a new destiny for them. Last night, she'd come to him, seduced him, offered her love not to the man who'd tried so hard to protect her, but to the man Brad had tried so hard to keep hidden from her.

He turned and looked up the stairs. It was time he put a stop to this comedy of errors. It was time he

started to live like crazy today. It was time he claimed
his Daisy Rose.

"SHH." Brad cautioned her to be quiet as he eased shut
the bathroom door and leaned heavily against it. "We
need to talk before the wedding."

"Really?"

Her eyebrows were set at a haughty angle, and she
didn't look all that happy to see him. But she looked
beautiful, and he thought, perhaps, he should begin this
apology by telling her so. "You look like a bride," he
said.

Her pupils flared. "That's it, Brad. Don't think for
two seconds that I am going to walk out of this bathroom and down that makeshift aisle by the garden. I
don't care how much your moronic boss has invested
in bringing in a string quartet, or how much the florist
charged him to set up that arbor. I don't care if Carson
is the top photographer in the nation and has, at the
insistence of his greedy, arrogant little wallet, agreed
to take my wedding portrait. I don't even care that my
daughter is wearing a *real* diamond pendant, courtesy
of Ames Publications, or that she has a veritable bucket
of rose petals to strew in front of me. I am *not* going
to marry Hubby Bee in a sham of a ceremony to keep
you from having to admit you're a wonderful writer
who just happens to be using a woman's name as a
pseudonym!"

He blinked. "Wow," he said. "You must have been
working on that speech all morning."

"Don't patronize me, either. I'm turning in my overalls and resigning my commission. You can tell Ames
and your family that I ran off with the gardener guy,

for all I care, but it's finished. Over. Stick a fork in me, I'm done.''

She was breathing hard, and he found the rise and fall of her breasts fascinating. He found the tilt of her chin and the anger in her eyes and the curve of her lips equally charming. ''Would you consider just walking outside with me? Just as far as the garden?''

Her frown was a work of art. ''I just told you, I'm not taking another step as your gooey Daisy Rose.''

''Gooey?'' How had he been with her so many times in the past and never realized how deeply, insanely he loved her?

''I'm upset. And I'm getting all mixed up.''

''That's okay because I have a plan. Tim came up with it.''

''Tim?''

''Okay, so it's really Hubby Bee's idea. But please, Zoë, just go with me to the garden, and I promise you won't have to do anything else. And you know I always keep my promises.''

Suspicion flared in her eyes, but faith won out. ''To the garden,'' she clarified. ''But that's as far as I go.''

He smiled, wondering what he'd ever done to deserve her faith in him, but accepting it finally for the miracle it was. ''That'll be far enough,'' he said, and took her hand.

THE STRING QUARTET played Mozart, and Lark danced like an ungainly sprite as Zoë walked beside Brad down the porch steps to the garden. She was an idiot to let him draw her into another round of Let's Pretend. Still, she did feel a little like a bride in her flowing blue dress with the cluster of baby's breath in her hair. At the opposite end of the garden path stood the minister under the canopy of a lovely, if hastily assembled, arbor. He smiled at their approach and signaled to the crowd to stand for the bride's entrance.

Crowd was something of a misnomer, although the camera crew added bulk to the gathering. There was an elderly couple on the back row sitting next to Lloyd, and Brad's family was up front in folding chairs. Granite Ames, of course, had the best seat in the garden with a good view of the arbor and the pond in the distance. Tweedles, Dee and Dum sported new collars and leashes, and even Elmer looked spiffy—well, at least alert—as he edged his way toward the flowered arbor from the far side. It was exactly the sort of wedding Daisy Rose would have wanted. If, of course, Daisy Rose had been real.

Brad's arm flexed beneath Zoë's hand, and she looked up at him, trying to make it clear that she'd meant what she said and said what she meant—the rose bush was as far as she was going this time. He stopped before they reached it and squared his shoulders.

"I, uh, have an announcement," he said, pitching his voice above the music.

All eyes were already on them. Except for Elmer's, which were holding steady on the arbor. Zoë sighed and moved to step back, away from Brad, but his free hand came up to cover hers and keep her beside him. "I have something to say, and then, maybe, we'll see about having a wedding. Okay, here goes. There's been one name mentioned more than any other in the last twenty-four hours—Daisy Rose—and I think it's time you all met her. She's a lot of people, really, but mainly she's the *nom de plume* for a columnist who has been too shy, too frightened, too stupid to reveal her true self. Until now."

Zoë watched Brad, half afraid he was going to reveal himself, half afraid he wasn't.

"I'm ashamed to admit," he began hesitantly, "that I'm responsible for keeping her under wraps and not letting her step forward and claim her identity as…a man." Brad inhaled sharply. "That's right, ladies and gentlemen. Mom, Dad, Kellen, Chris…Mr. Ames, sir. I am Daisy Rose, and she is me. She's part fiction and part fact, and I expect every one of you to support her—me—today and every day after this. Any questions?"

There was shock and doubt in the Kenneally row, but Granite Ames hopped out of his seat and hustled down the aisle with an expression of doom on his face. He stopped only a few feet from Brad and turned a hard stare on Carson, who was standing to one side, talking to Annelle, oblivious to the drama by the rosebush. "Hey, Picasso!" Ames called. "What am I paying you for? To stand there and flap your jaws? Get over here with that camera and take some pictures!" He brought his gaze back to Brad, and by association, Zoë. "It's about time you owned up to those columns, Bubb," he said. "I was running out of ideas to force you into admitting it, you big lummox!"

Brad blinked. "You knew?"

Ames laughed heartily. "Well, I didn't just fall off a turnip truck, you know. Besides, Lloyd knew it was you, and even though you swore him to secrecy, he's not exactly a hard nut to crack, if you know what I mean. What I don't know is how you talked Zoë Rose into pretending *she* was our Daisy. Not that I'm at all upset about that. And not that I don't still have big plans for all the characters on Lazy Daisy Acres, you understand. The readers will have to be told the truth, but I think they can handle it. We may lose a few, but with the publicity we'll gain many more. It'll work out for the best. Now, I'm willing to let the two of you have a little time to think about where we go from here, and more say in the direction we wind up taking. Providing, of course, that you go through with this wedding today. I can't be promoting a couple who sleeps together outside the bonds of holy matrimony, if you get my meaning.''

The music had stopped, and, suddenly realizing it, Lark stopped dancing and tossing rose petals. ''Hey!'' she said. ''Hey! I thought we were gettin' married!''

Brad's parents had been talking to each other, but they suddenly got up and came down the aisle. ''Brad?'' His mother pinched her mouth into a disapproving frown. ''Does this mean you're a writer, or a columnist?''

''Both, I think, Mom.''

She nodded, still obviously uncertain as to what it meant to her son. ''Will you be covering some sports events for the newspaper?''

Zoë felt the muscles in his arm tense under her hand, and she gave him a reassuring squeeze.

''Probably not, Mom. I'm not much interested in sports these day. I've taken a real interest in farming.''

''Farming?'' his father muttered. ''Not much challenge there. Or money.''

''I'm not planning to quit my job, Dad. Just where I live. And *how* I live.''

''Will you still want to go to the football games with me?'' his dad asked. ''At least, sometimes?''

Brad nodded. ''Yeah, Dad. I still like sports. I just like other things, too.''

''Daisy Rose is going to make enough money to buy

a football team," Ames predicted jovially. "If she ever wants one, that is."

"Well," Brad said on a sigh of relief. "This has turned out better than I expected. Elmer!" he shouted. "Get away from there!" Elmer had reached the arbor and had a flower already picked out.

"Elmer!" shouted a new voice, stern and unfamiliar. Zoë's gaze followed Brad's to the elderly man who was standing between two chairs and whose attention was on the mule. "Elmer," the man repeated. "Get on. Get on, now."

The mule stopped, looked stubbornly at the man, then, with what resembled the expression of a pouty child, ambled off toward the pasture gate.

"Mr. Renfroe," Brad said, recognizing the man and moving forward to greet him and the gray-haired lady beside him. "Mrs. Renfroe. What are you doing here?"

The man slipped his thumbs under his suspender straps and faced Brad. "We've come back to take back the farm," he said. "Turns out we changed our mind about selling it."

"You can't do that."

"Says in the contract for sale we can. Says we don't have to pay back the down payment you give us, either."

"Now wait a minute," Brad said. "Wait just a minute. That can't be right."

Mr. Renfroe pulled a folded paper from his pocket and tapped it with a gnarled finger. "It's in there, and you signed it."

"Let me take a look at that." Ames snatched the paper away from Brad. "I told you to pay attention to what you were signing, Bubb."

"Hey!" Lark yelled from beneath the arbor. "I want to get married!"

"Caspar, this ain't right, and you know it." Mrs. Renfroe stepped out and took the paper from Ames's hands. "I'm sorry, Mr. Kenneally. This contract may be legal, but it's not right. A few years back, Caspar got the idea that we should take ourselves a little vacation. It started out to be a simple arrangement whereby we got a little money and somebody took care of the place while we were gone. But in just a week, they were so frustrated at all the work they'd had to do, they paid us to come home early. We never meant no harm and we sorta thought of it as renting out the place, although that's not what it says in that there contract. We're not keeping your down payment, and if you want your Corvette back, it's parked out by the road."

"Now, Mother," the old man fussed. "Look what you've gone and done."

"I did what was right, Caspar, and you know it."

"Now, Alphie, we got a legal contract, and it says we can have the place back. He didn't have to sign it. We've not done nothin' wrong."

"Wait a minute," Ames interrupted. "That's misrepresentation, pure and simple, and I've got a whole passel of lawyers who can prove it. We're not giving up our Lazy Daisy Acres without a fight. No, siree. Especially not since I'm giving these two—" his head bobbed in the general direction of Zoë and Brad "—another forty acres on the north side over there as a wedding present." He winked at Zoë. "Thought we might want to expand the garden," he said.

The old man looked stricken. "Well, where will we go? What will we do?"

The old woman took his arm. "Florida," she said. "We're goin' back to Florida. And if he gets to keep the property, by golly, we'll be keepin' that Corvette."

Brad offered his hand. "It's a deal."

Caspar looked at his wife of more years than he could remember, looked at the place he'd lived in at least as long, and scratched his head. "What about Elmer?"

"It's his home," Brad assured the Renfroes. "Besides, I couldn't get him to leave if I whispered in his ear from now until the next century."

"Whisper in his ear?" Caspar Renfroe had obviously never heard of that bit of folklore. "You'd do better to talk stern to him and let him know you mean business."

Brad laughed. "I'll try that."

"Hey!" Lark shouted again, bucket of petals at her feet, hands on her hips. "When are we gonna start eating the wedding cake and smoochin'?"

"Hold your horses there, Daughter Lark." Ames rubbed his hands together as he turned once more to Brad and Zoë. "Enough interruptions. Let's get on with this wedding so we can start the party. Everybody get back in place." He waved a hand at the musicians. "Play something perky," he instructed. They did. One look had Carson snapping the shutter release with rapid-fire precision. Another got everyone, including the Renfroes, back in their seats. "Okay," he said to Brad and Zoë. "You're all set. Let's rock and roll."

Brad looked at Zoë, then at his boss. "I'm sorry to disappoint you, sir, but there's not going to be a wedding. Zoë and I…well, she's only willing to go as far as the rosebush with me."

"What?" Ames's glower returned, set full on Zoë.

"You're not gonna keep everybody waiting while we move the arbor to this end of the garden instead of that one, are you?"

Zoë laughed, new happiness bubbling inside her. "No," she said. "Actually, I'm just reconsidering my position. I think I may have misunderstood the original proposal."

Brad grabbed her hand and held it tightly, hope shining in his eyes. "You did?"

"Well, I agreed to walk only as far as the rosebush with *you*. I might consider going a little farther for a man like Daisy Rose."

He kissed her, right there, a short distance from the wedding arbor and a promising happy-ever-after. "Zoë Rose," he said when he pulled back from the kiss. "I know this is sudden and I know it probably sounds like the dumbest idea in the world, but would you consider marrying me now, instead of later?"

"Why, Hubby Bee," she said, laughing in reply. "I'd be delighted. I thought it was you who wanted to wait."

"That was your bodyguard. I fired him."

"Really?"

Brad smiled wryly. "Well, he'll be back, but I'm putting him to work protecting the apple trees."

"Mom? Uncle Brad?" Lark's voice was weary with waiting. "Are we *ever* gonna get married?"

Zoë looked up at Brad, her heart—so recently his— in her eyes. "Yes, Lark. We're getting married in just a minute. Right after we finish smoochin'."

When planning your garden, Friend Neighbor, remember to incorporate room for growth, because the unexpected can and often does occur. Just like a visit from the stork, that pretty little flowering vine you forgot you planted last summer can return next spring to catch you by surprise. Daughter Kate is thrilled with the idea of being a big sister to not one, but two babies! (Due any day now.) She's impatient for our twins to get here, and so, I'll confess, Dear Friends, are her father and I. Last night, as the three of us rocked in the porch swing, looked at the moon and anticipated our new arrivals, I couldn't help wanting to share our joy with you and letting you know that here on Lazy Daisy Acres, we're living like crazy today....

HARLEQUIN®

A M E R I C A N · R O M A N C E®

presents

CAUGHT WITH A COWBOY

A new duo by
Charlotte Maclay

Two sisters looking for love
in all the wrong places...
Their search ultimately leads them
to the wrong bed, where they
each unexpectedly find
the cowboy of their dreams!

THE RIGHT COWBOY'S BED (#821)
ON SALE APRIL 2000

IN A COWBOY'S EMBRACE (#825)
ON SALE MAY 2000

Available at your favorite retail outlet.

HARLEQUIN®
Makes any time special ™

Romance is just one click away!

online book **serials**

➤ *Exclusive* to our web site, get caught up in both the daily and weekly online installments of new romance stories.

➤ Try the Writing Round Robin. Contribute a chapter to a story created by our members. Plus, winners will get prizes.

romantic **travel**

➤ Want to know where the best place to kiss in New York City is, or which restaurant in Los Angeles is the most romantic? Check out our Romantic Hot Spots for the scoop.

➤ Share your travel tips and stories with us on the romantic travel message boards.

romantic reading **library**

➤ Relax as you read our collection of Romantic Poetry.

➤ Take a peek at the Top 10 Most Romantic Lines!

Visit us online at

www.eHarlequin.com

on Women.com Networks